Sweet Tea
and
Secrets

Also available by Joy Avon

In Peppermint Peril

Sweet Tea and Secrets

A TEA AND
A READ MYSTERY

Joy Avon

CROOKED
LANE

NEW YORK

Published in the United States by Crooked Lane Books, an imprint of The Quick Brown Fox & Company LLC.

Crooked Lane Books and its logo are trademarks of The Quick Brown Fox & Company LLC.

Library of Congress Catalog-in-Publication data available upon request.

ISBN (hardcover): 978-1-64385-023-8
ISBN (ePub): 978-1-64385-024-5
ISBN (ePDF): 978-1-64385-025-2

Cover illustration by Brandon Dorman
Book design by Jennifer Canzone

Printed in the United States.

www.crookedlanebooks.com

Crooked Lane Books
34 West 27th St., 10th Floor
New York, NY 10001

First Edition: June 2019

10 9 8 7 6 5 4 3 2 1

Chapter One

B ook Tea's door opened, and a group of women came out, talking and laughing. The relaxed expression on their faces suggested they had spent a quiet few hours on the high tea offerings and were now energized to tackle anything that came their way. Book Tea had that effect on people. The delicious treats with bookish clues, the perfect tea blends, and the mystery books lined up along the oak-paneled walls created a safe haven where guests could sit back and enjoy, letting the stress of their everyday lives wash away.

Still, as Callie Aspen watched the door close again upon all those inviting delights, nerves wriggled in her stomach, and a small voice in the back of her mind whispered, *Are you sure you made the right decision?*

Last time she'd been here, it had just been for the Christmas holidays. Some time off from her busy life as tour guide for Travel the Past, a company that specialized in trips to historic venues.

Heart's Harbor had always been her hideout for the holidays and as a kid in the summers, a place where she could play hide and seek, build forts, and watch the stars light up in the skies. Those happy childhood memories, in combination with the warmth and coziness of Book Tea and the new friends she had made during her Christmastime adventures, had convinced her it might be time to say goodbye to the life she had built so far and start over completely. Now Heart's Harbor was becoming her full-time home. Her apartment in Trenton was empty, waiting for another tenant to come and move in. And her position at Travel the Past had been taken by an eager young history graduate who couldn't wait to take her first group to Vienna later this week.

Callie's furniture was en route to Heart's Harbor, and in the back of the rental car were her suitcases packed with clothes and other personal things that she hadn't wanted to trust to the movers.

Everything that had formed the basis of her life for the past few years was over and done with, and she was about to start over, here, in the town of her fond childhood memories. No more taking groups past buildings, explaining about architecture and royalty; now her days would be spent baking cakes and organizing bookish tea parties. She had looked forward to this moment as she had taken careful steps to change her life, but now, standing here watching the tearoom, she wasn't sure what lay in store for her. Could she just leave everything she had built for something so completely different? The last time she had been here, in December, the air had been full of snow and sleigh bells, the houses lit up with colorful lights, and the warmth of the Christmas season wrapping itself around her, making her long for togetherness and family. For a steady life in one place, instead of all the traveling.

Now, however, in the sun-drenched brightness of a June afternoon, she wondered what on earth she had done. Was she really cut out for small-town life? Would she miss her colleagues at Travel the Past and her groups of history-loving people who drank in every word she said? Would a few weeks here show her that she had made a terrible mistake?

Maybe it would have been better to keep her apartment and take a leave at the company, to see if this was really what she wanted to do?

Why had she burned all of her bridges?

Shaking her head with a rueful grimace, Callie walked to the door and opened it. Inside the tearoom, an invigorating scent of ginger tea was in the air. Several tables were filled, and voices hummed on the air.

From the back, something small and furry came running for Callie, and she squatted to pat Daisy, the Boston terrier she had inherited from her boss's mother and who had been part of her reason to want to move here. All of her traveling wouldn't have allowed her to keep the dog. But giving up Daisy had seemed impossible. Just feeling the soft fur under her fingertips and seeing the trust in the dog's eyes as she looked up at her, Callie knew she had been right about that. Daisy was hers.

She lifted the dog in her arms and carried her past the tables filled with women who threw adoring glances at the cuddly terrier, to reach the doors leading into the kitchen area. Great-Aunt Iphy stood at the counter, scooping fresh raspberries onto chocolate cake. She didn't turn her head as she said in a tone of full concentration, "If you could just get me the whipped cream from the fridge."

Callie guessed that her great-aunt had taken her for one of her helpers, and lowered Daisy to the ground. She put a finger to her lips to indicate that Daisy shouldn't betray her presence.

As if she understood right away and played along, the Boston terrier stayed perfectly still.

Callie went to the fridge and got out the bowl of whipped cream. She put it on the counter beside Iphy, who was fully focused on arranging the raspberries.

"Thank you," she muttered in a distracted tone.

Callie stood beside her, watching the creation take shape, grinning to herself as she wondered how long it would take her great-aunt to notice it wasn't one of her helpers beside her. As usual, Iphy looked impeccable in a cream blouse and long, flower-patterned skirt. Her pumps were the same pale blue as the flowers on the skirt and the thin gauze shawl around her neck. Her hair was made up into a neat bun at the back of her head, secured with a pearly clasp.

At last Iphy was satisfied with the arrangement on the plate and looked up. "You can take this to table . . ."

Her eyes widened as she took in Callie. "You're here! Why didn't you call to tell me it would be today?"

"I wanted to surprise you."

"You're staying now, right? This is *the* move?"

Callie nodded, smiling despite the nerves in her stomach.

The move was exactly what worried her. The finality of it all. No turning back.

Iphy reached out and wrapped Callie in a hug that was surprisingly tight and strong for a frail elderly woman. "Welcome home, Callie. I can't tell you how happy I am to have you here at last."

Callie hugged her great-aunt back, for a moment thinking that she might have done the right thing after all. Iphy needed her to help out both at Book Tea and in the preservation of majestic Haywood Hall, a rambling old house on the outskirts of town, inhabited by Heart's Harbor's oldest resident, rich widow Dorothea Finster.

That was, everybody had believed Dorothea to be rich until the presentation of her new will at Christmastime had revealed that she was deeply in debt and needed others to help her preserve the house. Callie had agreed to help out, along with Iphy, and she realized now that the house that had fascinated her as a little girl was part of the new life she was going to build there in Heart's Harbor. That was amazing in itself. No matter how much she might miss traveling to historic sites, there was a historic site right here for her to preserve. Her own contribution to keeping town history alive.

Iphy held her shoulders and smiled up at Callie with laughter wrinkles around her clear blue eyes. "It's not too busy. I can sneak out and show you the cottage I got for you to live in. It wasn't easy. Everything gets rented to tourists in the summer. But I found you something I know you'll like. It does need a little work."

Callie froze. "What do you mean *work*?" She didn't intend to spend her sunny summer days trapped in a fixer-upper.

"Well, Mr. Neville, the elderly gentleman who owns it, used to do repairs himself, but he isn't up to it anymore, so he just let the place sit empty for a bit. I heard about it and thought it was a shame for such a nice house to be vacant just because of a few minor things. The wallpaper isn't very pretty anymore, and the paint is chipping. Could be a bad plank in the porch here and there. I had someone look it over before I decided to take it. It doesn't need major repairs. You won't have a leaky roof on your hands or bad plumbing."

"Phew. That's a relief. Although wallpapering isn't my strong suit either."

"I know, and I put up a little notice at the community center to ask someone to help out with it. We're a strong community here—we'll have someone in no time. Mr. Neville was delighted when I came to see him with the first rent check, saying the house needed a heart again. You'll be that heart—I just know it. You wait and see." Iphy patted Callie's arm. "Do you want to go look at it or not?"

"Absolutely. Should we take my rental or your station wagon?"

"I think the station wagon would be better. The dirt road leading to the cottage isn't . . . well, it could be better."

Callie frowned. Her feelings about the cottage were like a quickly changing tide: one moment she couldn't wait to see it; the next she heard something that made her wonder if she'd made a huge mistake. "It isn't in the middle of nowhere, is it? I'm not easily frightened, but I don't like isolated places."

"Nonsense. It's perfectly close to the lighthouse. It's no longer manually operated, but the cottage where the lighthouse keeper used to live is still inhabited. The couple living there organizes treasure hunts on the beach." Iphy waved her out of the kitchen.

"Treasure hunts?" Callie queried as she followed her great-aunt, with Daisy hot on their heels.

"Well, it's more like beachcombing, but to make it exciting for families with kids, they call them treasure hunts. You have an hour to walk along the beach and collect as many interesting items as possible. Whoever has the most, or the most spectacular find, wins a prize. The kids all get a beachcombing diploma, and then they can roast marshmallows. The couple also maintains a little museum of the best finds inside the lighthouse. You can explore the lower parts of it. You're not allowed to go up to the higher sections as it can be dangerous. It's quite a drop, you know."

Callie didn't like heights and nodded with a shiver.

Outside Book Tea, the bright sunshine pierced her eyes a moment, and she lifted a hand to shade them. On the other side of the street, a man in uniform was circling a car, apparently trying to determine whether it was allowed to be parked there.

Callie felt her heart skip a beat, thinking it might be Deputy Falk, with whom she had worked to solve some unpleasantness at Christmastime. At the tea party where Dorothea Finster had planned to reveal her new will, a valuable heirloom had vanished, and someone had been murdered. The crimes had touched Dorothea's nearest and dearest, unsettling the atmosphere in town so close to Christmas Eve.

Callie still wasn't sure how she had managed to clear everything up, but she would never have been able to do it without Iphy, other Heart's Harbor residents who had lent a friendly hand, and of course Falk, who had, despite his doubts as to whether citizens should be involved in a criminal investigation, shown an open mind to their suggestions and who had, in the end, even saved her from the killer.

It was odd how two people could go through something so emotional together and feel like they had forged a special bond, and then January rolled around and they went back to their normal lives. Callie had emailed Falk a couple of times to tell about her travels, but he had either not replied or just sent a few sentences that hadn't suggested great enthusiasm. Maybe he was really busy or disliked emails, but either way Callie felt like whatever there had been on that wonderful Christmas Eve when they had traveled in a sleigh together, and had laughed and talked like they were old friends, had vanished completely. She had even felt a little silly for being excited about seeing him when she moved to Heart's Harbor and possibly getting to know him better.

Good thing he had no idea what she had been thinking. No embarrassment there.

Callie quickly got into her great-aunt's station wagon and strapped herself in, but couldn't resist throwing another look at the busy deputy when they drove past. It wasn't Falk, but his colleague, whom she had only seen in passing at the police station when she had been there for the murder case.

She wanted to ask Iphy how Falk was doing these days, but she knew Iphy had a nose for what she called "affairs of the heart" and Callie wasn't eager to draw her great-aunt's attention to anything potentially romantic, or there would be no end to the well-meant suggestions about how to best handle the situation.

* * *

It wasn't a long drive to her new living quarters, and Callie was glad to see there were houses strewn along the road right until they turned into the dirt road that Iphy had called "not too good." That had to be the understatement of the century: the station wagon shocked and groaned as it traveled slowly across the uneven surface, with Iphy zigzagging to avoid the deepest potholes.

"Can't the town do something about this?" Callie asked with a desperate look out the side window.

Iphy sighed. "The new mayor has been busy catching up with other matters, I suppose. He stepped into a hotbed of suspicion and distrust after the discoveries made and . . . well, the council was decimated as well."

Callie felt a twinge of guilt at what she had set off with her investigation into the murder around Christmas, but then it hadn't been possible to solve it without digging into town secrets. Well-kept secrets that had involved an ever wider circle of people as the investigation had progressed. To change the subject, she said quickly, "I can already see the lighthouse."

"Your cottage is to the right here . . ." Iphy turned onto

an even smaller road, which led to an open space where a gray stone cottage stood. It had a wooden porch, several windows, and a cute low roof that gave it a bit of an English country–style vibe. Callie immediately saw the potential, but she also saw the porch step that sagged, the chipped paint everywhere, and the chimney that had twigs sticking out of it as if birds were nesting in it.

She glanced at her great-aunt. "You're sure we're not at the wrong house?"

"Very funny. With a little care it will turn into a very nice place."

"Yes, I do realize that, but I don't really see when I'll have the time to . . ." She fell silent when a figure suddenly appeared around the side of the house.

The man came from the back and was holding a notepad on which he scribbled with a pen. He was tall, blond, and in his forties, Callie guessed, dressed in a faded red T-shirt and stonewashed jeans, with beige sneakers that had seen better days.

Iphy braked and squinted at the figure. "I have no idea who that is. You?"

Callie shook her head. "I thought you knew everyone around town."

The idea that a stranger was prowling around her new house didn't settle well with her. She got out of the car, put Daisy down on the grass, and marched up to the man. "Hello there. What are you doing here?"

"Making a list of what needs to be done. Judging by the outside, of course. I don't have a key, so I can't get in."

He had a pleasant, deep warm voice, but Callie wasn't about to be impressed by it, or by his keen blue eyes. She said, "Of course you can't get in because you have no business here. This is *my* new home."

Her sharp tone didn't faze him. On the contrary, he broke into a smile. "Oh, perfect. Then we can talk about it right away."

He reached out his hand. "Quinn. I saw the notice at the community center, asking for a handyman to get this place into shape again. I'm a pretty good painter. My wallpapering is rusty, I admit—haven't done that since my college days when my mother declared that a room without wallpaper was like a freezer without pizza. I do love pizza, so I listened to Mom. Can't guarantee I can get it on without the occasional bubble, but I will certainly try. I work fast, neat—"

Callie raised a hand to stop the flood of words. "I'm not really sure yet that I actually want to hire anyone to do the work. My great-aunt put up that notice at the community center."

Quinn looked her over. "You're going to spend these gorgeous June days inside, in the fumes of drying paint and wallpaper glue? When you could let me handle the headache, literally, and enjoy the sun and the beach?"

He had a point there, of course. Callie seemed to remember that the scent of drying paint didn't do wonders for her head.

Quinn continued, "If money is a concern, I can assure you my hourly rates are very fair." He looked down at Daisy, who had circled his legs and was now waiting for attention.

Crouching down, Quinn patted her. The Boston terrier grunted in satisfaction and pressed her head to his leg.

Quinn looked up at Callie. "We can even agree on a flat fee. Whatever you want to do."

Callie was tempted. After all, she had enough to do in the run-up to the big Fourth of July tea party that Iphy had casually mentioned to her over the phone, before the move. It was supposed to be an event for the entire town and all of the tourists as well, focusing on events from Heart's Harbor's rich history. The program wasn't fully planned out yet, and things like that always took more time than you calculated at the start.

Quinn said, "Look, I can imagine you're not eager to hire a perfect stranger, but I took the liberty of peeking in and saw it's all still empty. I can work best when nobody is around, so maybe you could stay in town for a few days while I get everything done. With your great-aunt?"

He nodded at Iphy, who had also gotten out of the car and closed in on them. She answered his smile with a wide grin of her own. "Hello there. Delighted to meet you. So you can do some work here, get it into livable shape again?"

"I was just writing down a thing or two." He waved the notebook and pen. "But if you happen to have a key on you, we can look inside, and I can give you my estimate right away."

"Let's do it." Iphy produced the key from her pocket. Daisy looked up at her as if she expected a treat was forthcoming.

Callie wanted to protest as she wasn't quite sure she wanted to see her new home in the presence of a perfect stranger, but she also knew her great-aunt couldn't be stopped.

And Quinn was right: with the house empty, it was the perfect time for a checkup and some changes.

They went up the porch steps, Quinn unnecessarily pointing out the rotten one, and then, while Iphy opened the door, he tapped Callie's arm to draw her attention to the hooks in the porch's wooden ceiling. "Perfect for hanging baskets. If you need a ride to the nearest nursery, let me know. I'd be happy to come along and help you carry all the plants."

Iphy pushed the door open and gestured. "Voilà. Come on in. Welcome to Sea Anemone. That's the house's name but Mr. Neville assured me you can change it if you like. I had the distinct impression that if you like it here, you could offer to buy the cottage, and he wouldn't mind at all."

Callie hemmed. She had no idea yet how the house looked, or whether she'd even like to live here, so for the moment she was perfectly happy to rent it and think about something more permanent later.

Inside there was the pervasive smell of a space that had been closed up for a long time. Cobwebs threaded from the coats rack to the opposite wall, and their footfalls disturbed the dust on the floorboards. Daisy sneezed and shuddered.

Callie grimaced, but Quinn said, "I'll open all windows while I'm painting. The house just needs some air. It's a nice little place if you ignore the dirt."

Callie had to agree with him that, while it looked quite compact on the outside, there was a lot of room indoors, with a hallway that led straight into the open living room with a gorgeous fireplace. Daisy ran over and lay down in front of it as if she wanted to say, *My place is right here.*

The kitchen sat to the left, with some modern appliances already in place. And upstairs there were two bedrooms, so Callie could even have people come stay. The window in the room she immediately designated for herself gave a lovely view of the garden below. Left to itself, it had grown a bit wild, but she could see the potential. Rose beds, maybe growing her own herbs? Wouldn't it be wonderful to step out at night with a basket on her arm and snip off some parsley, or mint for tea? The image itself seemed the very epitome of country living.

In the bathroom with cute lavender tiles, the tap was leaking and the air was rather damp, but Quinn assured her he could fix that as well.

From the doorway Iphy said, "I hope you like it. I paid three months' rent in advance. And Mr. Neville was so happy he had found someone to live here, after all that time. It's not his fault he wasn't up to keeping things neat and tidy anymore. After his wife died, he just lost a bit of spark. But the idea of having someone restore the place put the twinkle back in his eye."

Callie exhaled. In her mind she was already buying towels with sprigs of lavender embroidered on them to go with the bathroom tiles, and changing the curtains in the living room and finding the perfect painting to hang over that hearth.

"I think that with a little work it could be great. Are we really allowed to make changes?"

"Of course," Iphy said, "just as long as it doesn't change the structure, so you can't knock down a wall or change the roof. But small changes like painting and repairs of the porch aren't a problem."

Callie turned to Quinn, who had been looking around and taking more notes. "Can you give me that estimate now?" She held her breath, cringing inwardly at what the figure might be.

But when he held out his notepad to her, she blinked at the scribbled numbers and refocused to see if she had read them right. Then she looked up at him. "That little?"

"Well, of course you need to buy all the materials: the paint you like, the wallpaper you want, a new tap if I can't fix this old one. These figures are purely compensation for my time and effort."

"Still I think it's very modest." She studied him with a frown. "Are you sure you're figuring on enough hours? I mean, you will finish it and do it right, and not leave me hanging halfway through?"

"Of course. This is what I charge for delivering you a completed job."

"Well, I guess it's a deal, then." Callie reached out and shook his hand. "I'll decide as quickly as possible what colors of paint and what kind of wallpaper I want." She looked at Iphy. "The only problem right now is that my furniture is en route here. It should be here tomorrow. If I can't put it here, where do I put it?"

"I think the old stables at Haywood Hall are empty. I'll ask Dorothea about it," Iphy said.

"Isn't Haywood Hall that old country house?" Quinn asked. "I saw a mention in the newspaper the other day that there's going to be a Fourth of July party there. Highlights from local history or something?"

Iphy nodded enthusiastically. "The theme is Living History. The Historical Society will present life on the coast through the ages, and some demonstration dancers will come in to do Golden Age dances. As we have plenty of space at Haywood Hall, we'll even bring in a small plane from the forties so people can have their picture taken with it. Aviation enthusiasts, in authentic pilots' uniforms from the era, will tell stories of Heart's Harbor's contribution in World War Two. There will also be a sweet tea competition, where participants share their family recipes, and a professional jury will choose the best sweet tea, which we will then put on the menu at Book Tea for the rest of the summer season. We have something for everyone really, but personally I'd love for us to have something spectacular to present right before the big fireworks start."

She looked at Callie. "I thought you could arrange that."

"Me?" Callie was taken aback. "But I just got here today. And the party is in three weeks' time."

"I thought you could come up with something. You've worked all these years telling people spectacular tales about events in the past."

"Yes, but then we were in Vienna or Paris. Here—"

"We're just in Heart's Harbor?" Iphy wagged a finger at

her. "Don't talk disparagingly about your new hometown. People won't like you any better for it."

Although her tone was light, Callie suspected that she meant it. Iphy expected her to turn up something sensational to wow the townsfolk with.

"Maybe newspaper archives can give you a starting point?" Quinn suggested. "Some big headline from the past that grabs your attention?"

"Yes." Iphy clapped her hands together. "That's such a good idea, Quinn. Why don't you help us, not only with the house but also with the tea party preparations?"

"Well, uh, I don't know . . ." Quinn fidgeted with the notebook in his hands. "I guess I—"

"Excellent. That's taken care of then." And with that, Iphy left the room.

"You'll have to forgive her for her take-charge attitude," Callie said to Quinn. That's just how she is. She's really sweet, and the town depends on her to come up with the good ideas."

Quinn held her gaze as if he was trying to see past her upbeat tone. "You've just been stuck a job to complete at short notice, and a handyman to update your new house, and now she's also getting the handyman involved in said job. Are you okay with that, or do you just want to run away screaming?"

Callie had to admit the butterflies in her stomach were fluttering harder now with the realization of all she had to tackle here. Her old life had been comfortingly familiar. She could have done her trips on autopilot, being so settled into her routine. Here everything was new, and she knew people would be watching her to see how she did. The Fourth of July celebrations would be big, and . . .

What if she couldn't meet all the towering expectations?

"Just think about it, okay?" Quinn said. "No pressure. I'd just enjoy the chance to learn a little more about this town and what happened here."

"So you're not a resident?"

Quinn shook his head. "Just passing through." He scribbled something on a page of the notepad, tore it off, and gave it to her. "My cell phone number, so you can call me to discuss the work. If it's okay with you, I'd like to keep the key on me so I can start working here right away. I can repair the porch step and get started on some other things without needing paint."

"I guess that's fine." It felt odd entrusting someone she didn't know with the key to her new home, but it was still empty; nothing of hers was there.

They caught up with Iphy, who handed over the key and thanked Quinn for dropping by. At the car, she said to Callie, "I want to go to the lighthouse now so you can meet Dave and Elvira. They're your next-door neighbors, should you ever need anything." She raised a hand in a wave to Quinn, who had pulled a mountain bike from beside a bush and pedaled off.

"You see, in a town like ours you'll always find someone to help you in a heartbeat."

"But Quinn is no local." Callie buckled up and cuddled

Daisy. "In fact, I'm not even sure if Quinn is his first or last name. He was rather vague about why he was here too."

She glanced at Iphy, who turned the ignition. "Are you sure we can trust him?"

"I don't see that he can do much harm."

Chapter Two

C allie loved landmarks of any kind, whether church towers, turrets on an old mansion, or lighthouses. She always admired the craftsmanship that had gone into building up to a certain level and maintaining a balanced and beautiful structure that was also functional.

The Heart's Harbor lighthouse was black and white with a beacon on top, encased in a metal construction that was painted black as well. The keeper's cottage huddled at its foot, looking a little like her new home, and Callie could now see in real life, instead of just in her imagination, what cute curtains, flowering plants and a bench to sit on at night could do for a place.

A woman with grayish streaks in her brown hair was on her knees, filling a wooden chest, and only turned to them when they were almost all the way up the path. She rose to her feet and put her hand against her throat. "Oh. You startled me. Unless we have groups coming for the beach combing, we rarely see people here."

As she caught Callie's incredulous look, she added, "The

beaches where tourists go for sunbathing and swimming are on the other side of town. The beach here is a little too rocky, and the wind can suddenly breathe across it and make you want to turn up your collar. Even in summer it's just not the best place to take your kids for a family outing that involves going into the water. But if you want to scour the sand for finds, well, I dare you to show me a place that is better suited to it."

Callie smiled. "You advertise it well."

The woman swiped a lock of hair from her face. "I've lived here for almost thirty years now. If it bored me, I would have been long gone. But the sea is just something . . . special. It's never the same. And this lighthouse always reminds me you need a beacon to feel secure. To know where you're going. Even if at some points you don't know where you are."

Callie reached out her hand. "I'm moving in to the cottage nearby. Mr. Neville's Sea Anemone"

The woman nodded. "Oh, what great news! It has been empty for too long. I'm happy someone's moving back into it."

"I just wanted to introduce myself. Callie Aspen. And this is my dog, Daisy."

"Elvira Riggs. Hello, Daisy." Elvira leaned down to pat the Boston terrier. "My husband has been here for all of his life. His father was keeper before him, and his grandfather before that. It's really a family thing. When they decided to move away from manual operation, we stayed on and came up with the beachcombing activities."

"Sounds like a summer thing. You can't have it easy in winter."

Scratching Daisy behind the ears, Elvira shrugged. "All small businesses with seasonal activities struggle when it's not their season. But we have other things we can do. I translate books, and Dave restores old boats. In fact, sometimes in the summer, when all the families with kids drive me a little crazy, I can long for the quiet winter season, when the rain lashes against the windows and I'm at the computer all day long looking for the perfect words to translate that one elusive expression."

Callie could just picture the scene. "What languages do you translate into?"

"From," Elvira corrected. "I translate French novels into English. Mainly historical novels, where the French can be quite challenging. All kinds of garbs for instance or furniture or professions. But I enjoy those challenges. And when I have another chapter finished, I make myself a fresh pot of tea and look outside at the raging sea, and I just can't help thinking I have the best life ever."

Callie hoped that she would feel that same way once she was settled into her new life here in town.

Iphy said, "I just wanted to ask you and Dave to keep an eye on Callie at her new place. I mean, she can take care of herself of course—after all she used to travel the world, but it's always nice when there's someone at hand."

"Of course. I do know the cottage has a bad porch step. Could Dave perhaps—"

Callie raised a hand to ward off the friendly offer. "That's very kind, but I just hired someone to do repairs and help me with painting and wallpapering."

"Oh, that's fine then." Elvira stood up straight again and raked back her hair with both hands. "Can I offer you a drink?" She smiled at Callie. "I think you'd like to see the lighthouse from the inside. Our little museum of finds?"

"Definitely, but some other time would be great." Callie glanced at Iphy. She figured her busy great-aunt wouldn't want to stay away from Book Tea for too long. And when she moved in to the cottage nearby, shortly, she'd have plenty of opportunity to go see the finds.

Elvira accepted her decision without offering again and turned back to the wooden chest, leaning over it and stuffing something into it a little better. Daisy followed her as if she wanted to see what was inside, and only came to Callie after she had been called a couple of times.

As the three of them walked back to the car, Iphy whispered, "People thought that Dave Riggs would never marry. He sure took his time looking for the right woman. But once he met Elvira, it was a done deal. She moved in with him from one day to the other. They met and married somewhere abroad, I think."

"Oh. How unexpected for a man so attached to his lighthouse to even travel abroad."

"It had to do with lighthouses, of course. Dave collects footage of them from all around the world. Most of it he gathers through contacts with other collectors and historical societies for the preservation of historical landmarks. But he does travel every once in a while to see some rare lighthouse in person. I think he must have met Elvira on one of those trips."

Callie nodded, glancing back over her shoulder at the busy woman. She had been friendly enough, but still as she saw her there, working on her own, she also seemed solitary, like the lighthouse, not afraid to weather the storm alone.

When they reached the station wagon, they found a police car parked right behind it. A tall, dark-haired man was standing at the back and leaned over to the ground.

Callie focused better and realized the man was exchanging his shoes for knee-high rubber boots.

"Deputy Falk!" Iphy called.

Falk looked up. He only pretended to be surprised, Callie guessed, as he must know her great-aunt's station wagon very well and had to have recognized it the instant he parked his own vehicle right behind it. Or did his surprise not extend to her great-aunt but rather to finding her in town? "You blocked our way out," Iphy said.

"You can make a turn there." Falk gestured to the left. "I have to look for a missing dog."

"Missing dog?" Callie echoed.

Falk sighed. "Elderly couple was walking him when some kids shot off a firecracker in the dunes. The dog got a scare and ran off. They think he's still wandering on the beach. They even wanted us to use a search helicopter to spot it. They were very disappointed when I told them we can't put a helicopter up just to look for a dog. I mean—don't get me wrong—I understand they're concerned for their dog, but we have to look at how we use our resources. The sheriff's out of town, took his wife to Venice to celebrate their fortieth anniversary, and he won't appreciate me spending the town's money on a search for a runaway canine. In fact, had he been here, he would probably have told them to go look themselves or just put up a few posters asking for information. He'd say the dog will turn up somehow. Get hungry, go to a house looking for food maybe."

Callie nodded. "I understand. But you don't share that opinion? You're here, ready to look. Still, it can't be very efficient if you go on foot, looking for a dog that might be miles off."

Falk rolled his eyes. "I know, but the woman was so upset that I felt I had to do something. Besides, we had a call from someone that they saw a black and white dog running around just a little farther down that beach."

"You know what?" Iphy said. "Callie can help you. Two pairs of eyes spot more than one. You can drop her at Book Tea later, right? Bring Daisy, Callie. Her presence might attract the other dog."

Callie wanted to protest and say she doubted this would work, but Iphy got into her station wagon and started the engine before she could argue.

As she turned away, Falk looked down at Callie's shoes. Although not towering heels, they weren't exactly beach-proof either. He sighed. "Want to borrow my boots? I can put my shoes back on. They're more suitable for plowing through the sand than yours."

Callie felt awkward intruding into his mission like this. "I had no idea I would be plowing through any sand. Iphy told me she only wanted to show me my new house."

Falk glanced at her. "You got a house here now?"

"Don't tell me you didn't know I was coming to live here." Callie itched to point out that she had written to him about it, but thought that it might sound sad and needy. He had decided not to reply to her last email, so that was his choice.

"Of course I knew that," Falk said. "Peggy told me how Iphy couldn't stop talking about it."

"Where did Peggy hear Iphy talking about it?" Callie asked as she balanced on one leg to exchange her shoe for the rubber boot Falk had placed ready for her.

"At Book Tea of course." Falk sounded surprised. "Didn't you know Peggy works there a couple of mornings a week?"

"No. I thought Peggy was still doing those call center calls from home. The job she got just before Christmas?"

"Yeah, that too." Falk leaned against the police car. "She's been taking on everything she can get."

Callie glanced at his guarded profile. She knew Falk had trouble with his widowed sister trying to do everything by herself, refusing his help with finances and with the raising of her two young sons. Falk adored Jimmy and Tate, but Peggy seemed to feel like Falk pretended to know better than she did how to raise them, and wasn't too keen on that. Callie supposed that Peggy's struggle to prove her independence to her brother also had to do with her still trying to find her feet after her husband's unexpected death. Working through her grief and finding some sort of life again for her boys and herself.

"You know what?" she said. "I heard there's this beach-combing activity. A kind of treasure hunt. I think we should try it some time. With Jimmy and Tate."

Falk didn't reply. Callie felt like she was sixteen again and eyeing the boy she had a terrible crush on who didn't seem to notice she existed.

"If it isn't a good idea, you can just say it," she said, then added to make it sound less odd, "I mean, maybe you've already done it?"

"No, not at all."

Callie had wrestled her leg into the other rubber boot and straightened up. "Let's go find that spooked dog then."

They went down to the beach, Daisy running ahead of them, slipping in the sand and holding her head low against the wind that came across the water.

"I can see why Elvira told me this beach isn't popular with tourists." Callie struggled to clamber across the rocks that separated the higher area from the waterline. "It's wild."

Falk reached out a hand to her. "Be careful, those boots can be slippery when the rocks are wet."

Callie wanted to ignore his hand, but as she felt her foot slip away, she grabbed it anyway. It closed around hers in a warm, safe grip.

"What kind of dog is it?" she asked, navigating the rocky patch.

"A border collie mix. The couple just got him the other week. He had to be rehomed after his owner moved into a retirement home with a no pets rule."

"Oh, and instead of letting him get used to his new home quietly, they took him on a trip?" Callie looked concerned. "For all we know, he could be on his way back to where he used to live."

"That's going to be a long hike." Falk stared ahead of them across the stretch of beach. "Do you see something moving there? Oh, no, I think it's just a piece of paper that got caught between the rocks."

Callie walked beside him as they tried to conquer the wet sand and scan their surroundings for a runaway dog. It struck her how close this was to the mental picture she'd had at first, when envisioning her new life here. She had lain in bed at night dreaming of beach walks with Falk, Daisy frolicking around them, of him holding her hand. Of them stopping to sit on the rocks for a while and staring out across the sea until the sun set.

She hadn't wanted them to dive into some crazy whirlwind romance, but she had expected to feel some kind of closeness to him. Not the alienation she felt now, as if she could sense he wasn't happy that she had come. Had he realized when the Christmas season was over that their attraction had just been a superficial thing? Something he regretted?

"So how are Jimmy and Tate?" she asked, just as he asked, "How are the Fourth of July party preparations coming along?"

"You first," she said, and Falk shrugged. "Tate didn't do too well in school this year, but considering he's still getting over his father's death, they decided to let him go into the next grade anyway. Else he'd lose contact with his friends. Jimmy's okay, I guess. I can never read him quite like I can read Tate."

"Maybe it's easier since Tate is younger and shows his emotions more? And the Fourth of July thing is coming along fine, I guess. Iphy just saddled me with a chore to do, and I'm not quite sure how to handle it yet. She wants some big event from history explored, or something . . ."

"Explosive?" Falk supplied. "I mean, the Fourth and fireworks is a good combination."

"Yes, well, I guess I should just follow Quinn's advice and dive into the newspaper archives."

"Who's Quinn?" Falk asked immediately, an edge to his voice.

"A guy Iphy found via a note at the community center. He's going to paint the cottage I'm moving into. Sort of get it all set up so I don't need to do anything."

Falk glanced at her. "So you're going to settle here? It's not just for the summer vacation?"

"No. I resigned at Travel the Past, and my apartment is going to be rented to somebody else soon. I came out here with most of my stuff packed into a few suitcases, and the rest will follow shortly." As she said it, her throat constricted again. Had it been the right decision? Could she make it work? "I thought that . . . well, never mind."

Falk squinted as he stared ahead to where sand was swirling in the air. "Is that a digging dog?"

"Could be," Callie agreed. They hastened their steps.

Daisy was still ahead of them, like the wet sand and the wind didn't bother her at all. Spotting the flying sand, she ran straight into it. They heard excited barking.

"What if he's unsure and nips her?" Callie asked Falk worriedly.

Falk gestured at her. "You wait here, and I'll go catch him."

But Callie followed along, her heart pounding for little Daisy's safety.

When they reached the spot, they saw Daisy sitting low, staring into a cavity in which the other dog had apparently disappeared. They could hear some sort of sound coming out of the dark hole, like ragged breathing.

"Great," Falk said. "What do we do now?"

Callie put her hand in her pocket. "I've got dog treats. I could coax him out and maybe then you can grab his collar?"

Falk looked doubtful. "If I make a fast move, he might get spooked and bite you. Let me have the treats, and I'll try to catch him by myself."

"No way." Callie had already lowered herself beside Daisy and put a treat on her hand. She reached it out to the opening and cooed, "Here, boy."

"His name is Biscuit."

"Here, Biscuit. Hey, good boy. Come and have a little look. Here's a treat for you. Yes, a nice little treat. Oh, look, Daisy wants it too. If you don't show yourself, she's going to get it."

"As if he's going to care." Still Falk leaned forward, his posture tight, like he expected the dog to suddenly burst from his hiding place and make a run for it.

Callie ignored his tension and continued, "That's a good boy. You can't stay here. It's getting darker and colder. You have to come with us. Yes, good boy."

Callie unconsciously lowered her voice when she saw something move and a snout peeked out a moment, only to be retracted again.

"Good boy. You come get your treat." She moved her hand back a little. "They have an excellent sense of smell," she said to Falk. "He seems curious too. Maybe he's not afraid anymore and was just running because he didn't know where his people had gone to."

The snout appeared again, sniffing, taking in all of their scents.

"Good boy," Callie cooed. "Come and get it." She moved back a little more.

Now the snout came out and part of the head, with a floppy half-hanging ear. Bright amber eyes studied her.

Callie didn't dare speak and just moved her hand to better show the dog the treat.

He tilted his head, his nose moving. Even his eyebrows moved, as if he wasn't sure and was assessing potential dangers.

Callie brought her hand a little closer to him. He didn't shrink back but kept in place, every muscle tight.

"Don't get any closer," Falk whispered. "He's uncertain and he might nip you."

"I know."

The border collie shook his head and made a low sound. Callie moved her hand up and down, not bringing it closer to him. He came out farther, still watching her with those yellowish eyes, like he couldn't decide what to make of her.

Then his snout touched her hand, and he very carefully took the treat. She heard it break under his strong teeth.

"Good boy," she whispered, not making any move to grab his collar. "Good boy." The dog crouched and watched her, apparently waiting to see if any more treats were forthcoming.

"Hey." She reached out her empty hand.

He sniffed it.

She gave him a quick brush over the side of his head. He didn't show any signs of aggression, but instead wagged his tail. She brushed the other side of his head. Then she pulled out another treat and gave it to him.

He devoured it and sat up on his rear, barking. Callie reached out and brushed his head again, catching hold of his collar. He let her, not pulling back.

She exhaled slowly. "I counted on him being familiar with unknown people touching him, since he's been rehomed recently and might have lived in a rescue or shelter for a while. Dogs do see different volunteers there, and . . . Have you got anything to put him on?"

Falk handed her a leash. Callie took it in her hand and kept talking to the dog in a friendly tone while she moved it into her other hand and brought it close to his head.

He let her clip it onto his collar without any protest.

"Good," Falk said, with a small hint of tension still in his tone. "Now you better walk him back, in case he doesn't like me. Some dogs have bad experiences with men and can get wild when they feel intimidated."

Callie rose to her feet, the leash in both hands. She knew border collies were strong and swift, and she had no intention of letting smart Biscuit get away from them again.

"Some dogs also react badly to a man in uniform," Falk said, following the proceedings with sharp interest.

"He doesn't seem to be concerned at all. Look, he's wagging his tail at you. Just give him a pat."

Falk looked doubtful, but then he squatted and reached out his hand. "Hey, boy. How you doing?"

Biscuit stretched out his snout, sniffed Falk's hand, then stepped forward and licked him on the neck. Falk tilted his head up with a huff to avoid being licked full in the face as well. "I guess he likes me," he said ruefully, ruffling the dog's fur.

Callie laughed softly. "I think it's more than that."

Falk got to his feet again. "We'd better get back to the car so I can inform the owners that their dog has been found. I doubt I'll have very good reception down here on the beach."

They walked back, side by side, Biscuit pulling on the leash and Daisy daring him into games by running away from them and then coming back.

At his police car, Falk put the border collie into the back seat and called the station while Callie wriggled out of his rubber boots. She was kind of sorry their time together was over so soon, but luckily the dog was found now and going to be reunited with his owners.

"I see." Falk's expression set. "I see. Well, you tell them anyway. They deserve to know."

He disconnected and said to her, "It seems the wife got a terrible scare when they lost the dog. Her husband told my colleague that they might consider giving him back to the rescue. That this trip had shown them that Biscuit is not the right dog for them."

Callie dropped the rubber boots in the trunk and closed it. Through the rear window she saw Biscuit, his ears up, his face happy and relaxed. Her heart clenched for him not understanding how the nice people who had taken him home were going to return him to the shelter.

"I guess he'll find another home," Falk said, the doubt thick in his voice.

"Let them think about it. Why don't you take him for the night? In the morning they might see things in a different light."

Falk looked at her. "You think so?"

"Like the husband said to your colleague, his wife had a shock when the dog ran away, and now she's not sure if she can handle him. But in the morning it won't feel the same. They'll want to keep him—believe me. But if you drop him off with them now and he's excited to see them and all wound up, she might feel like he really is too much. Come on, give the dog a chance to stay in his new home with his new family."

"All right. But if he destroys anything in my cabin . . ."

"You don't have things that can be destroyed. No vases with flowers, no cute little pillows. It's dog-proof!"

Falk rolled his eyes but didn't object anymore. Together they drove back into town.

Chapter Three

The next morning Callie awoke in the bed in her great-aunt's spare room, where she had woken up so many times as a kid, eager for the summer day ahead. The same bright sunshine winked outside the window, and the excitement of old grabbed her right away.

She got up, hugged Daisy—who was over the moon that her human was living with her full-time now—and showered and dressed. She hesitated over whether to apply any makeup: in her job as a travel guide, it had been mandatory to look your best for the company, and she did like a brushed-up appearance. But here in Heart's Harbor, she'd be working on her new home; taking long beach walks; helping out Iphy, behind the scenes of Book Tea, with the administration, and Callie didn't really see a big role for makeup there. Nevertheless, she decided that a little mascara never went amiss and also dabbed just a bit of gloss on her lips.

With her hair dancing loose on her shoulders, she ran down the stairs and found her great-aunt in the kitchen. Iphy pointed at the table where a plate held buttered toast.

"Still warm—I took it out of the toaster when I heard your steps on the landing. I've also pressed some fresh juice."

"Delicious. This is just like a hotel." Callie peeked over her great-aunt's shoulder to see what she was doing at the counter. On a tray, Iphy had placed marzipan in different colors and was using a knife to cut out squares for a creation that looked like a box. Callie frowned.

Iphy glanced at her. "Can you tell what it is?"

"Not really."

"I was afraid of that. For the Fourth festivities, I wanted to make some decorations that aren't just fireworks or flags. So I thought about picnic baskets. But somehow it doesn't look quite right yet. What are you up to today?"

Callie made a face. "I'll probably have to go pick out paint and wallpaper. Not my favorite chores, to be honest. I don't have the patience to go through a million choices. My apartment in Trenton came with its set color scheme, and I only had to throw in my own furniture."

Iphy shook her head. "I thought you'd appreciate the chance to create your own little place."

Callie clutched her knife a moment, about to cut up the toast. Was she really the type to enjoy choosing flowered pillows for her sofa and spending nights in a rocking chair on the porch? Wouldn't she soon miss the bright lights of the big cities she had traveled to, sparkling company, new people? Change, challenges? What Elvira Riggs had told her about spending entire winter days alone in her cottage, translating books and sipping tea, was that cozy and comforting or just kind of claustrophobic?

Suppressing the nerves fluttering in her stomach, Callie chewed on the toast and swallowed it down with a big gulp of juice. "Look, getting the house ready isn't my first concern. Your project for the Fourth is. I need to dive into the town's history to figure out this sensational event you want. What kind of thing did you have in mind?"

Iphy started to say something, when a knock resounded at the back door. Callie sat up straighter, and Daisy barked, running after Iphy, who went to see who was there. She came back with Quinn in tow.

He was wearing a light blue shirt today and beige pants, making him look more like a real estate agent than a handyman. He leaned down to pat Daisy as he said to Callie, "All set to go digging? I thought I could come with you to the newspaper archives and have a look. That way it goes faster."

Callie wanted to say he should be working on her cottage, but realized that as long as he hadn't scraped off all the old wallpaper, she didn't need to worry about new stuff. She nodded her assent. "Sure. I'm almost done with breakfast."

Iphy protested that she was still boiling the eggs and Callie hadn't even had coffee, but Callie was on her feet already, eager to do something and shake the melancholy and doubtful twinge inside. Working on the Fourth of July tea party would take her mind off things.

She said goodbye to Daisy, who couldn't come to the library, and followed Quinn out the back door and around the Book Tea building onto Main Street.

The owner of the general store was just putting his ice cream sign in place while his wife organized the stands with colorful postcards, brochures on regional tourist activities, and magazines about fishing and boating. The coastal vibe was present everywhere in Heart's Harbor.

Quinn gestured to the library. "Fortunately, it opens at eight thirty."

"Oh, you've already been there?"

"Checked on it last night. I was in town to have dinner."

"I see. Where are you staying anyway?"

"At the campgrounds. I should probably cook macaroni and cheese in a pan over the open fire, but I'm not much of a cook."

"Well, once you're done with the house, I'll have to treat you to dinner. The Golden Chef is a really nice place along the highway. They have excellent fish."

They entered the library, and Callie was immediately gripped again by the hushed silence that reigned in the building. Behind the reception desk, the librarian was typing away at a keyboard, but even that sound seemed to be subdued, consciously quiet to maintain that solemn atmosphere.

Quinn made no attempt to approach the librarian, apparently leaving it to Callie, as the local, to phrase her request. She asked for the newspaper archives, and the librarian rose at once, clinking the keys on her key ring. Rounding the reception desk, she came over to them and gave Quinn a once-over. "Back again?"

"I've never been here before. You must be confusing me with someone else."

"That could be," the librarian said briskly. "Your clothes don't look like the clothes of the other gentleman I saw.

Well, we do see a lot of people during the summer season. Follow me."

She led them to a door in the far wall, which she unlocked with a click that gave Callie a jolt of excitement. What spectacular old event might the newspapers be able to unveil?

A spiral staircase led down into the library's basement. Instead of it being a low-ceilinged, claustrophobic room where things stood packed up in crates, it was a high affair with arches and bright lighting, and two long tables where people could sit to do research, while all the old newspapers were carefully conserved along the walls, in filing cabinets marked with dates.

Callie looked around with an appreciative sigh. "What a beautiful research room."

"Yes, we're quite proud of it. But not a lot of people use it. So I'm delighted you want to have a look. Is there anything in particular you're looking for?"

"Some event from town history that made waves." Callie grimaced as she realized how general this sounded. "I guess we'll just have to see if we can hit on gold."

"Yes, I can't really help with such a broad query. But feel free to search right from the beginning." She gestured. "I'll bring down some coffee later on. But please keep the cups on the separate table over there, as we don't want anything to get stained or otherwise damaged."

"We'll be very careful," Callie assured her.

The librarian left, and they heard her steps click back up the staircase; then the door through which she had brought them in closed. On the other side of the door, the click wasn't exciting, but rather sort of menacing. Callie shivered involuntarily. This place did feel a bit like a dungeon.

To shake her uneasy feeling, she marched to a file cabinet and looked at the dates. "I'm in the sixties here. No idea if there's anything worthwhile. Maybe we should focus on the early twentieth century to see if any big inventions were made here? Something that helped the car industry? Or the first fridge, maybe?"

"I think people love something having to do with a famous person. As this is a seaside resort, maybe celebrities came here?" Quinn opened a file cabinet and started to look through the contents.

"I wouldn't exactly call it a seaside resort. I do know the Cliff Hotel is quite old. Maybe it had celebrity guests in the twenties? It could be fun to do an item on them, after the exhibition dancers have done their fox-trot and two-step. Those dancers could even be the ensemble cast as they come dressed for the era. Then we can ask some people from the local theatrical company to play the celebrities. And the dancers come with their own quartet, so if we could discover that some jazz singer came here, I could ask Heart's Harbor Harmony, our local choir, if they can deliver a soloist to perform as that singer."

Callie's mind was buzzing with ideas, and she rushed to the cabinet containing newspapers from 1928 and browsed the headlines. Lots of shipping incidents, cost of fish, a mayoral election gone wrong . . . Nothing really attention grabbing.

She closed the cabinet and moved back to 1926. She felt a certain pressure to deliver something big, for Iphy's sake, but also to prove to the town that her arrival here could be an asset for the community.

Quinn said, "Hey, listen. What do you think of this? *'TV Personality Monica Walker Vanishes from Heart's Harbor.'*"

"Vanishes?" Callie echoed.

"Yeah. It seems that she came here for a few days off, and then she was never seen again."

"Sounds kind of grim." Callie looked at him. "She could be murdered for all we know. I don't think people will really enjoy that." She didn't want to tell him they had had a murder right before Christmas, and it had been hard to solve it, especially because of all the emotions attached.

"No, I read here that they assumed she had a secret lover around these parts and they took off together. The public was really passionate about the case and called in tips. Places where she was supposedly seen, etcetera. But it didn't turn up anything. They assumed she had sailed off, because a local fisherman reported his boat missing. Maybe stolen."

"They think that Monica Walker and her alleged lover stole a boat and vanished with it?" Callie was intrigued in spite of her misgivings about the potential of this story for their Fourth of July tea party. She had always been interested in how people could start a new life somewhere under a different identity.

"Yes. It was a fisherman from Heart's Harbor. His boat never turned up again, although people looked for it in harbors all along the coast."

"Hmm." Callie leaned against a file cabinet. "It must have made waves at the time, but I don't see how we can really turn it into something for the Fourth of July party. I mean, we don't know any facts. Where did she go, with whom did she leave? It would just be speculation about this supposed lover and all. Rehashing of what the newspapers said at the time."

"Not necessarily." Quinn looked at her. "You could do a call for information. You could ask people if they remember something. Maybe you can hit on new information and crack the case."

"After so much time? When did this happen?"

"In 1989."

"Right. Think about it. People won't remember much aside from what the news covered. And they certainly won't be able to offer anything worthwhile."

"Aren't you in the least bit intrigued by the thought we might find out something?" Quinn looked down at the newspaper he had been studying. "I think it would be amazing to delve into such an old case and discover what happened."

"I think it would be a very difficult exercise that would probably yield absolutely nothing in terms of results. How can I sell that to Great-Aunt Iphy?"

Quinn sighed. "Oh well, if you feel that way." He pulled up another newspaper from the same cabinet. "*Pumpkin Harvest Better Than Ever*'? *'Who Stole Farmer Graves's Truck'*?"

He glanced at her. "Not exactly fodder for an exciting reveal on the Fourth."

Callie came over to him. "Let me read those bits about Monica Walker for myself."

Standing at the cabinet, she looked at the photos of a

lively, handsome woman in her late twenties and read about how the public had loved her for her role in the glam soap opera *Magnates' Wives*, in which Monica had played the wife of an aviation mogul who had married her only so she would give him the son that his first and second wives had been unable to give him.

Callie grimaced. "This sounds rather like the history of some European royal families, where matches were made purely for the sake of an heir or to combine lands and power. People tend to call that old-fashioned and even despicable, but from what I read here, marriages for motives other than love remain popular when people have assets to protect."

"I suppose the series was exaggerated," Quinn said. "People love to watch others having a completely different life. Money, opportunity. Power, manipulation."

He shrugged. "That's probably also why Monica Walker was so popular. Because she represented that life everybody wanted to have."

"It says here that she was supposedly away for a few days to relax by the seaside. And she stayed at the Cliff Hotel. That's still there. It's a lovely vintage hotel. We could go there and ask if they know anything but I doubt there's anyone still around who also worked there in 1989. It's simply too long ago."

As she said it, Callie stared into Monica Walker's vivacious eyes. Somehow that picture resonated with her. As if the woman was silently asking her for help.

But that was nonsense, of course. They couldn't find out what had happened to her—not after so much time.

"It can't hurt to put out a call," Quinn said. "Via the newspaper that ran the stories about the disappearance at the time. I bet you, the editor-in-chief will love it."

"They love any story in summer, when there's nothing to write about," Callie agreed. "However, I'm worried we'll be seen as sensationalist for picking up on such an old story. What can we really hope to uncover?"

Quinn shrugged. "Come up with something better, and I'll drop this in a heartbeat."

The librarian brought them coffee, and Callie was surprised to see how much time this had already taken. She didn't feel like digging through stories about pumpkin harvests for much longer. Quinn might be right that a little call for information couldn't hurt. It would, in any case, draw attention to the historical theme of their Fourth of July tea party and maybe induce more people to attend.

She took another swig of the strong mocha coffee and was about to say something, when the librarian popped up again with an apologetic expression. "The deputy is looking for you."

Falk appeared behind her. Looking straight at Callie, he said, "You have to help me with that dog. I didn't sleep a wink last night because Biscuit kept walking through the house, scratching at things. The couple who brought him here have decided they don't want to keep him, and of course I can let them take him back to the shelter where they found him, but they're really not in a happy mood, and I don't want the dog to get even more excited than he already is. You told me I had to take him in for the night. Now he's completely crazy about all the changes, and he's probably wrecking the police car as we speak." Falk raked back his hair. "Look, I have a job. I can't take him along, and he obviously can't stay at my cabin alone. What do we do?"

Callie's mind raced to come up with a solution in which they could keep Biscuit for the moment. She looked at Quinn. "I have an idea."

Quinn hitched a brow at her. "Yes?"

"We'll look into Monica Walker on the condition that you look after Biscuit while you work on my house. We can decide later what to do with him as a more permanent solution."

Quinn wanted to protest, but Callie said, "You're a big, strong guy, so you should be able to get a little cooperation from a young dog."

Falk didn't seem pleased that Callie was calling Quinn big and strong, but before he could speak up, Callie said in a cheerful tone, "Done deal then. We're through here, so we'll go to the *Herald* now to ask the editor how he feels about doing a call for information. You can get Biscuit, Falk, and leave him with us."

Falk sucked in air as if he wanted to start a discussion, but then he said, "Okay," and walked off. The librarian who had hovered at the back of the room darted after him.

"Why do you feel obliged to help him?" Quinn asked Callie. "He's a police officer; he can solve his own problems."

"I did land him with the dog. I suggested he could take

care of it overnight. You see, the owners got Biscuit in a rehoming situation, and they're not happy with him. He isn't the right fit for them, but the poor dog can't help that. I'm worried that this whole thing is just making him traumatized. We have to keep him happy and open to a new family situation as soon as one turns up."

Quinn sighed. "I see. I don't have anything against dogs. I just don't know if I can watch him when I'm doing chores."

"I'm hoping that some exercise will get him tired enough to be calmer when you're working. You could take him to the beach and have him run, play fetch with him. I mean, you can't wallpaper for hours without getting sore. A break here and there is a good idea."

Quinn grinned at her. "Now you're talking."

Outside the library building, Falk was waiting for them at his police car with a very bouncy Biscuit on the leash. Callie took the leash from Falk's hand and leaned down to pat the dog's rough head. "Hey, boy. Good morning. Have you had a nice walk?" She looked up at Falk. "Did you walk him?"

"I took him out before I left the cabin for work, but no, I didn't have time for much of a walk. Maybe you can do it together?" Falk glanced cynically at Quinn. "See you later." And he practically dove into his car.

"He's rather protective of women, isn't he?" Quinn observed.

"What do you mean?" Callie asked, taken aback by the plural used.

Quinn shrugged. "I was at a job last week, and he came breezing in, asking me a ton of questions and acting like I was trespassing, when the lady of the house had hired me to do the jobs. Irritating habit of his."

Callie felt her heart clench at the idea that Falk was involved with other women around town, or maybe just being nice to women in general, while she had thought at Christmas . . .

How stupid.

Quinn gestured in the direction of the newspaper building. "Shall we?"

Callie dragged along Biscuit, who was trying to dig underneath a towering oak tree, and together they crossed the street and made for the invitingly open door of the *Heart's Harbor Herald.*

* * *

Inside the building, a group of teens was standing at a white-board while a woman was writing names underneath photos that had been taped to it. *Victim*, Callie caught in passing, and *witness*. What on earth was that?

Quinn was already at the office door of the editor-in-chief and knocked.

"Enter!" a baritone voice called.

Quinn opened the door, and Callie followed him in, pulling Biscuit along before he could grab at a crinkled piece of paper on the floor.

A tall man with a head full of white hair was standing at

his desk, a half-eaten apple in one hand, a phone in the other. He gestured at them that he would be done in a minute, and Callie looked around the office. The walls were lined with shelves filled with file folders and books, and between the two tall windows several frames held certificates of awards that either the paper or its reporters had won. In a corner a golf bag leaned against a metal filing cabinet. Callie noticed that this cabinet was secured with a combination lock.

The man put down the phone and waved his half-eaten apple at them. "Good morning. How may I help you?" He cast his eye over Biscuit. "If you're collecting money for a good cause, like a shelter or something with dogs, I'm sorry to say we can't run a fundraiser in the paper. That decision was made a long time ago, to ensure I can live in peace with everyone in town. I can't support one cause and not another, but if I gave all of them space in the paper, I wouldn't have room left for any news. You understand?"

"Perfectly," Quinn said. "We're not here to ask for money. We're here to discuss something that might even get you some money."

Callie cringed at the way he presented their idea.

The man raised a brow. "And you are?"

Callie reached out her free hand, planting her feet firmly on the floor so Biscuit couldn't pull her off balance. "Callie Aspen. I help my great-aunt at Book Tea."

"Ah, yes, Iphy—how is she this fine morning?" The man shook her hand. "Joe Jamison, but you probably already saw that on my door." He turned to Quinn. "Not a local, right? I think I did see you around town lately?"

"I'm helping Callie redo her new home. And we're look-ing into an old story to see if it's something to share at a Fourth of July party where town events will be highlighted. I think you might be able to help us. Monica Walker."

Jamison's expression changed for the briefest of moments. The joviality vanished like a cloud passing across the sun, and something flickered in his eyes. Worry? Distrust?

"I'm sorry." He seated himself in his desk chair. "The name doesn't ring a bell. Does she live here?"

"No, we have no idea where she lives. She was a TV star in the eighties, and she was last seen here in town."

Callie rushed to add, "The *Herald* wrote extensively about her disappearance. Weren't you already with the paper then? I think my great-aunt mentioned to me once that you have an impressive forty-year career with the paper."

"Yes, yes, started as a boy getting lunch for the journal-ists. The sounds in here fascinated me, the typewriters and the faxes. Like news was made here, not just recorded."

Jamison gestured around him with his big hands. "I got a small job reporting sports, then I transferred to local news."

"You must remember the Monica Walker case then," Quinn said.

Jamison shook his head. "I was often out of town in summers."

We never said the disappearance happened in the summer, Callie thought silently.

She studied Jamison's face closely, the way he leaned back as he sat, how he held his hands. Was he lying? If so, why?

"Can we talk to someone who worked at the paper on that case?" Quinn asked. "I know it's a long time ago, but—"

Jamison waved a dismissive hand. "I don't remember the names of each and every person who worked at the *Herald* over time."

"But surely you have lists? And"—Quinn dug out his notebook, the same one he had used to make an estimate for Callie's cottage—"I know the name of the reporter who worked on the Monica Walker case. Let me see where I wrote it down."

He scanned the notepad. "Ah, there it is. Jamison. Hey, what a coincidence. You had a family member also working at this paper? Your father perhaps? Or an older brother?"

Jamison's face turned pale. "I don't like your tone. And I don't recall that you told me your name. I don't know what you're after, but I'm not going to cooperate. Please leave my office."

Quinn wanted to say something, but Jamison turned away in his swivel chair. The leather back looked like an impenetrable wall he put up between himself and them. His voice was hoarse when he spoke: "Just go."

Biscuit whined as if he didn't understand the sudden change in atmosphere, and Callie made for the door, ushering out the confused dog.

Quinn followed her, whispering, "He was lying about not knowing anything. He worked on the case himself."

"As you very well knew when you came here," Callie hissed back. "Why did you play it this way? He's upset now, and I can see why. How can we do a public call when you alienate the man who has to help us with it?"

"Like he runs the only newspaper around! And why not use TV? You can ask for information to be mailed to a special email address we'll set up. We could buy a prepaid phone and use that number, but I think it could be useful to have email addresses. Better than phone calls, which can come from booths."

Callie stopped. They were outside again, in the bright sunshine, with the sound of voices from tourists and their playful kids wafting around them. She said to Quinn, "What is this to you? Playing detective?"

Her heart was beating fast. Falk wouldn't like this. She had to stay away from it.

Quinn lowered his voice and spoke earnestly, "Look, you just saw how he responded to our questions. He knows more about it than he's telling us. Isn't that the best proof that we're onto something? You could get an explosive story for your party."

"The party is supposed to be fun for everybody. Unite the town. Not drive people apart." Callie handed Quinn the leash. "You look after Biscuit for a few minutes. I'm going back in to apologize to Jamison. You were very rude."

Quinn called after her that he hadn't been rude at all, but Callie didn't listen. She marched through the room where the teens were still listening to the woman who was filling the whiteboard with notes about some criminal case, and knocked softly at the door. She couldn't hear very well if there was a reply, as it was simply too noisy, so she pushed the handle down and stepped in.

Jamison sat at his desk with his head in his hands. Looking up at her, she noticed the sheer panic in his eyes. He tried to sit up and maintain a stern attitude, but it was obvious he was undone and not quite sure what to say or do.

Callie rushed to say, "I'm sorry about this. Quinn is working on my cottage, and he suggested to me that we could look into some big event for the Fourth of July party that Book Tea is setting up at Haywood Hall. He took me to the newspaper archives in the library, and that's where we found the Monica Walker story. It does have certain appealing aspects. Supposing we could still find out what happened to her? But I had no idea it was somehow . . . sensitive. In that case, we can leave it alone."

"*He* won't let go." Jamison leaned back in the chair and studied her with a weary look. "He's been to my house and talked to my wife. Innocently, of course, over coffee after he had done a little job for us, repairing a leaky faucet. But he asked a lot of questions about how long we had lived here, and so forth, that I really didn't like. I even fought with my wife about it. She defended him, saying he was just a nice handyman who meant no harm."

Callie got a cold feeling as she listened to his revelations, but she didn't speak up.

Jamison said, "I wasn't happy when he came in with you. I'm not sure what he's after."

Callie sighed. "I can't tell you either. I was under the impression that we hit on the Monica Walker story in the archives by accident, but I can't vouch that Quinn wasn't aware that it was there and that he didn't consciously lead me to it." She recalled the librarian remarking that she had seen Quinn at the library before, which Quinn had denied. Had he been there? Had he lied?

Jamison held her gaze. "So what does he want?"

"I don't know. He didn't tell me."

Jamison gestured to a chair. "Sit down." He leaned on his desk, holding her gaze. "Yes, I reported on the Monica Walker story. It was hot news at the time. I interviewed people at the Cliff Hotel, where she had been staying, and at the marina. Talked to the fisherman whose boat was allegedly stolen on the night on which she vanished. I never had a good feeling about the case. I can't explain that, but some people who work with news can tell you the same thing. You have a sort of gut feeling about the outcome. And my gut feeling wasn't good."

He knotted his fingers. "I was somehow certain that something had happened to her. That she had maybe met someone here who . . . put the squeeze on her? Threatened her? She was in the tabloids all the time, you know—she was interesting to people. She had ended a high-profile relationship just a few weeks before she vanished. Did her ex do her in? I can't say for sure that I saw him around town during those days when she stayed here, but he was an actor, a master of disguise. With a wig, makeup, I doubt his own mother would have recognized him."

Callie listened, fascinated in spite of her misgivings about this story.

Jamison said, "I started the assignment with a vague hope I would find her and interview her and show the world that I existed. That the case would be my big break into journalism away from this little town. But you see"—he gestured around him—"I'm still here today."

"So you never found her? Or any trace of her?"

Jamison scoffed. "We never even found that boat that vanished along with her, and I can tell you it was a pretty big thing."

He leaned back and sighed. "It was an odd case. People concluded she had simply wanted out of her life, the pressure it put on her. That she used her so-called 'break' here to disappear. I can't say whether that's possible or not. In the eighties it was easier to just start a new life somewhere. You didn't have all that technology we have today, so I can't say whether she could have slipped away, changed her identity, and is now quietly living someplace, acting like she was never Monica Walker."

"You looked into it at the time. What did you believe?" Callie swallowed before adding, "Do you think someone hurt her?"

"Initially, yes. There was the ex I told you about, and there might have been some crazy fans too. You know, people who think they own a celebrity?"

Callie rubbed her cold hands together. This wasn't the revelation she had been hoping for. "I'm sorry about that. I guess we should just forget about looking into this any further. It's not suitable for our Fourth of July tea party. We want to keep that a family-friendly affair."

Jamison leaned on his desk. "But later my opinion changed. I started to believe she had run away of her own accord. I can't tell you any details, as I promised I'd protect the source, but I had every reason to believe Monica Walker survived. Maybe even is alive today."

Callie stared at him. "But you said earlier you didn't have a good feeling about the case."

"That was my inner conviction, a gut feeling as a journalist. However, you can't argue with irrefutable proof."

"Proof? You have proof about Monica Walker's disappearance?"

"I had a source. I . . ." Jamison stared into the distance for a moment. He seemed to be considering a difficult problem. "Like I just said, I doubt that this Mr. Quinn will give up. He came to Heart's Harbor for a reason. I would appreciate it if you don't tell him what I just told you. And if you continue to work with him . . ."

"What?" Callie stared at Jamison.

"I want to know what he's after. You can tell me, if you stick to him." Jamison leaned closer. "Just pretend I didn't tell you anything worthwhile. Go to another paper or a local TV station, and ask them to cooperate. Take testimonies from people who claim to know something about that last night Monica Walker was in town. See if you can make the puzzle fit."

Callie held his gaze, trying to read the emotion in his eyes. "Why? What do you think can come of that?"

Jamison sighed. "It was a big case at the time, and it left a lasting impression with me. If this man, Quinn, is determined to dig up old dirt, he'll do it anyway, with or without my cooperation. But I would like to know what he can turn up and, most of all, why he's so interested in this old story. He might have plans to harm our town. If you keep an eye on him, you're doing all of us a big favor. Also the police. I know for a fact that Falk is already onto this Quinn character. He seems to think he's up to something, but he can't put his finger on it."

Callie sucked in air. Falk had acted hostile seeing her with Quinn in the newspaper archives at the library. But if he was really interested in Quinn's actions around town, he might welcome her involvement if she could tell him a thing or two. Why not try it, at least for a while? She had already engaged Quinn to work on her cottage and could hardly go back on her given word unless she wanted to reveal to him that others had slandered him.

Was she even sure that Jamison was telling the truth?

Was Quinn really the problem? Or Jamison himself? Did he know much more about the old disappearance case than he was willing to tell? Wasn't it odd that he had mentioned a vengeful ex who was a master of disguise, suggesting someone had been lurking in town, maybe to hurt Monica Walker, but then went on to assure her Monica had run away to start a new life somewhere and that he had proof of that?

Callie took a deep breath. "Okay. I'll continue my search with Quinn. I'll keep Falk posted on everything we find out. He's best positioned to judge what should be done about it."

Jamison shifted his weight in his chair. She couldn't quite determine whether he was relieved about her idea for handling it or upset at the suggestion that Falk would be in on all they discovered and even able to act on what they would learn.

Callie rose to her feet. "I'd better get back to Quinn, or he will think it's suspicious."

*   *   *

Outside Quinn had found a sunny spot on a bench and was sitting there quietly, Biscuit at his feet.

Callie walked over and smiled. "You calmed him down."

Quinn looked up at her. "I jogged a few times around the block with him. He just has a lot of energy. You took your time in there."

"Jamison isn't happy about our plan, and he tried to talk me out of it. But I explained that we want to do something special for the Fourth of July, and that he can understand. I have a feeling he's just frustrated that he couldn't crack the case when he reported on it, and he's worried he'll look foolish if we figure out now what happened."

It surprised her how easy it was to lie and how Quinn seemed to believe her right off the bat. He nodded. "I wouldn't be happy either in his position. But it can't be helped. Now we have to decide what paper to go to next. Or should we go the TV route?"

"It seems you have all of this worked out." Callie stroked Biscuit. She was angry that Quinn had led her to the Monica

Walker story on purpose, that the whole thing had been a setup on his part, while he kept smiling innocently at her. Did he take her for such a fool?

But she couldn't let him know she was onto him. "Should we take your car? I do assume you have a car around here?"

Quinn got up and nodded. "Sure. Follow me."

Chapter Four

"You're on in a few moments," the friendly student assistant said to Callie.

The TV station had been delighted about the idea of asking for information on a cold case, and Callie had been dragged through makeup, received some instructions on how to look best on camera, and studied her lines, all while listening to Quinn's advice, calling Iphy to tell her to watch the show, and trying to keep Biscuit out of mischief. Fortunately, everybody seemed to love the perky border collie and was willing to keep an eye on him while she would be on TV.

The station had a daily live lunch program where people could call in with questions and ideas, and Callie's appeal would be a part of it.

"Walk over there, please, and take the seat," the assistant said. "Remember to keep your chin up, and don't mumble. Speak clearly, as if you're addressing a crowd. You don't have to speak up, since you'll be mic'd, but pronouncing everything clearly is very important."

Callie nodded. Her tour guide experience had to come in handy now. Still, she had never been quite so nervous.

"Three, two, one—and you're on!"

"Hello, viewers." Callie tried to smile as if she was perfectly at ease. "My name is Callie Aspen, and I'm from the Book Tea tearoom in Heart's Harbor. On the Fourth of July, we're organizing a tea party at Haywood Hall, in cooperation with the Heart's Harbor Historical Society, to celebrate the rich history of our little town. Volunteers from the Society will show how life on the coast has changed across the centuries, and exhibition dance group Swing It! will demonstrate how Golden Age dance contests pulled crowds to our beautiful Cliff Hotel.

"You can have your picture taken with an authentic forties fighter plane from a private collection and learn more about Heart Harbor's own World War Two heroes. There will also be a sweet tea competition to celebrate family recipes, so if you have an old family recipe for the best sweet tea in the region, then bring your creations to the celebration, where they will be judged by an expert panel. The winning sweet tea will appear on the menu at Book Tea during the summer season, and the winner can bring five friends to an exclusive high tea at Book Tea. So dig through your recipe books and surprise us on the Fourth.

"But first, we need your help with something special. During our research into Heart's Harbor's illustrious past, we came across an unsolved mystery—something that made waves at the time and is still an intriguing story. In August 1989, TV star Monica Walker traveled here to stay at the

Cliff Hotel. As a beloved member of the cast for the successful TV drama *Magnates' Wives*, she wasn't just an actress, but a celebrity that garnered attention wherever she went."

Callie shifted her shoulders ever so slightly. "Therefore, it's all the more remarkable that Monica Walker disappeared from the Cliff Hotel, from Heart's Harbor, and wasn't heard of again. There have been persistent rumors that she left with a man she loved, to start a new life. We'd like to find out where Monica Walker is today. Wouldn't it be lovely if we could tell the people of our town that she lived happily ever after with the man she loved? The man for whom she gave up her glamorous life? If you know anything at all about Monica and her stay in Heart's Harbor in 1989, please contact us via email or phone."

She then gave the relevant contact information and ended her appeal with a heartfelt thanks to the public.

The assistant smiled at her. "Well done. You're a natural."

Callie rose from the seat. "Maybe, but I'm glad it's over." She felt her blouse sticking to her back. Her palms were covered in sweat, which she tried to remove by rubbing them together. This call for information was just the beginning. What would happen now?

She walked over to Quinn, who squatted, patting Biscuit, who didn't like to be indoors. Or maybe the bright lights and bustle unnerved him?

Quinn looked up at her. "I still think we should have given a special email address, not the address from Book Tea. Who knows what cranks might respond to this call?"

Callie hitched a brow. "If you think it's dangerous, you should have said so."

"I said to use a separate address or a prepaid phone, but you didn't want to."

"I don't see why I can't give the Book Tea address, since I just told people on air that I'm from the Book Tea team in Heart's Harbor." Callie held Quinn's gaze. "What do you know about Monica Walker that makes you so careful?"

"Nothing. I'm just helping you with this Fourth of July thing." Quinn shrugged.

A young man came running up to them. "Our phones are ringing off the hook!" he yelled. "People want to know if we're going to follow your quest to find the truth. They seem to want a TV show about it or something. Updates via social media maybe?"

"Not a chance," Quinn said, cutting him off. "We're going to do this very discreetly to protect the people involved. Once we have some results, we will, of course, share them. But we're not going to turn it into a media circus."

"I have to agree with Quinn there," Callie said quickly. "And we should be on our way now. Thank you for giving us time on the air."

She pulled at Quinn's sleeve to have him follow her.

Outside, Biscuit scratched in the grass, lifted his head to the skies, and yapped.

"I don't like being locked up either, boy," Quinn said, with a smile at the border collie.

Callie said to him, "You better drop me off at Book Tea and then get to the cottage to start on the repairs. Look after

Biscuit for me, and I'll be by later in the day to bring you some food and see how you're coming along."

"If you get an invite to a meeting," Quinn said, "with a witness in the disappearance, you're not going without me, are you?"

"Of course not. Now let's get back to our normal lives. I doubt that we'll hear anything relevant right away."

* * *

Back at Book Tea, Callie found her great-aunt on the phone, writing down something the caller was telling her. Iphy gestured that she would be with her in a minute, and Callie shrugged out of her thin coat, hung it on the rack, and headed into the kitchen.

She had barely washed her hands and poured herself some coffee when Iphy ran in. "Take this before another call comes in." She pushed three sheets full of dense handwriting into Callie's hands. "Some people didn't want to say their names or contact information, so you can't call them back. Oh, there it goes again!"

She ran off to tend to the ringing phone.

Callie stared in mute surprise at the paperwork in her hands. She began to read at the top of the first sheet. "'*Caller doesn't want to give his name. Saw dark car on the coastal road. Woman behind wheel, blonde like Monica Walker. Car at high speed. Reported to the police. Never took any action.*'"

She pursed her lips and read the next entry. "'*Mr. Miller is certain he saw Monica Walker two years after her supposed disappearance, while on holiday in Florida. She was on the beach with a small child. He went over to her and said, "Monica Walker?" The woman immediately picked up her child and fled.'"*

Hmm, maybe just because she thought he was trying to come on to her?

Callie quickly read most of the information on the first sheet, which consisted mostly of rather vague sightings of blonde women or suspicious vehicles that didn't strike her as particularly relevant after all that time had passed, when the door into the kitchen burst open and Falk appeared on the threshold. "Are you out of your mind?" he barked at her.

"Good afternoon to you too," Callie said sweetly, holding the sheets behind her back. "Is something up?"

"Yes, you could say that. You appeared on regional television, asking for information in a cold case, just handing out your contact information as if it's nothing and—"

"I'm preparing a Fourth of July festival about highlights from Heart's Harbor's history. Most people already know that. It's been in the paper and everything."

"Not connected with an unsolved crime."

"Crime?" Callie tilted her head. "So you're sure Monica Walker disappeared against her will? If she left of her own accord, it's hardly a crime."

"She went missing. A missing person is also a matter for the police, not for everyday citizens." Falk rested his hands on his hips. "What am I going to do about this?"

"I thought you'd be happy."

"Happy?" Falk's eyes shot sparks at her. "You think you're solving an old case for me?"

"No. I'm keeping an eye on Quinn. Jamison asked me to. He said you wanted that too."

"Why would I want that?" Falk looked completely confused.

Callie gestured at the kitchen table. "Please sit down so I can explain it to you. Coffee?"

Falk made a gesture of surrender with both hands and sat down. "You thought you were helping me?" he repeated cynically.

"It's a bit more complicated than that." Callie poured coffee for Falk and topped up her own mug, then sat opposite him. She explained how Quinn had turned up at her cottage the other day, offering his help with the repairs and the Book Tea party. How he had brought her to the newspaper archives that morning and had drawn her attention to the Monica Walker case.

How they had visited the *Herald*'s offices and gotten into an argument with the editor-in-chief, Joe Jamison, after which she had returned to Jamison's office alone, to offer her apologies for Quinn's behavior, and Jamison had told her a thing or two about the old case, asking her to look into it and keep an eye on Quinn and report back on his movements.

"He said you also wanted that," she concluded. Adding silently to herself that maybe, just maybe she should have checked that with Falk before she believed it and acted on it.

Falk threw his weight back against the chair with a sigh. "It's true that I don't trust Quinn Darrow. He turned up at Peggy's house, offering himself to do chores for her."

Callie watched Falk's tight expression. "And?"

"And nothing. He did the chores, she paid him, he kicked a soccer ball around with the boys and left. But she was kind of . . . I think she liked him."

Callie leaned her elbows on the table. "You dislike Quinn because Peggy liked him?" She had noticed before that Falk was rather protective of his widowed sister and her kids, but this was taking it too far.

"How do you even know she likes him? I bet she didn't tell you that."

"No, she never tells me anything. Neither do you. I look like an idiot when the other deputy tells me you're on TV." Falk grimaced.

Callie felt a flush rise to her cheeks. "It was all rather spur of the moment, and I thought you knew about it."

"You going on TV?"

"No, that Jamison had asked me to keep an eye on Quinn to find out what he wants in Heart's Harbor with the Monica Walker story."

"Oh, that."

"Yes, that." Callie leaned forward. "Did you or didn't you know about that?"

Falk seemed to consider his answer.

"Come on, don't be so reticent. Just tell me what you know," she urged.

"All right. Jamison gave me a call and complained about a guy who came to his house and did chores for his wife. Over coffee, he asked her questions about how long they had lived here, talked about what a beautiful town it was—you know how those things go—and while he was at it, he managed to turn the conversation to the year 1989 and Monica Walker's disappearance. Now Mrs. Jamison is kind of talkative, and she told him a thing or two about her husband having been so proud of investigating the case. Jamison told me, rather upset, that he wasn't proud of it at all, but that his wife had loved to hear highlights of his career, and he might have mentioned it to her in a certain fashion—"

"To impress her?" Callie ventured.

"Exactly. They were dating at the time, so he must have felt like he had to win her over or something. Now Jamison has asked me to look into this Quinn character and find out what he's here for. I can't just check on people at will. Although I was tempted since he'd also been to Peggy's."

"So you're telling me that you didn't check out Quinn?" Callie tilted her head. "You were tempted, but you didn't succumb?"

Falk took his time staring into his coffee mug.

Callie shook her head. "You did check. Come on, 'fess up. What did you do?"

"I called the Cliff Hotel to ask about possible fraud with credit cards. We're looking into some instances of it—a sure thing in summer, you know. I mentioned Quinn claiming that he had paid for something with a credit card that might be suspect. The receptionist told me at once that Quinn had paid cash, in advance, for ten days."

"Wait a minute!" Callie stared at Falk. "Quinn told me he was camping."

"No, he's not. He's staying at the Cliff Hotel."

"What? But to me he pretended like . . ." Callie was confused, running her finger over the tablecloth. Quinn had suggested he was living a simple life, staying at the campgrounds, eating out because he didn't want to cook macaroni and cheese in a pan. Now it turned out he was staying at a luxury hotel, where he could eat a four-course dinner every night, with fine wines from the hotel's famous wine cellar.

Falk said, "Why would a man check into a hotel and pay cash, in advance? It sounds to me like he's ready to leave at any moment, should some kind of problem occur."

Callie couldn't deny that. "But let's suppose that Quinn is here for a reason. He's looking into the Monica Walker case. Why doesn't he just investigate any leads on his own? Check the newspaper archives, meet with people, ask questions. Why did he agree to help me with the Fourth of July party, and why did he consciously steer me to the Monica Walker case?"

"There are two very good reasons for him to do that." Falk leaned heavily on the table. "First, he wasn't getting anywhere with his own investigation. Yes, he can check newspaper archives, but he won't learn much new from those. And if he asks questions, people might not want to answer or might not consider the topic interesting enough. Now that a TV station is asking for information, people are eager to share what they know."

Or what they think *they know,* Callie thought cynically, remembering all the useless observations Iphy had scribbled down for her on those three sheets she was hiding under the table.

Falk continued, "Quinn knows that he'll get a lot further if he can engage locals to do the digging for him. People like you, they trust you. And besides, Book Tea has a solid reputation. He can just lean back while you get him whatever he needs."

"Needs for what?"

"I have no idea. He could be a journalist or a writer working on a book about Monica Walker."

"Could be." Callie clenched the sheets in her lap. "Why didn't you warn me when we were at the library? I mentioned to Quinn that we could look into Monica Walker. You already knew Quinn had been to Jamison's house about it, so why not tell me not to get involved?"

"Because you mentioned going to the *Herald*'s offices to ask Jamison for help. I knew he didn't trust Quinn, so I was certain he would dissuade you from pursuing it further. How was I to know that Jamison, of all people, would tell you to go through with a call for information? It doesn't fit at all with his earlier anxiety about the Monica Walker story getting stirred up again."

"That's true." Callie sighed. "It's all very odd. And what's the second reason Quinn would use me to help him?"

Falk held her gaze. "You won't like this one."

The concern in his eyes put ice in her stomach. "What do you mean?"

"His other reason for letting you ask for information is that he knows there's danger involved. He's worried that someone won't like him digging into the old case and might take some kind of action. By using you as the face of the campaign, he ensures that any violent response won't find him."

"You mean, he set me up as a target?" Callie asked, her heart pounding.

"Possibly. Either way, I'm not keen on him staying in town. I could ask him to leave."

"If he's a paying guest at a local hotel and just going about his business, you can't make him leave. You know that, he knows that. Besides, don't you think it's interesting that Jamison asked me to keep an eye on Quinn? Why? If he's so sure the case was a dead end in 1989 and can't be solved anymore, why does he even want a new call for information to go out?"

"Maybe he wasn't sure at the time, and he never got over it. Maybe he thinks there can still be a resolution."

"He did mention to me he had proof that Monica lived, so maybe he believes we can actually find her," Callie said.

"Proof? What proof?"

"He didn't tell me. I had the impression it came from a source he's protecting."

"Someone in town?"

"Maybe. He didn't say. I guess he feels uncomfortable about Quinn digging and discovering he's known about it all along. I guess he hopes the source might now also come forward with this proof, and the case can be solved without him having to admit he knew more about it for all those years."

Falk shook his head. "I should go talk to him immediately and force him to tell me what he knows."

"He doesn't have to tell you anything. Besides, if he

believed that Monica is somewhere alive and well, he didn't break any laws. He didn't hold back information that could solve a crime. There never was any crime if she left on her own. In any case, the call went out, and I can't turn it back. People called the TV studio, and they've been calling here."

"Yes." Falk emptied his mug. "I heard the phone ring while we've been sitting here. Nonstop. How is your great-aunt going to work if this keeps going?"

"It will slow down, I suppose."

"Just don't go to a meeting with a supposed witness alone." Falk turned the mug around between his hands. "The new mayor is determined to get the town back on track by not allowing for any kind of irregularities. If he got wind of me going after a visitor to town because he happened to do some chores for my sister, it might cost me my job."

Callie's eyes went wide. "You have a reputation for doing an excellent job. Why would he be able to fire you?"

"I used an ongoing investigation to look into Quinn while I knew deep down he had nothing to do with the credit card fraud. I was using my work for a private matter. That was wrong. I knew it the minute I did it."

He looked at her. "But now you're involved with this Quinn character too, and I feel like . . ."

Callie's hear skipped a beat. What if Falk got into trouble, even lost his job because he was trying to protect her? "You shouldn't do anything that can get you in trouble. Okay? I know how much you love your job. I can take care of myself, honestly. I won't go meet people on my own.

Besides, I don't think we'll dig up anything of special interest at all, so you can rest easy."

Falk didn't respond. He was studying her with a probing look.

Callie pressed, "Please don't cross any lines for me. It really isn't worth it. I mean, your job is so important to you."

Falk turned away from her and left the kitchen without saying goodbye. She wasn't sure what was eating him, but he seemed different from the way he had been in December.

Or had she just been fooling herself, believing he liked her? Was he just a good cop and a man who cared for the people in the town, without attaching any special meaning to her or their connection?

Had she forgotten that he had barely responded to her emails as she had been getting ready to come out and live here? And when they had finally met again, he had asked right away if her stay was temporary.

Maybe he had hoped it was—just another holiday, seeing each other as friends, then they'd each return to their own lives again?

She shook her head with an impatient sigh. What Falk thought or wanted didn't matter. She had to refocus on handling the call for information about Monica Walker.

Most of all, she had to make sure she wouldn't get caught up in whatever game Quinn was playing here in Heart's Harbor, getting friendly with people, lying about where he was staying, what he was up to.

Thing was—and it gave her a chill to think about it—she was afraid that she was caught up in it already.

Chapter Five

Callie took a felt-tip marker and wrote on the cardboard to her left: *Dinner at the Cliff Hotel around seven (four witnesses). Wearing a gold top, black pants, and high heels.*

She stopped for a moment to rub her forehead. The calls had kept coming in, and Iphy had enlisted her to take them while she herself tended to her Book Tea guests again.

Taking the calls herself had enabled Callie to ask additional questions about details, and although some people couldn't tell her much, others had been quite specific about what they had seen at the time. They had also told their stories to the media back then, which made it easier to check to see if their memories had become blurred over time or were still as crisp and clear as ever.

Slowly a picture began to emerge of the night on which the TV star had vanished. Times, places. And particularly the moment after which everything had gone blank. After which Monica Walker had vanished from the face of the earth. Gone without a trace.

Callie startled when somebody knocked on the kitchen

window. She turned her head and stared out into the darkness. She could just make out a tall figure. Male?

She went to the door and opened it a crack, bracing herself for a hand reaching out for her to push past her and get inside. "Hello?" she asked in a trembling voice.

"It's me, Dave Riggs. You met my wife the other day. I work at the lighthouse."

"Oh yes, of course." Callie blinked. "I'm surprised to see you here in town. I heard you live on the beach most of the time."

"I do. I love water. I grew up beside it. I sat in boats even before I could walk." Dave smiled at her. "Can I come in for a moment?"

"Of course." Callie stepped back. She felt slightly silly that she had believed some menacing stranger was lurking at her door. It was just a friendly local. "I'm having some juice. Would you like some?"

"No, thanks. I won't stay long. I don't want Elvira to know I came here."

Callie hitched a brow at this rather curious statement. She gestured to the kitchen table so he could take a seat.

Dave glanced at her notes, and too late she realized she should have covered them up. She quickly overturned the sheets as she sat down to face him.

"That's why I'm here." Dave nodded at her paperwork.

"Monica Walker?" Callie asked in surprise.

"Yes. I already lived here when she vanished." Dave studied his hands. They were sun-tanned and muscled, with a scar on the back of the right hand.

"I know. Elvira told me that your family has tended the lighthouse for generations."

"That's right." He smiled a moment, before continuing with a serious expression. "I met Monica Walker the day before she disappeared. At the lighthouse."

"I see."

Dave shrugged. "There was nothing special to it. She wanted to see it and know how it was operated. I think she mentioned something about plans for a new TV series that would be set on the coast. She wasn't here to vacation, but to experience the coastal lifestyle."

Callie pursed her lips in disbelief. "From a series about millionaires' wives to one about a small-town idyll? That seems like a stretch."

Dave grinned. "You can say that again. She was a real beauty queen. Lots of makeup, fake lashes. Long nails. Dyed hair. I couldn't really picture her as a woman living by the sea and doing manual things. But I guess a good actress can play any part."

"So she was here to look into coastal life for a new series? Does that also mean she was going to quit *Magnates' Wives*?"

"Well, she did mention something along those lines. And that her bosses weren't happy about it. But she needed a change after her relationship ended. She was still quite upset about that; I could sense it." He stared at his hands.

Callie's mind raced. If Monica had really wanted to quit the successful series, that gave people a reason to be angry with her, maybe even to come after her to her quiet hiding place along the coast and threaten her to rethink her decision.

She tried to put it into words carefully, feeling Dave out rather than putting words in his mouth. "You met the day before she vanished. Did you notice anything about her that might give a clue as to her mood? Was she planning something? Or anxious? Worried?"

Could someone have followed her to Heart's Harbor?

Callie tapped her pen on the table. "It makes no sense, you know. If you tell me she was prepping herself for a new series, why would she run away and not let anyone know where she had gone to?"

Dave shrugged. "I have no idea. I just wanted you to know that she came to the lighthouse, in case people mention it. It might look odd. But there was no special reason for it. Just sightseeing."

"Were you alone at the lighthouse when she came to see it? You weren't married to Elvira yet?"

"I was, yes, but we had married abroad, and she still had to wrap up some things to be able to come live with me, so she wasn't in town yet."

"I see." Callie turned the cardboard with her reconstruction of the last hours back over and studied it. "And you have no idea what happened to Monica on that last day? What she did, who she met?"

"I know she dined at the Cliff Hotel that night." Dave rubbed the scar on his right hand. "I helped some friends with fishing, and when we brought in the fresh catch for dinner, I saw her walking through the lobby."

"What was she wearing?"

"A gold top, I think. Something glittery." He smiled

sadly. "I think she felt obliged to look glittery because people expected that of her. Must be very exhausting."

He pushed himself up. "Well, that was all I had to say. I'd appreciate it if you didn't mention this to Elvira. She's happy in her own little world. Better to keep it that way."

Callie looked at him. "Didn't she see the broadcast this afternoon, my call for information?"

"We don't have a television at home, but I caught it when I was having lunch at a roadside café. I was picking up some stuff we use in our treasure hunts."

"I see." Callie used her pen to push against the felt-tip marker on the table, rolling it away. "You can't hide the old case from her forever. She's bound to see some newspaper article about it. It will make waves, I suppose."

Dave sighed. "You know . . ." He shuffled his feet. "Elvira didn't have an easy life before she met me. She didn't believe in good people or good places. Heart's Harbor has been a very good place to her. I want her to keep feeling that way."

Before Callie could even respond, he walked to the back door and disappeared into the night.

Callie sighed. Maybe she should never have let Quinn talk her into this. What had they set in motion? How many people would be affected by this? And all probably for nothing.

Still, as she looked at the cardboard in front of her, with her reconstruction of Monica's last hours in Heart's Harbor, that provisional time line, she felt like something was staring her in the face. Something important.

But she couldn't quite make out what it was.

* * *

The next morning Callie came down with a head full of fluff from dreaming about glittery tops on dogs that ran away across a rocky beach while a boat came up from the sea with the letters *Monica* on its bow.

Yawning as she walked into the kitchen, she didn't find Iphy there. A few uncut oranges lay on the counter, suggesting Iphy had wanted to make some juice. Had a phone call interrupted her breakfast preparations?

In the far corner of the counter, on some plastic foil sat a tiny marzipan picnic basket with a bit of a bottle and a baguette sticking out. Iphy had created a woven look to the basket, and the bottle of green marzipan even had a tiny beige cork. "So cute!" Callie exclaimed. "I knew she could make this work. Iphy? Iphy!"

Itching to tell her great-aunt how perfect this was as decoration for the Fourth of July treats, Callie rushed into Book Tea and saw Iphy at the window, standing on tiptoe to look into the street. Her expression betrayed deep concentration while she angled her head for the perfect view. Callie grinned mischievously as she approached her softly and then suddenly put her hands on Iphy's shoulders. Iphy yelped and stepped back, almost on Callie's foot.

"Guilty conscience?" Callie asked with a wink. "I never knew you loved peeping."

"There's something wrong at the newspaper building." Iphy's tone was worried, her expression tense. "The police are there."

Callie's mouth went dry. "The police?"

She stretched her neck to look out at the angle needed to see the building in the distance, and indeed caught the flash of blue lights. The lights were only necessary in an emergency. *What was up?*

"I'll have a look. Okay?" Without waiting for an answer, Callie turned the lock on the tearoom's entry door, opened it, and headed out into the street.

Several people were gathering at some distance from the *Herald*'s building, talking and pointing. Callie passed them without stopping to ask anything.

At the building, the door was open, and she could look in. A woman stood in the room, her hands up to her mottled face. Callie walked in and asked her in a soft voice, "Are you alright?"

The woman looked at her and whispered, "He's dead. Our boss is dead."

Callie froze. "Joe Jamison? Dead?"

"Yes. I found him." The woman sobbed into her hands.

Callie left the woman to herself and closed the distance to the office quickly. She kept her hands clenched together in front of her so she wouldn't accidentally touch anything. This was a crime scene, after all.

She went in and saw Jamison's desk as she had seen it the other day, his swivel chair empty behind it. The file cabinet with the combination lock stood open. Falk leaned over to it, wearing thin white gloves, apparently intending to take something out of it.

He heard a rustle and looked up. "What are you doing here? Get out."

"I want to help you. That file cabinet was closed the other day. I think Jamison kept really important stuff in it. He was nervous when we talked about Monica Walker."

Falk straightened up. "I can figure out for myself what happened here. Please leave."

Callie held his gaze. "I need to know something." She ignored the shaking in her knees and the light feeling in her head. "Is Jamison dead because of the Monica Walker case? Did I . . ."

Her throat was tight, and she could barely get the words out. "Did I cause this?"

Falk looked her over. "I don't know that. I can't tell from a dead body on the floor what killed him or who did it or why. I just need quiet to work it out."

A dead body.

Jamison was lying there, dead! The man who had asked her for help. Who had also told her he had always had a bad feeling about the disappearance. A gut feeling. Had he been right? Had he died because of what he knew about the summer of 1989?

Callie couldn't believe it. "I feel terrible about this." Her voice shook. "I set this all in motion." She sensed how cold her hands were. Like she was freezing from the inside out. "My call for information . . ." She desperately wished she could turn the clock back.

Falk shook his head. "You didn't set it in motion. That guy Quinn Darrow did. And if we find his fingerprints on anything in this office, he'll be locked up before he knows what's happening."

The ferocity in his tone struck Callie. Moments ago he had said he didn't know who did it or why. Now he seemed to suspect Quinn and was looking for evidence to support this assumption. Fingerprints on the scene. But . . .

Callie said, "Quinn was here with me yesterday. He may have touched things. I can't remember exactly but it doesn't prove he was involved in this death."

"It's not just prints I want to look at. There's also something here beside the body that I think might give us a nice clue."

"What is it?"

"That's none of your business. I recall having asked you now, several times, to leave. Do you really want the other deputy to come in and escort you out by force?"

"No, of course not, but what's that on his desk?" She angled her head to get a better look. Paper, blue, a marked spot. "It looks like a map of some kind."

"Callie . . ."

"I'm going, I'm going." Callie backed away, still careful not to touch anything. Her disbelief and guilt mixed with determination to find out what on earth had happened here. What had Jamison known? What did Quinn know? Why hadn't they worked together? *Only one way to find out. Talk to Quinn.*

Or would that be dangerous?

Was Quinn the killer?

But why? Why would he kill Jamison? Jamison had been so adamant to Callie that she not tell Quinn what Jamison had told her, so if Quinn hadn't had any idea that Jamison knew more, why would he have wanted to kill him?

The locked file cabinet. It was open now. Did that mean anything?

Her heart pounding, Callie left the newspaper building in a hurry, brushing past the still crying woman who had found the body.

Outside, another police car had pulled up, and the deputy was securing the perimeter. He saw her and called out to her, "Hey, what are you doing? You're not allowed to be in there."

"I'm already leaving," Callie assured him. "I, uh . . . I gave Deputy Falk some pertinent information." It was a lie, of course, but she could hardly tell him she had needed confirmation that this death wasn't her fault. Her head was spinning, and she could barely think straight. "I'm going back to Book Tea right now. I don't want to hinder your work."

He looked like he didn't believe her for one single moment, but she flashed him a forced smile and was off again, back to Book Tea's familiar welcoming front.

Once inside, she leaned against the door and closed her eyes a moment. What a total mess! If only she had never let herself be dragged into it. As soon as she found out for sure that Quinn had led her to the Monica Walker story on purpose, she should have told him to pursue it on his own.

Iphy asked softly, "And?"

"Joe Jamison is dead. Murdered probably."

"What? At the newspaper building? How?"

"I don't know. I didn't see the body. Fortunately." Callie snapped her eyes open and faced her great-aunt. "I can't help feeling like it's all my fault. This whole Monica Walker thing. I even enjoyed it in a way. The call for information on TV, people responding with all of these clues, and I believed we might find her and present her at the Fourth of July celebration. A story like you might read in a magazine. All's well that ends well, right? Well, this ended in disaster!"

"Wait a moment." Iphy placed a soothing hand on her arm. "Jamison asked you to go through with the call for information. He wanted it to happen. Didn't you tell me that?"

Callie nodded. "Yes, he did. It somehow felt like he was looking for resolution. I can't quite explain it, but it was important to him. Very important."

"There you are. He asked you to do this for him, and you did what he asked. You wanted to help him. Now it turns out that someone isn't eager for this old story to be revived, and that person came after Jamison. After *him*, mind you, and not after you."

"Me?"

"Yes. Your face was on TV. If someone was just angry about the old matter getting attention again, they could have come after you. Why Joe Jamison? His name wasn't mentioned in your call for information."

Callie hadn't thought about it that way. "You mean, someone must have suspected he knew something and killed him to keep him quiet?"

"Exactly. We have to figure out who it is and why Jamison had to die."

Iphy's face scrunched up. "If Jamison wanted a new look at the case, he didn't know the solution. Or at least he was doubtful. He wanted confirmation. So what did he know that caused his murder?"

"Hopefully Quinn can tell us. I'm going to grab a banana from the fruit bowl, and then I'm driving out to the Cliff Hotel to find him. He's the only real lead we have, since he obviously knows a lot more than he ever told us, so I want to know exactly what he's looking for in our town."

Iphy followed her into the kitchen. "Are you sure that's wise? Falk won't like it if you tell Quinn that Jamison is dead before he has a chance to do so."

Callie picked up a banana and then looked at her great-aunt. "I think Falk believes Quinn already knows. I had the distinct impression he believes that Quinn is the killer. I want to know what Quinn's involvement with Monica Walker is before he's arrested and locked up. I might not get a chance to talk to him again and hear the truth. I'll confront him at the hotel with people around so he can't hurt me. I'll be super careful. Promise."

* * *

At the Cliff Hotel most people were still in the breakfast room. On a long table, baskets of rolls, plates of scrambled eggs, brie and other cheeses, cold cuts, and towering fruit bowls invited the guests to come choose whatever they wanted. Waiters brought coffee and tea while a woman in white refilled a basket with croissants. They smelled like they were fresh from the oven.

Acting like she belonged there, Callie walked among the tables, looking for Quinn's tall figure and blond head, but couldn't find him. At last she asked someone from the staff and heard that he hadn't been there the night before. They had no idea where he had gone and even if he would be back.

Perplexed, she left and considered her options. Maybe he really was at the campgrounds like he had told her?

But if he was sleeping in a tent, why had he taken a room at a pricey hotel and paid for it in advance? None of this made any sense.

Callie drove out to the campgrounds and talked to the proprietor, who directed her to the area where Quinn's camp was supposed to be. Campers had spaces to themselves, but they weren't far apart, so she could be sure that if she screamed, someone would hear her. As an extra precaution, she clutched her phone in her pocket, her finger poised to hit the call button.

She found a small red tent pitched underneath a couple of trees. A wobbly canvas chair was outside beside a gas stove for cooking. Closing in on the tent, she heard a deep snore.

She leaned over and listened better.

"That's not me," a voice said behind her back.

Callie almost jumped a foot off the ground and spun around to see Quinn standing with a paper bag in his hand. He held it up to her. "Not many luxuries when you're camping, but I do love fresh bread. Want some?"

Callie shook her head. She nodded at the tent. "Who's in there?"

"Biscuit. He has a mighty snore for such a small dog."

Callie had to laugh despite her tense mood.

Quinn gestured at the canvas chair. "You sit there, and I'll sit on the ground." He plopped down into the grass and crossed his legs, tearing open the bag and taking out a croissant. It smelled just as inviting as the ones at the Cliff Hotel had. Callie's half-empty stomach growled.

Biting into the fresh croissant, Quinn chewed with his eyes closed, as if in pure bliss. The morning sun shone on his face, and Callie wondered for a moment if she could be staring at a murderer. A pleasant-looking, friendly-acting murderer who would be willing and able to kill again as soon as he understood what she was here for.

Falk had warned her not to do anything alone, and here she was, all alone, with Quinn. Within screaming distance from other people maybe, with a phone in her pocket to use, sure, but still . . .

It was a lot lonelier out here than it would have been in the Cliff Hotel's breakfast room.

She really needed to think things through better next time.

If there was a next time.

She spied around casually for something heavy to strike him with, should he attack her, but there was nothing suitable in sight.

Quinn said, "You could have called me. I gave you my cell phone number."

"Yes, that's probably the most convenient when you have two places to stay and can't tell people where you'll be at any given moment. I was at the Cliff Hotel, and they said you hadn't been there all night."

Quinn hitched a brow. "Do you think I can bring a dog like Biscuit into the Cliff Hotel? He'd wreck the room. I had to find another place to stay."

Of course. That made perfect sense. Still, she was determined to confront him with what could euphemistically be called "incongruities" in his story. "You told me you were camping here before you even had Biscuit."

Quinn looked her over as if her stern tone confused him. "Why the third degree?"

Callie shrugged. "I felt like a fool asking for you at the hotel when you weren't even there. People know me around here, and I care what they think of me." She nodded at the croissant in his hand. "Any good?"

"Delicious. Now what are you here for? A hot lead from the calls about Monica Walker?"

"Well, I do have a lot of information now."

Quinn surveyed her. "Really? Something we can work with?"

"I have no idea since I don't know what you're after."

"Finding out where Monica Walker disappeared to."

"At what cost?"

Quinn froze. He narrowed his eyes. "What do you mean?"

"Well, I don't see any clear reason why it would matter at all to you what happened to this woman who was a TV star thirty years ago. If she ran off to be with a man she loved, or to escape the paparazzi or whatever, do we really have to go after her and trace her? If she was trying to get away, then wouldn't being found again just make her unhappy?"

Quinn seemed dumbfounded by the suggestion. He held her gaze, his blue eyes flickering like a computer when it's processing information. "You think she doesn't want to be found?"

"That's possible." Callie took a deep breath. Without telling him about Jamison's murder, she wanted to provoke him into betraying his agenda. "We're looking at this as a nice little search of the past to enliven our Fourth of July party, but it might not be so easy for her."

He waited a moment. "Or for others involved."

Now it was Callie's turn to be puzzled. She tilted her head. "What do you mean?"

"If there was a man she vanished with, what about him? And what if somebody from town helped them get away? Think of the boat that vanished as well."

"The fisherman reported it stolen."

"Maybe he was told to do so. Maybe he was even paid to do so. What do we know? If it turns out he lied about the theft, he might get into trouble."

Quinn seemed to relax now that he had the lead in the conversation. He took another bite and chewed. Then he swallowed. "Well, whatever the case, we've started now, and we can't turn back. Whether Monica Walker wants to be found or not is not for us to speculate about."

"Are you with the press?" Callie sprung the question out of the blue, hoping to surprise and trap him.

But Quinn looked genuinely confused, then began to

laugh. "Excuse me? You think I'm some journalist who needs a big cover story?"

"Isn't that possible?"

"I can't prove I'm *not* a journalist, can I?" He leaned back, putting both of his hands flat in the grass. The paper bag rested beside him. "What do you want to see? The press card that I don't have?"

Falk wasn't going to like this attitude. Quinn would be behind bars soon. She had to corner him and wring some answers out of him before he was locked up.

"You seemed to know Jamison." Before Quinn could protest, Callie added, "I know you did chores at his home. You talked to his wife. About Jamison's work on the Monica Walker disappearance."

Quinn shrugged. "Is that forbidden?"

"No. But it is a pretty big coincidence that that particular topic would just *happen* to come up, after all those years. I would think there are more natural things to talk about over coffee—the weather, activities around town. The grandchildren you saw in a photo on the mantelpiece. You get my point? You led the conversation to it. You wanted to know more. So, did you contact Jamison again? Maybe last night? Have a meeting with him at the newspaper building?"

"Certainly not. Why? The information was coming to us now. From witnesses, people who knew a lot more than Jamison ever did. He didn't want to help us at all."

If Quinn believed that, he might not have killed Jamison. But maybe it was an act of anger? A need to lash out at a man who had insulted him?

And what had that map on Jamison's desk been for?

Callie said, "Have you taken a boat out since you've been here?"

"No. I'm not very good with boats. Why all of these questions?" Quinn studied her. "Do you think I'm taking action on all this behind your back?"

Callie smiled. "Well, you did lead me to this story on purpose. The woman at the library said she had seen you before. You denied it, but it proves you've been there before. You knew exactly what I would find and that it would pique my interest. You used me."

Although she said it in a pleasant tone, putting it into words made her realize how angry she was about it all. The hot lava streaming through her stomach took her breath away. She wanted to just reach out and grab and shake Quinn. He had used her, and now there had been a murder. Someone had died because they had stirred up a hornets' nest.

Quinn said tightly, "It's for a good reason, Callie. You'll see."

"I want to see now. Tell me. Explain it to me."

"No. Not now. We need more first."

"So you admit you used me?"

"I admit that I knew that there was an interesting story in those archives, and I helped you find it. You wanted something big for your event: now you have it." He added after a few moments' thought, "I also knew that you and Iphy had helped find a valuable family heirloom that disappeared during a Christmastime tea party you hosted at Haywood Hall.

So I thought Monica Walker's story would appeal to you, and you might have the skills to help me figure it out. When Iphy put the notice up on the bulletin board that she was looking for a handyman, it made sense to apply. I could do your chores, and you could help me with Monica Walker's disappearance. Win–win."

Callie swallowed hard. "Did you also hear about the other thing that happened at Haywood Hall while we were catering the tea party there?"

"I heard there was a death, yes, and that you figured out who had done it. Which only goes to show you're really good at sleuthing, so"—Quinn made a gesture with his hand—"I was even more convinced I needed your help."

"And you couldn't have just asked for it? You had to go through this whole cloak-and-dagger routine, offering yourself as handyman to Iphy and then leading me to the Monica Walker story at the library?"

"I thought you'd be more likely to help me if you knew me a bit. I could hardly turn up out of the blue at Book Tea and ask for your help. Why would you get involved with a perfect stranger? However, if I was already working on your cottage, it would look more . . . natural."

"And innocent?" Callie pressed. "Did you have any idea that our call for information might be dangerous?"

"Dangerous?" Quinn echoed. He sat up and frowned at her. "Have you gotten weird calls? There are always people who use something like this to do a little heavy breathing. That's why I told you to use a separate phone number for it."

He fell silent. Callie perked up as she heard sirens in the distance. That was fast.

Quinn also turned his head to listen. "What's that?"

"Time for me to leave." Callie shot to her feet. But Quinn was faster. In a heartbeat he was up from the ground and grabbed her by the arm.

Chapter Six

Quinn hissed to her, "Did you turn the police on me? What did you tell them? I'm not a criminal."

Callie winced in pain under the pressure he was exerting on her arm. She tried to look calm as she countered, "If you're no criminal, you have nothing to fear."

"No?" Quinn huffed in frustration. "I know Jamison didn't like me asking questions. Now you asked the police to come here, and what for? I don't get it. I'm taking care of your dog for you."

"It's not my dog!" Callie struggled to be released. "You used me and never told me what this is all about."

"Let go of her!" a voice called. "Back away from her right *now*."

Quinn turned to Falk, who was holding his hand on his weapon, ready to pull it from its holster.

Releasing Callie, Quinn raised both his hands in an apologetic gesture. "I was only asking her why she called the police on me."

Falk closed in on Quinn. Once he reached him, he jerked

Quinn's hands down and behind his back, putting the cuffs on. "I'm arresting you for the murder of Joe Jamison."

"What?" Quinn turned deathly pale. "Jamison is dead? Murdered?"

"What a nice little act," Falk said in a scathing tone. "Isn't that what Callie already told you?"

He glared at Callie. "You should be happy I'm not arresting you as an accomplice."

"Why? What did I do?"

"You came out here to warn him. He might have fled."

"Callie didn't tell me anything about any murder," Quinn protested. "She was just mad at me for using her to get information in the Walker case."

"You're a journalist," Falk spat.

"Yes, I admit it."

Callie stood rooted to the ground. *He admitted it.*

Her mouth went sour. She had just trusted the totally wrong person. And once word got out about Jamison's death, the media would pounce on it, relating it to the Walker case and the recent call for more information. People would assume she had known Quinn was a journalist and had worked with him to get some sensationalist story. They'd hate her for it. This was a nightmare.

"Come on. You can tell your story at the station." Falk dragged Quinn away to his car that was parked out of sight.

Callie turned to the tent and opened the zipper. Biscuit came to her right away, dancing around her. She put him on the leash and went after the deputy and his prisoner. She was sure that Falk wouldn't listen to anything she had to say right now. She was also sure she wanted to say absolutely nothing to defend the stone-cold liar that Quinn had turned out to be.

But deep down inside, she just wasn't sure he was a killer. She somehow felt like there was more to it than that.

* * *

Falk beat her to the police station and was already inside with his prisoner when Callie arrived. She pushed through the double glass doors, keeping Biscuit beside her. He wasn't very upset about Quinn's disappearance from the camp site but seemed to think it was some sort of game they were playing: *Look for Quinn.*

Inside the station, he sniffed the floor and barked, pulling Callie to the left as if he wanted to say, *"Here is the trail—just follow me and we'll have him in no time."*

Callie followed him as far as the little corner where visitors could sit. Biscuit wanted to continue, into the corridor that led to the interrogation rooms, but Callie called him back. "We're going to wait for Quinn here," she said softly, brushing Biscuit's head.

He looked up at her. She expected he would try to pull into the corridor anyway. But he seemed to sense that she was tense and serious, and lowered himself onto his bottom beside her. He whined and pushed his head against her leg, and she sat down in a chair and sighed, rubbing his ears.

What a mess. Falk would never trust her again. He

believed she had actually rushed out to warn Quinn and help him escape arrest. Of course she hadn't intended any such thing, but . . .

Her conversation with Quinn hadn't yielded anything useful either. Especially not when she took into account that he had probably been lying about every single thing he told her. Imagine him laughing off the suggestion he could be a journalist and then admitting to Falk outright that he was.

Callie leaned back against the plastic chair, feeling thoroughly humiliated. She wanted to rush in there and tell Quinn he had used her not just when he had suggested the Monica Walker case to her as if it was all a big coincidence, but all over again that morning. With his nice little act of knowing nothing about Jamison's death. How could he!

The doors opened, and a woman walked in. Her blonde hair was pulled back in a ponytail, and in her jeans shirt and pants she looked like a cowgirl.

Callie rose from her seat and waved. "Peggy!"

Peggy turned her head and saw her. "Callie! What are you doing here?" She closed in on her. "Are you here for my brother? Is he in?" Her voice sounded eager.

Callie nodded. "He's interrogating someone. Do you already know about—"

Peggy lowered her voice, glancing toward where the other deputy was typing away at a keyboard. "The murder? Yes. I came to Book Tea to discuss some details for a tea party with Iphy. Then I saw all of the commotion. Is it true that . . ."

She took a deep breath and glanced around again, as if she was worried about being overheard. "Is it true that Ace thinks Quinn has something to do with it?"

Callie tilted her head. She had never called Falk by his first name yet, as everyone always called him by his last name, which fit him quite well. For a moment she felt sad at the idea she might never get to call him Ace, as their friendship seemed to have dissolved and he was livid at her for her part in the current trouble. She said quickly by way of a distraction, "Well, he has Quinn in there right now, so I suppose that means he does believe Quinn had something to do with it. But how do you know Quinn?"

She knew of course that Quinn had done chores for Peggy and had played soccer with the boys, but she wanted Peggy to tell her side of the story.

Peggy sighed. She gestured to the seats, and they both took plastic chairs, side by side. Peggy leaned over. "Quinn came to town and was looking for small jobs to do. I miss having a man around the house, and I asked him to do some chores for us. He really hit it off with the boys. They love him."

Peggy swallowed, knotting her fingers in her lap. "I was a bit worried about that, you know. Quinn is only here for a while, and Tate and Jimmy might get attached to him and be upset when he leaves again."

"That's always a risk, of course."

Peggy continued, "Ace didn't like Quinn from the get-go and suggested to me that he might have an ulterior motive.

Some reason to be in town. Like conning people or something. I told him he was a total idiot."

Callie cringed at Peggy's brutal assessment. "Falk is just worried for you and the boys. After all, it's possible for a con man to come to a small town in summertime and—"

"Yes," Peggy said, cutting her off, "but Ace won't give me an inch to move. I do have my own life. It's so Ace to think that the moment I hire a handyman, I'll get conned. Of course I won't. I know what I'm doing."

Callie thought of how Quinn had probably been lying about everything he had told anyone here in Heart's Harbor, and her heart clenched for poor Peggy when she found out about that. She didn't deserve more misery in her life.

And how about the boys who liked Quinn so much? Could he really be a coldblooded con man who used people, including widows and children, to attain his end?

Peggy continued, "I told Ace that I could hire whomever I wanted, and he was not amused. I bet you he's only grilling Quinn now because he doesn't like him." She fidgeted with her watch's band. "He has nothing to do with the murder. He didn't even know Jamison."

"I'm afraid that isn't exactly true." Callie held Peggy's gaze. It might be better if she broke the bad news to Peggy herself. Peggy wouldn't believe Falk, and it would be bad if she had to hear it through the town grapevine. "I was in Jamison's office the other day with Quinn because we wanted to ask how much Jamison knew about the mysterious disappearance in 1989 of a TV star. Quinn thought it would make a nice item to speak about on the Fourth of July tea party that Iphy is setting up."

"And?" Peggy's eyes were wide and questioning, not understanding how it all fit together.

"When we got there, I had the impression Jamison and Quinn had some sort of tension between them. I also know for a fact that Quinn did chores for Jamison's wife. Jamison wasn't happy that Quinn was asking a lot of questions."

"He's just a nice, open, considerate man. He doesn't ask questions because he's after money or anything."

"Peggy . . ." Callie put her hand on the other woman's arm. "Please hear me out. Quinn hasn't suggested this Monica Walker thing to me by coincidence. He's here to look into that case. He's a journalist. He's after a story, and he . . . well, I can't put it any other way than that he used me to get at what he wanted."

"I don't understand."

"He let me do the call for information on television and gather all the clues that came in so he could use them."

"But I thought that you yourself wanted something spectacular for the tea party."

"Of course, but Quinn didn't tell me honestly that he was with the press or how much he actually knows about the case. I'm worried he knows much more than he told me, and because I was so ignorant, I stuck my head into a hornets' nest. Especially now that Jamison is dead."

"I don't see what his death has to do with it. Maybe Jamison simply had a heart attack."

"I didn't see the body, but I don't think it was a heart attack. It must be foul play or else Falk wouldn't be taking action now."

Peggy scoffed. "Ace just wants Quinn to be involved. Then he can tell me with a smug smile that he was right all along saying Quinn couldn't be trusted. But I don't believe it."

She continued in a pleading tone. "Callie, you also met Quinn. He's perfectly nice. He doesn't have some hidden agenda. He came here to spend a quiet summer in a small town. He told me he was raised in one, and this brings back so many good memories for him. I saw in his smile that he meant it."

Callie wasn't sure what to say.

Should she cruelly dispel the notion that there was any good in Quinn?

Or accept that maybe he was a man with two faces, a nice side and a business side where he was ruthless in pursuit of the story he wanted?

"Tell me this," she said to Peggy. "Can't a man be charming and at the same time use that charm to get things his way? Yes, I admit that Quinn has a very disarming way of asking something and that he is really very nice. But that can also make him the kind of man who—"

"Manipulates women." Peggy crossed her arms over her chest. "Sure, that's what Ace is going to say. He's going to argue that we were both blinded by Quinn's smile and never saw that he was a con man."

Callie felt a little irked to be included on that list, but she had to admit that she had the same instinctive need to defend

Quinn that Peggy seemed to feel. Maybe he was the sort of man who wrapped women round his little finger and always got away with everything?

Peggy said, "We have to help him. We have to prove he has nothing to do with Jamison's death."

"But how?"

"Well, for one thing, we could find out where he was at the time of the murder. Maybe he has an alibi."

"If he does, he'll be telling that to Falk right now."

Peggy looked up when they heard a thud. "Is that the sound of a door?" Just then Falk popped out from the corridor. He saw them together and froze a moment, tilting his head as if to assess why they were there.

When Callie and Peggy both rose and came toward him, Falk lifted both hands in a defensive gesture. "I have nothing to say about it, ladies."

"Are you going to charge Quinn?" Peggy asked. "Have you checked whether he has an alibi? Does he even have a motive? He barely knew Jamison. Why would he want to hurt him?"

Falk said, "He told me a thing or two I'm going to check on."

"When?" Peggy put her hands on her hips. "Have you already locked him in a cell? Do you enjoy this?"

Falk's eyes flashed. "He's still in the interrogation room. With a colleague who's keeping an eye on him, so don't get any thoughts into your heads."

"I don't intend to help him escape," Callie rushed to assure Falk. "I only came here to explain to you what I was doing with Quinn when you found us together." She felt Peggy freeze at the mention and hoped her newfound ally wouldn't rush off in anger at this revelation.

Falk said, "I really don't want to hear it right now, Callie." He reached up and rubbed his forehead as if he was already tired, though his working day had only just begun. "I can't think of any valid excuse for entering a crime scene, asking me questions, and then rushing off to inform the main suspect of what happened."

"But I didn't tell Quinn about the murder. I only wanted to know why he hadn't told me that he knew more about the Monica Walker case. He led me to it for a reason. I need to understand why."

Falk scoffed. "Money, a promotion at the paper. His name splashed across the front pages. Does it really matter?"

"What matters," Peggy said, "is that you're working on a case when you're prejudiced! You never liked Quinn, and now you're looking for ways to involve him and keep him here."

"I don't have to look for ways to involve him. He *is* involved. He went to Jamison's house and talked to his wife. He needed information and he tried to get it from Jamison's own family. How low is that? Then he tried to put pressure on Jamison via Callie. Taking her to the newspaper offices, mentioning the case was about to become hot property again. Jamison felt cornered. You told me that yourself."

The latter was said to Callie.

She had to admit he was right about that. "Jamison was agitated, yes, and he did ask me to keep an eye on Quinn and find out what he was really after, but—"

"And you agreed to that?" Peggy exclaimed. "You let yourself be used that way? To spy on Quinn?"

She stepped back as if she couldn't stand to be near Callie. "I understand perfectly now. I don't have to expect anything of either of you. Goodbye!" And she marched off.

"Peggy!" Falk called after her. "Peggy, don't be silly."

But his sister had already walked out the door.

"I don't want to know what she's up to," Falk said between gritted teeth. "I'm only glad I have Quinn here, and she can't get into any trouble with him."

"But if he's not the killer," Callie said, "and Peggy starts poking around . . . She just told me she wanted to find a way to clear Quinn of the murder charge."

"What?" Falk ran to the doors. A few moments later he came back in, shaking his head. "She just drove off. I'll leave a message on her phone. Meddling is dangerous."

"So you don't really believe Quinn's the killer? You think he or she is still walking around free?" Callie asked.

"I just told you I'm going to check on some things that Quinn told me. Until I know more, I'm not drawing any kind of conclusion. I don't even have an accurate time of death yet."

"But the medical examiner will have told you whether Jamison was killed this morning or late at night. Surely he didn't spend the entire night in his office, so it has to be one of those."

Falk looked her over. "Clever," he said in a cynical tone.

Callie pulled her shoulders back. "I just want to help. Jamison confided in me. He asked me to keep an eye on

Quinn because he was worried. Now he's dead. I feel like I let him down."

"Nonsense. You did nothing wrong."

"What about that map on his desk? Is it related to the Monica Walker case?"

"I'm not giving out any kind of case-related information. It's too early. And even if I decide to do so at some later time, it will be to people who are supposed to know it. Not to a citizen who—"

"Is just a pain in the neck?" Callie added contritely.

Falk sighed. "Look, Callie, you did a good job in December. I admit I couldn't have figured it out without some of the information you supplied to me. But this is different. It has nothing to do with any friends of yours like it did back then. You have no reason to get involved."

"But I do. Peggy is set on defending Quinn. If she starts investigating on her own to clear his name, she might get into danger. I can keep an eye on her for you."

Falk scoffed. "Is this some kind of emotional blackmail?"

Before Callie could say anything, he added, "If it is, it's working. I can't stand the idea of Peggy sticking her nose into this. It's too dangerous. She has two small children to consider."

"Right. So let me do the investigating. I can tell her I'll share everything with her. Iphy will also agree it's better that way. Come on. Please?"

Falk rubbed his face again, apparently none too eager to give her carte blanche.

Callie pleaded, "Look, I also have a ton of information

about the Monica Walker case that people called in after my TV appearance yesterday. I think there are might be valuable bits and pieces in there that can help with the Jamison murder now. Provided both cases are connected, of course."

She gave Falk a probing stare.

He looked away from her, then returned her gaze and sighed. "All right then. Yes, I do think they're connected somehow. I don't think that Jamison happened to die just as the cold case he once worked on was opened up again."

"Good. That's one thing we agree on. How about this deal? I'll give you everything I know in exchange for an open mind on your part about Quinn. I'm personally mad at him for the way he used me and how he lied to me, even right before you arrived on the scene. He told me when I asked about it that he was no journalist. Then to you he suddenly admits he is."

Falk shook his head. "There's something about the whole story he gave me that doesn't gel. That's why I have to look into it."

He pointed a finger at her. "You know what? You go to Book Tea and get all that information you claim to have. Then come back here. I should know a little bit more by then. We'll sit down and talk about it. How does that sound?"

Callie was a little miffed about his word choice—"claim to have"—like she had lied about it or exaggerated its importance, but she nodded her assent readily enough.

This was her ticket into the investigation, and she intended to use it the best way she could.

Chapter Seven

At Book Tea, Callie was relieved to see Peggy's car parked outside. As she came in via the back entrance, she already heard Peggy's indignant voice explain to Iphy, "Callie is in cahoots with Ace. That's the last thing I would have expected of her. I don't know what to do now. I want to help Quinn. But if I can't trust Callie, can I even trust you? Whose side are you on?"

Iphy responded in a calm tone, "I think you misunderstood Callie. And of course you can trust me. I liked Quinn from the first moment I laid eyes on him. I'm a pretty good judge of character, and while I think he was a bit furtive about a thing or two, I can't picture him as a killer. I think we should help him—at least look into ways to brush up his image with your brother. So he can be released again."

"Good. But how do we do that?"

Callie entered and said quietly, "I think I can help there."

Both women turned to her, Iphy with a welcoming smile, Peggy with a hostile stare.

Callie quickly explained, "I'm here to pick up the notes

collected after the public call for information yesterday and give them to Falk in exchange for an inside look at the investigation. It will give me some leverage to plead for Quinn."

Peggy pursed her lips. "You don't trust Quinn yourself."

"Quinn lied to me. Several times. Or at least he twisted the truth. I want to know why. If we're going to defend him against a murder charge, we'd better make sure we know we're defending someone who's truly innocent."

Peggy seemed to want to protest, but Iphy nodded at her. "Well put."

Peggy hesitated and considered Callie's words. At last she said with a sour expression, "I suppose you're right. We would look pretty stupid if he turned out to be guilty anyway. But I can't see how he could be. Why would he kill Jamison?"

"We can't know that," Iphy said, "because we have no idea why Jamison was killed. I assume the murder was meant to silence him. He investigated the Monica Walker case at the time. The topic made him jumpy. That suggests he knew more than he ever told people."

"But why?" Callie tilted her head. "Why keep your mouth shut about something for almost three decades? He was a journalist at the time, just starting his career. If he could have cracked a case that made waves, he could have built his name fast. He might even have had a chance to go to New York or the West Coast. Why keep silent and stay here? I mean, I don't want to demean his career, and it's lovely he became editor-in-chief of the *Herald*, but it's not exactly the résumé he must have dreamed of when he started out."

"Not all people are quite that ambitious." Iphy stared

ahead thoughtfully. "Maybe he knew some facts that could be incriminating but weren't vital to revealing Monica's whereabouts. Maybe he decided he wasn't up for a fight with the person who would be incriminated and could sue him for slander. Or maybe it wasn't until he heard what Quinn was digging into that he put two and two together and saw a pattern, a clue that he hadn't seen before. Maybe only then he started to suspect a certain concrete person of involvement in the old disappearance."

"But," Callie said, "if that person then came and killed him, we have to assume he or she is in Heart's Harbor."

"Indeed. So perhaps we're dealing with a local who helped Monica disappear and who is now eager to keep that story under wraps."

Callie stared at her. "When you say 'disappear', do you mean alive or . . . dead?"

"To be honest, I'm not sure. When you first mentioned this case to me, I thought it was very possible she had sailed off to wedded bliss with a man she loved, leaving all of the pressure and paparazzi behind. But right now, I'm not so sure. Would it really matter after thirty years if we found out where Monica Walker is today? That is, if she's still alive. If we found out that she had died and could even recover a dead body . . ."

Iphy clicked her tongue. "Then we'd have a case again, right? A murder case."

"But even if someone feared that a new look at the events could turn up the fact that Monica died, why would he or she be worried that the cause of death and the perpetrator could still be established? I mean, after thirty years there can't be much left of a body."

"That depends." Iphy frowned hard. "I think I read in the newspaper once that archaeologists had found a skeleton and could establish that the person had died an unnatural death. I don't remember how exactly, but I can imagine that, for instance, damage to the skull can still be seen even after a body has mostly decayed."

Callie nodded. "Yes, of course. Damage to the skeleton could give some indications. So you think that someone who knows how Monica died wanted to prevent a discovery of her body and an investigation into the cause of her death?"

Iphy spread her hands. "It's a mere possibility. You never know how people will react to an unexpected turn of events. Maybe someone got upset about the call for information and agreed to meet Jamison at the newspaper building to talk about it. They got into an argument, and the unknown person killed Jamison. It doesn't necessarily mean that whoever killed Jamison also killed Monica Walker."

"Of course not. But why would someone be upset about the call for information if he or she wasn't involved in Monica's disappearance?"

"I have no idea. Maybe a local person knew some things at the time, and Jamison persuaded them to stay quiet about it? Maybe the person feels bad about it now and approached Jamison again? Or maybe a local saw something at the time that never made sense and suddenly saw the light? You don't know how the human mind can work."

Callie considered these options. "Either way we have to

keep this in mind: if Quinn isn't our killer, then the killer is still free. And if the killer is a local who is somehow connected to the Walker case from 1989, we have to be very careful about who we share any information with. Because if that person is really so eager to keep this all in the past . . ."

Peggy had listened in silence to their conjectures. Now she asked in awe, "You really think he or she might come after us too? To kill us?" Her eyes were wide.

Callie assured her. "You don't need to do anything in this case. Falk would also rather—"

"Yes, of course." Peggy's eyes flashed. "I bet he told you to scare me out of my wits with the suggestion that there's a murderer on the loose who might come after me, so I won't help Quinn. But I'm no coward, and I'll do anything to get Quinn released."

"Peggy," Iphy said in a soothing tone, "your shift is starting soon. The murder will be the talk of the town. Keep your ears open, and note everything you hear. In the previous case, gossip shared in Book Tea helped us along as well."

Peggy looked doubtful. "Really?"

"Really." Iphy smiled at her. "Let Callie go to Falk with the information she's gathered already. She has more leeway with him than we do, you know."

Callie's cheeks flamed at her great-aunt's semi-innocent tone, but she rushed up to go collect her information and return to the police station to exchange it for something hopefully worthwhile.

* * *

When Callie got back to the station, Falk informed his colleagues that he would be back soon and left the station with her. Having expected to talk in Falk's office, Callie was quite stunned at this sudden turn of events. He ushered her to his car and drove off, taking a few dirt roads that seemed to lead nowhere. Then suddenly they were at a vantage point with a stunning view of the sea below. Falk produced a thermos and two cups and poured steaming coffee for them both.

"I need to clear my head every now and then. At the station there's always calls coming in, people stopping by to complain about something, a colleague with a question or stacks of paperwork to fill out. If I want to have a breakthrough, I need the quiet to see the bigger picture, a perspective that I lack when I'm too close to the case. This is my hideout."

Callie's eyes were a little teary from the strong wind blowing in her face. At least she told herself that that was the reason and not the fact that Falk was showing her something personal, even though he had every reason to distrust her or even hate her for having rushed out to Quinn right after she had left the murder scene.

She knew she'd had her reasons, but considering objectively how it must have looked, she knew it seemed bad. And he should hate her for it.

But for some reason he was giving her coffee and sharing these private moments with her. It threw her off balance and made her forget she had wanted to be strong and bargain with what she held.

Falk said, "Quinn is no journalist."

"What?"

"I said Quinn is no journalist. I have no idea why he claimed to me that he was while telling you he wasn't, but he did tell you the truth. He's no journalist, so his interest in the Monica Walker story isn't professional."

Falk sipped his coffee. "He tried to convince me of that all during the interrogation. He even claimed he had a wager with a colleague that he could turn up new evidence, something that would get him a lot of money."

He glanced at her. "Sounded believable and was enough to get me even angrier at him and the trouble he's caused in our town. For a bet? But a few phone calls proved that he's not known at the newspaper or the websites he claimed to be working for. Not even as a freelancer. In fact, I can't find any evidence anywhere online that he's ever published anything. He doesn't have a website or blog, doesn't showcase his clippings anywhere, isn't on networking sites either, so how on earth would people find him to hire him? Of course, he could still be writing a book or something that he's keeping close to his chest. All I can establish is that he has no journalistic track record to speak of. Question is, of course, why would he be so eager to sell me this truckload of lies?"

"Because he has another reason for being here, and he doesn't want you to find out about that. He must have believed you would readily accept the journalist angle and not check on it further."

"Exactly. I checked his records, and I ran his fingerprints through the system. He isn't known to us. So if he is a con man, he never got caught."

"There's a first time for everything, I suppose."

"Yes, of course, but the typical pattern is that they get caught or someone does file charges, and they move on to another state. Quinn is in his forties already. Is it possible he would never have been caught? Can he have a clean record if he's really a confidence trickster? I doubt it."

"Maybe he had a nice job, got fired, and then started to make a new career out of using his charm."

Falk looked at her. "Are you suddenly seeing the light about him or only trying to placate me?"

Callie shrugged. "We're standing here together. Do I need to placate anymore?"

Falk laughed softly. "I don't forget that easily, Callie. I don't want to ruin this case with a prejudice. And I don't want to invest all my energy into feeling cheated."

"I didn't do anything to deceive you. Honestly." Suddenly Callie's throat was tight. She had come here to Heart's Harbor believing she and Falk were friends at the least and potentially even a lot more. He was the one who had been acting differently toward her since she'd returned, cold and distant. Acting like he didn't remember how it had been between them at Christmas. It confused her and made her do things she might otherwise not have done. Oppose him, seek confrontation.

"If Quinn is a criminal," Falk said, "we have no records of it. Nothing to hold him on. And as far as the Jamison case goes, Quinn's prints are in the office, but you already told me that he was there, and he even told me that himself, so I can't really use that. Next to Jamison's body on the floor was a disposable paper tape measure, like handymen use. Of course those are quite common, but this one had Quinn's fingerprints on it. If he lost it in Jamison's office, it's quite coincidental that it ended up right beside Jamison's body."

"Could it have been planted on purpose, to lead you to Quinn as the alleged killer?"

"It's possible of course, but how would the killer have secured a tape measure with Quinn's prints on it?"

"He did odd jobs for lots of local people."

"True, but if someone had already snatched the tape measure when Quinn was doing a job at his home, they must have planned to kill Jamison ahead of time. No argument in the office, no blow struck in anger. Premeditation, going so far as to implicate an innocent man in the crime. Why?"

"I don't know. I'm just trying to explain the discovery of Quinn's tape measure beside the body. It does incriminate him. If you also have prints on the murder weapon . . ."

"We don't know what the murder weapon was. Judging by Jamison's head wound, the weapon must have been blunt and heavy. The killer might have brought it along and taken it with him."

"Or her." Callie looked at his profile. "Or do you think the murderer was so strong that it couldn't have been a woman?"

"It might certainly have been a woman." Falk glanced at her. "Jamison was struck down while his head was in a low position. Probably when he was going through the file cabinet to find something. When you strike a blow that way, it takes less force than when you have to reach up."

"I see." Callie tapped her coffee cup. "Could the killer have picked up the weapon in the office? Someone who had been there before could have noticed the presence of a convenient weapon at that time. Something heavy to strike with and maybe even make it look impromptu? If the killer wanted to incriminate Quinn, the scene could have been set up for you to conclude it happened like this: Quinn comes in, argues with Jamison, grabs a weapon at hand, bashes him on the head and runs off with the weapon but loses his tape measure."

"I'm not excluding any possibilities yet, so I certainly considered whether the weapon came from the office. But Jamison's secretary was in shock after finding the body, so I didn't want to take her into the office to have her check if anything was missing. But as soon as she's up to it, I'll do that. If we know what we're looking for, it will be easier to find it."

"There's a lot of water around town. If the killer removed the weapon because fingerprints were on it, it might have been thrown into the ocean. It has to be heavy, you just said, so it would sink right away."

She eyed Falk with a frown. "It did strike me when I was in Jamison's office that there was a combination lock on that file cabinet. Like he didn't want anybody getting in there. But can we seriously believe he was hiding something in there relevant to the Monica Walker disappearance? That he had it in there since 1989 and never did anything with it? It seems like such a long time."

"I agree. My colleagues are checking everything in the cabinet and making a list for me."

Falk pushed himself up on the balls of his feet. "Isn't the quiet here the best? I can always think better when I'm here."

"It's beautiful. Thanks for showing this to me." After a pause she added, "And that map on the desk? Did it come from the file cabinet?"

"It might have."

"Does it have anything to do with Monica Walker?"

"Could be." Falk glanced at her. "I don't know yet, and once I do know, I will share it with people who need to know."

"I'm not trying to interfere. I'm just thinking . . . Monica vanished and so did a boat, right? A boat that a fisherman claimed was stolen? Did Monica sail away to wedded bliss, as Iphy puts it, on that boat? Or did the boat vanish to suggest that she left? Maybe she never left. Maybe—"

"She died here around town? Maybe, but I can't start digging at random. Besides, there have been a bunch of building projects in the last few decades. The site where she was buried might now be the new mall."

"I see." Callie finished her coffee. "That was delicious. Thanks." She handed him the cup. Their fingers touched as he accepted it. She wanted to ask him why he hadn't answered her emails and why he had been acting so different since she had moved back, but it seemed odd to ask. What if he said he didn't understand what she was talking about? It would be so awkward. Falk said, cutting through her thoughts, "What do you have?" He held her gaze. "Remember, I told you that Quinn is no journalist and how Jamison was killed. Now it's your turn."

"I know, and I have something for you." Callie reached into the bag she had slung over her shoulder when leaving Book Tea. "I received a lot of calls the other day. Some information was so vague and pointless I just couldn't do anything with it."

"Now you can experience firsthand how we have to work in an investigation when we ask the public for tips. There's just so much fluff going around, of course from well-meaning people who sincerely believe that they're helping the case, but it can be hard to dig out what's real."

"Yes, I do see that now. However, I did manage to put together a time line of Monica's actions during the last hours she was still seen around town. I have it here." She handed him the cardboard.

Falk studied it. "Aha. Her outfit could be important if we do at some point come across . . . you know."

"Clothes decompose, right?" Callie asked with an unconscious shiver.

"Yes, but sequins don't. Neither do high heels." Falk studied the time line more closely. "I see she was in public places. She could have been seen there by some disturbed fan or admirer."

"Who then came after her and killed her?"

"Well, imagine the fan asks for an autograph, and Monica doesn't feel like it. There's an argument, a struggle. She could have taken a tumble, hit her head. The fan was shocked and, to conceal what he did, hid the body."

"And stole a boat to make it look like she left? It sounds too well planned for someone who killed on impulse, almost by accident. If the stolen boat was part of the plan, it must have been better prepared than that."

"Yeah, you're probably right. That doesn't quite fit. Yet." Falk held up the time line. "Is it okay if I keep this?"

"Of course." Callie didn't tell him that she had an identical one back at Book Tea. "If you think it might help."

Falk lowered it with a sigh. "I hope it can. Look, despite what I think of Quinn, I realize that I might be focused on an innocent man right now. That, whatever he wants with the Monica Walker story, he did not kill Jamison. I owe it to him, and to justice in general, to do the best I can. But it's not going to be easy. There are too many unconnected dots."

Callie took a deep breath. She wondered if she should share with Falk that Dave Riggs had turned up at Book Tea the other night and had acted kind of weird, claiming Elvira couldn't know anything about him meeting Monica Walker the day before she had vanished. Could it be that Dave had been smitten with Monica? Could he be a killer? Of both Monica Walker and Jamison?

Jamison, who might have known or suspected that Dave had been involved back then?

Callie shivered as she considered that her next-door neighbor might be a murderer. Had been for three decades, while peacefully living with his wife and tending to the lighthouse.

Falk said, "Well, thanks for this, but I have to get back to the station. I want to have another talk with Quinn now that I know he lied to me about being a journalist."

"Are you going to keep him locked up?"

"I don't know yet. That probably depends on what

forensics can come up with on short notice. And how he reacts to new questions. If he keeps working against me, I could hold him just for obstructing the case."

"Don't hold him just for the sake of holding him."

Falk slapped the cardboard against his thigh. "I'm not sure he's guilty of anything, but I'm not certain he's innocent either. You keep that in mind when he gets out again. We have no idea what he actually wants."

Chapter Eight

A t Book Tea, all the outside tables were taken. The neat red-and-white-checkered clothes on them moved in the mild breeze that tempered the sun's warmth. People sat talking over maps to plan a bicycle tour or a boating trip, while enjoying their teas with bookish treats. In passing, Callie saw that the Hound of the Brownievilles was quite popular: brownie bites shaped to form a dog figure running across grass made from marzipan.

Some kids were sampling Grimm Tales, a plate with several cookies in fairy tale shapes and with colorful frosting forming cute details.

Peggy stepped out the door just then, carrying a tray with lattes and cappuccinos, while in the kitchen Iphy put the final touches on a large cake. With her tongue between her lips, she attached tiny marzipan roses to the trellis on a miniature cottage. "Where Darcy asked Elizabeth Bennet to marry him. For a birthday party of Austen-mad friends who will arrive in, say"—she checked the silver watch on her slender wrist—"twenty minutes. How did it go with Falk?"

Callie made a so-so gesture. "It seems Quinn lied about a lot of stuff. Like an elaborate smokescreen almost. Falk is not amused and is looking for a way to keep Quinn locked up. He thinks he could be dangerous."

"He wants to keep him away from Peggy," Iphy concluded.

Callie nodded. "That too. I must admit it's off-putting that Quinn lied. I mean, why would he do that?"

"We'll have to ask him as soon as he's out again." Iphy put the cake in the fridge. "Can I get you some coffee?"

"No, thanks, Falk gave me some." Callie didn't tell her great-aunt it hadn't been at the station. The amazing beauty of his private hideout still struck awe in her: the sea; the horizon with the thin clouds, like a panoramic oil painting; the red kite from some local kids, a lone dot against the azure skies; the boys' excited cries carrying far on the clear air.

She could understand so well that Falk needed that place to create clarity in the muddle in his mind whenever a case was developing in three different directions at the same time and he wasn't sure what leads to follow and what to dismiss. He didn't have time to go after everything, especially not with the sheriff out of town.

Iphy said, "I'm so sorry for Jamison's wife. I gave her a call to express my condolences."

"And?" Callie studied her great-aunt. She knew her well enough to be certain that while Iphy meant it when she said she was sorry for the new widow, she had also been eager to learn something—anything—that might help the case. After all, it was also in Mrs. Jamison's interest to find out who had hurt and killed her husband.

121

Iphy stared at the floorboards in deep thought. "She was very upset about Quinn's arrest, blaming herself for having told him things about her husband's involvement in the Walker case. She seems to think it's directly related to his death. She told me, in tears, that ever since it came up again, her husband hadn't been himself. That he had slept badly and had stayed away from home late at night."

"Like last night?"

"Yes. She went to bed around eleven thirty, and he wasn't there yet. This morning, when she woke up, she thought he had already left for the office again. He often left while she was still in bed. He usually made her coffee and brought in the newspaper, laid it out, ready for her on the counter. This morning there was no coffee and no newspaper."

Iphy looked up with sadness in her eyes. "Strange how little things can tell us something is wrong even if we can't put our finger on it just yet."

"Does she believe Quinn killed her husband?"

"I'm not sure. She seemed to like him. I asked her outright if she knew of anybody here in the town who might have been involved in the case at the time and who might be able to help out now. She said that the former owner of the Cliff Hotel might be able to tell us something. He sold the hotel years ago, but he still lives around these parts. We might go and see him."

"That's a good idea. But can you leave? The birthday party is about to arrive."

"I know. I thought you might go alone. Take Daisy and Biscuit for cover."

"Cover?" Callie asked, surprised.

"Yes, I heard from Mrs. Jamison that the former owner of the Cliff Hotel—Mr. Bates his name is—is a keen artist, and he likes nothing better than doing pet portraits. I thought you could ask him if he could do a portrait of these two. He'll need to take a picture of them to work from. You can have a look around his studio and maybe turn the conversation to the murder."

Callie grinned. "That sounds pretty devious, but doable. I'll go right away. Where is this studio of his?"

Iphy wrote down the address, and Callie left, with the dogs, to find her artistic source.

Mr. Bates's pet portrait studio turned out to be a half-wooden, half-brick villa situated among pines, with hydrangea bushes in pale blue and pink set close to a cute outdoor seating arrangement. Callie knocked on the door and studied the miniature portraits of two dogs that were attached to the doorframe underneath the wooden banner reading "Bates Studio."

Barking from the inside suggested these were the artist's own pets, guarding the studio.

Callie picked up Daisy and tried to keep Biscuit behind her, to avoid any confrontation, as soon as the door opened. But when it did, she just saw a friendly-looking man peering back at her. He had a shock of white hair and light blue eyes. His appearance was rather unkempt, his shirt full of paint stains, and his bare feet were stuck into oversized, threadbare slippers.

"I locked up the dogs in the bedroom," he explained.

"They don't like intruders in their home. Ah, what a cute Boston terrier. Very distinctive face. Oh, and a border collie. They can be hard to capture. I don't want just the energy, but also the intelligence and the loyalty. They are a misunderstood breed. Come in, come in."

Callie followed him through a hallway full of antique trinkets, ranging from a marble umbrella stand to a coat rack created from deer antlers, into a living room with large windows that gave the room extra light. Several easels carried portraits of dogs, horses, and even a goat, each at different stages of completion. The floor was partially covered with paint-splattered sheets, and there were half-full paint pots, used brushes, and discarded pencil and charcoal sketches everywhere.

Biscuit tried to attack a bronze statue of a bear, and Callie gave him a sharp order to sit down and stay.

Biscuit looked up at her with an innocent expression.

Callie didn't smile. Her heart pounded as she worried the eager dog would knock something over, damaging the artworks of this kind gentleman. She might be able to pay for the canvas and paint but could never repay the long hours he had spent creating these stunning likenesses.

"Do sit down." Mr. Bates gestured to a faded velvet couch full of cross-stitched pillows. "Throw off any pillow you don't need. And the dogs are welcome to sit on it as well. That's what it's for."

Callie put Daisy down on the couch and grinned as the Boston terrier snuggled against a pillow and made a satisfied sound. She pulled Biscuit to her and had him sit, brushing his back and scratching him behind the ears. She told Mr. Bates how she had come to be in possession of Biscuit, while the man poured her some sweet tea from a large jug without even asking if she wanted any. The ice cubes in the jug tinkled against the glass.

"Very sad," Mr. Bates said. "People feel sentimental when they are in a shelter, and they want to give the dog a better life. But they don't understand that it will take effort to change things around. Dogs can be like naughty little children. They need to be told what they can and cannot do."

He handed her a glass of sweet tea. "Secret recipe."

"Really? You have to come to the Fourth of July party at Haywood Hall, then, and participate in the sweet tea contest. The winner will receive a high tea for six at Book Tea, and their creation will be put on the menu as well." Callie sniffed and took a sip. "Very refreshing, with a spicy undertone. Does it have a name?"

"Not really, but I could think of one. The Fourth of July, you say? What time does it start?"

"The party starts at four PM, and the judging for the contest takes place between six and seven. We expect a lot of entries."

"I see." Mr. Bates settled himself in a chair that was as faded as the couch, and stretched his legs. The threadbare slippers had paw prints on the soles.

Biscuit looked at the man's feet. His ears turned forward. Bates shuffled with his right foot and then suddenly flipped the slipper up in the air. Biscuit jumped forward, pulling away from Callie so abruptly that her tea sloshed over the rim of the glass. Biscuit grabbed the flying slipper in mid-air and shook it.

"Well done," Mr. Bates said with a grin.

Callie put her glass down on the side table and snapped her fingers to lure Biscuit to her. "Give me the slipper, boy. That's a good boy." She shook her head at Bates. "You shouldn't get him all wild."

"I don't mind wild dogs. There's not a lot they can break here."

"They could ruin your artwork!"

"They usually have a lot of respect for it, as if they know it means something to the people I'm making it for. Dogs are very sensitive." He nodded at Daisy. "She's reproaching your young friend for being so wild, but I can see in her eyes that she also feels sorry for him. She knows he doesn't have a home."

"I'm hoping to find him one." Callie bit her lip, realizing she had secretly counted on Quinn keeping him. There had seemed to be some sort of instant connection between the two of them, and she'd thought Quinn would have time to work with the dog and gain his full trust.

But Quinn was at the police station right now.

Quinn might even be a killer who might never be free again.

Mr. Bates studied her with interest. "Are you staying here for the summer?"

Callie wanted to tell him she was moving back here to

help her great-aunt run her tearoom, when she suddenly thought that maybe a little white lie would take her further as it could start the topic she was here for. "Yes. At the Cliff Hotel. I think you owned it once? They told me about you there."

As she said it, Callie hoped that the current employees at the Cliff Hotel did tell guests about the former owner and his new vocation as pet portrait painter. Otherwise, Bates would be onto her lies in a heartbeat.

To her relief, he nodded. "Yes, they often send clientele my way. It keeps a connection alive. Although it was ages ago that I sold the hotel. I have nothing to do with it anymore. So if you have a complaint about anything, from the cooking to the bedding or the mattresses, you'll have to turn to the receptionist."

"No, it's fine. Luxurious, really. I just can't imagine being in charge of such a wonderful old hotel. It must have had so many famous guests over time."

"Oh, yes. We had musicians, politicians, movie stars." Mr. Bates settled better into his chair, wriggling his bare toes.

Biscuit stared at his foot, and Callie made sure to hold on to his collar tightly so he couldn't make a move for the toes this time.

Mr. Bates said quietly, "I suppose you think I can tell you something about Monica Walker?"

Taken aback, Callie stared at him.

"Surely you didn't think you could remain incognito when your face was all across the TV screen just a day ago."

Mr. Bates spoke in a teasing rather than reproachful tone. "I bet you're not staying at my former hotel either. You told the viewers you were with Book Tea, on Main Street."

"That's right." Callie felt a fiery flush settle in her cheeks. "I'm sorry. It seemed like a nice conversation starter. I just wanted to . . ."

She figured that honesty might be the best policy from here on out and so explained with a rueful sigh, "I'm in a bit of a pickle right now. I made that call for information the other day, and this morning someone was murdered. The two things might be related."

Mr. Bates studied her. He didn't seem very shocked at the mention of murder. "Who died?"

"Joe Jamison, editor-in-chief of the *Heart's Harbor Herald*. He was also the local reporter on the Monica Walker case at the time she disappeared."

"Oh yes, I remember him all right—buzzing about the hotel like an obnoxious fly, asking all of my guests impertinent questions. Where they were on the night of the disappearance, if they had seen something, maybe overheard a conversation. They were there to vacation, not to accommodate the press. Even if someone famous had disappeared without a trace."

"Have you ever felt like"—Callie searched for the right words—"Monica didn't leave of her own accord? That maybe she was kidnapped or something?"

"I can't imagine that." Mr. Bates sounded certain. "I spoke to her hours before she was last seen. She was lively, happy, even sort of excited, like she was about to do something she had been looking forward to for a long time and couldn't wait. When I heard she had vanished, I was certain she had run off with a lover."

That was in line with what other people had told her and what the general opinion about the case had been—Monica eloping. "But why the secrecy? Why not just say she wanted to quit the series?—"

Mr. Bates gestured with both hands. "She would be hounded still. She wanted peace and quiet, a normal life. I remember her putting it exactly like that. I came to her hotel room door, you know, with some bouquets that had been sent to the hotel for her. Admirers and fans often sent her flowers and packages with gifts. Perfumes, even jewelry. Quite expensive too. Monica looked at the cards attached to the bouquets, and she said to me, 'Will it never end? No, it probably won't. Not as long as he knows where I am.'"

Mr. Bates held Callie's gaze. "That suggests she wanted to disappear, does it not?"

"Yes, definitely." Callie's heart was beating fast with excitement at this revelation. 'As long as he knows where I am.' To whom could that refer? She leaned forward. "Who sent her those flowers? Do you recall?"

"Well, of course we weren't in the habit of reading the cards that came with flowers for our guests. But I have to admit that after her odd response to the bouquets, I was rather curious. She didn't want them and told me to throw them in the trash."

"What a waste."

"Indeed. So after she had closed her door again, I did

look at the cards. They were all from the same sender. And all had the same message. *'You are my life. R.'"*

Callie shivered. "Sounds creepy. I mean, sending multiple bouquets and with such a card attached. The same message over and over. I can imagine how Monica might conclude that it would never stop."

Patting Biscuit, Callie thought of the stalker theory she and Falk had been discussing earlier. "Do you know who sent the flowers? What 'R.' stands for?"

"No. But they were delivered by a local florist. I thought the staff there might know more about it, have a name or a credit card number, maybe. I told the police about the bouquets after Monica vanished, and they promised to look into it. But whether they ever followed up with that florist to track the mysterious 'R.' or not, I have no idea."

Mr. Bates pursed his lips, a sign, it seemed, of his doubts.

He pointed at her with a fleshy hand. "Jamison had heard about the flowers from another hotel guest who was in the corridor when I was at Monica Walker's door with them. Jamison wanted to know what florist had delivered them as well. I bet you he followed up on it. And if he ever got his hands on a credit card number, I'm sure he traced it to find out who it belonged to."

Callie tilted her head. "But it must have come to nothing because I can't remember having read or heard anything about flowers and a mysterious admirer in the newspaper reports about the disappearance. Of course I only read a few, at the library archives. There might have been more on it published later?"

Mr. Bates shrugged. "I wouldn't know about that. All I can tell you is that Jamison was acting like a man with a mission around my hotel. He dined there—we took non-guest diners even back then, you know—to be able to listen in on conversations. He believed he would hit on a major clue that way. His behavior annoyed me so much that I informed the police about it. But they said there was nothing they could do, that Jamison was entitled to dine at the hotel. That they could only act if he caused damage, broke into someone's hotel room, or hurt someone. He was too smart to go that far, of course."

Callie's mind raced to fit all of this information into a meaningful whole. What had Jamison hoped to learn? Had he believed someone close to Monica was in the know about her disappearance? Had there been people with her that the police had asked to stay at the hotel until they knew more?

But the newspaper reports she had read hadn't mentioned staff. Hadn't featured interviews with such people, although you'd expect them to be the first to be in the limelight after the disappearance of their employer. "Was Monica staying at the hotel alone?" she asked Bates. "You'd expect her to have staff with her, like a personal assistant or a makeup artist or somebody like that? A manager maybe, or a secretary who kept her diary?"

"No, she was all alone. She told me it was a vacation, far away from work."

"But people knew her face and recognized her. I mean, how could she ever really be away?"

"But she could." Bates held her gaze with his curious

light eyes. "She vanished. She left a hotel room full of suitcases, her ID—everything. She simply walked into the night and she was gone. Never found again. So despite her familiar face, she wasn't recognized at all as she made her big escape."

Callie studied the man, so relaxed in his chair. He had obviously known quite a bit about Monica. Had he liked her? Felt close to her? Perhaps thought she was somehow put in his path? Had he gone after her to ask her for a date or something like that, and she resisted and . . . ?

Callie wet her dry lips. The idea that she could be sitting here, chatting amiably to Monica Walker's killer, was surreal.

"Drink some more tea." Mr. Bates smiled, gesturing at her glass.

Callie stared at the liquid that had gone over the rim and shook her head. "I have to keep Biscuit under control. You say Jamison was very persistent to get to the bottom of the case. When did he stop? Because he did stop. He never solved it, and he had to let it go eventually."

"Yes, that was quite unexpected." Mr. Bates's thin white brows drew together in a thoughtful frown. "Just the day before, I'd seen him in the parking lot, looking at cars, writing down license plates and even measuring tires. What would our guests think of such behavior? I told him I was completely fed up with him and would have him arrested if he showed his face again. It was an idle threat, of course, as I already knew the police weren't going to do anything about his snooping."

Bates huffed. "But to my surprise, Jamison never did come back. Not the next day or the one after that. I didn't dare hope he had let go. I kept expecting to see him again, hiding behind some potted palm to spy on people at the elevators, but after two weeks I had to conclude that for some reason it was over. Maybe his boss at the *Herald* had given him some other story to pursue? I don't know. I was just relieved that he was letting us run our hotel in peace."

Callie thought about this for a moment. "But Jamison stayed around town. He became editor-in-chief. You must have met some time, socially. Have you never asked him why he let go of the Monica Walker case?"

"Not really, no. I was curious, of course, but as Jamison always had a temper, I was worried that questions might strike him as provocations, taunts that he hadn't been able to solve the case. What if he dug in again, to prove to me that he had been right all along? That was the last thing I wanted. No, I knew how to keep my mouth shut."

Mr. Bates suddenly sat up and rubbed his hands. "Shall I take a picture of the dogs now? I think they would look best in two individual portraits. Yes, two."

He rose to his feet and went to a cupboard to pick up his camera. "I will start with the cute little lady. Just leave her there."

He came over and sat on his knees to snap pics of Daisy, who seemed fast asleep on the cushy sofa.

Callie wanted to protest that she didn't want a portrait of Daisy asleep, then remembered it was the terrier's favorite activity and grinned to herself. Bates had read that exactly right.

The snapping of the shutter woke Daisy up and,

immediately curious, she sat up, tilting her head at Bates, who kept clicking away. After what had to be sixty pictures from all angles, he turned to Callie and Biscuit with a satisfied sigh. "Fifty percent done. Now with him I think we need to go out so I can get some action shots. You can throw a toy for him."

Callie nodded mutely. Mr. Bates was a force in his own right, and she didn't want to go back on her order for the pet portraits now. She just wondered how expensive they would be and who was going to pay for them.

*   *   *

"Three hundred dollars," Callie called out as she raced into Book Tea's kitchen with both dogs trotting behind her. "Not in total—each! I guess it will be worth it in the end, since Mr. Bates is extremely talented and I loved what I saw in his studio, but he didn't seem to know all that much about the old disappearance case. He did meet Monica in the flesh and . . ." Callie fell silent when she saw that Iphy was on the phone. Her great-aunt gestured to her to take a seat and wait a minute for her to wrap up the call.

Callie filled two bowls with water for the dogs, since she figured they must be thirsty after their photo sessions, and then sat down to listen in on what Iphy was saying.

"I see, Irma. Yes, you did the right thing to call me. I'll take care of it. You needn't worry. No, that's completely fine. Thank you so much. And do drop by some time to try the new treats. Yes, I can make them dairy free for your granddaughter. Of course. Just let me know in advance as I have to prepare them separately. Thanks again. Bye!"

Iphy disconnected and looked at Callie. "That was Irma. She runs the campground store. She sells fresh products to the campers so they don't have to go shopping at the mall. So convenient when you find out at eight PM that you have no noodles."

"Yes, yes, what did she say?"

"That Quinn came tearing in and is packing up."

"What? So Falk released him?"

"Yes, and he's about to leave town. That's not a good idea, of course." Iphy checked her watch. "I can leave for an hour. It's quiet now. Peggy and the others can manage on their own. We're going to stop this foolish young man from making the biggest mistake of his life."

Callie wanted to point out that Quinn was hardly a young man, but to Iphy everybody was young. She had to smile. "What do I do with the dogs?"

"Leave Daisy here, she'll find something to do. The helpers can look after her. But bring Biscuit. I hope the dog can convince Quinn that he has to stay, even if we can't."

* * *

At the campgrounds they left the station wagon at the reception building and continued on foot, zigzagging between pitched tents and playing children to reach the spot where Callie had talked to Quinn earlier that morning. She was a little disoriented because of the trees everywhere and things looking so alike, and led Iphy astray once, but then she noticed how Biscuit was pulling on the leash and just followed the border collie.

He ran with his tongue out of his mouth, his tail wagging, as if he couldn't wait to be reunited with his new human.

Callie's heart ached that the dog would be disappointed again in someone who disappeared from his life, leaving him behind. How many disappointments until his trust would be ruined beyond repair?

They came into a clearing where no tent or canvas chair or gas stove had been left—just imprints in the grass. Biscuit pulled them farther along to another clearing where a car stood. Quinn was just closing the trunk.

Callie called out, "Quinn! Don't leave."

Quinn started and clearly wanted to get into the driver's seat quickly, but Callie let go of the leash and Biscuit ran for him. Through the open car door, he jumped in, straight into Quinn's arms and licked his neck and face. Quinn didn't fight him off but just wrapped his arms around the dog and hugged him.

Callie rounded the car and stopped at the sight of the two of them. Quinn's expression was so sad. She reached out and touched his shoulder gingerly. "You can't just leave. You have to stay and prove you're innocent."

"How? Deputy Falk claims he found my fingerprints at the scene. Even on a tape measure lying beside the body. And Falk claims I'm the only one Jamison was afraid of."

"He can't know that." Iphy had come up to them and stood with her hands on her hips. "Mrs. Jamison told me over the phone that her husband hadn't been himself lately. Maybe he was being pressured by somebody. Blackmailed even. What do we know? It could have been a local. Someone who was involved in the Monica Walker case in the past."

Quinn sighed. He rubbed Biscuit's back. "I can't stay now. It all went wrong. Somebody died. That's all my fault."

He looked up at them. "I didn't kill Jamison. You have to believe that. And if I had known somebody was going to get killed over this case, I would never have come here in the first place. But I did come, and somebody did die, and I just don't know what to do but run away."

Callie expected her wise great-aunt to have some response to that, but Iphy said nothing.

In the deep silence, they could hear the pines rustle overhead. A blue jay chattered.

Biscuit pushed himself close to Quinn.

Quinn stared ahead without seeing anything. "Running has always been my solution to everything in life. When I found out that my parents weren't really my parents, I ran. I didn't want to talk to my sister, who isn't really my sister, you know. I ran off to Asia and backpacked for two years. Then I came back, and I couldn't leave it alone. I should have. My mother told me on her deathbed that I should never try to find my real parents. That it wouldn't make me happy. But I didn't listen to her. I felt like I deserved to know the truth."

He looked at Callie with burning eyes. "She was right. My mother, who wasn't my birth mother, but who cared for me for all of my life. To protect me she told me to leave it alone. Because she loved me, she told me not to try and find out. But I had to do it anyway."

He banged his fist on the steering wheel.

Biscuit whined and licked his neck again.

Callie stood motionless, processing the implications of what Quinn was saying. He had come to Heart's Harbor to look for his birth mother? But why had he believed Jamison could help him with that? And why hadn't he simply told her the truth?

She didn't dare ask anything right now as Quinn was so emotional and might clam up. They had to give him space to share in his own time.

Quinn continued through gritted teeth, "I've made mistakes in my life before, but never something this big. I mean, Jamison is dead. He can never come back. When he refused to tell me anything, I thought he was a pompous fool. I thought he was in my way. But he was just protecting me. Like my mother. He knew it was dangerous."

He banged the wheel again. "*I* should be dead now. That killer should have come to silence *me*. I was the one asking questions, throwing up dirt, digging into secrets. Not Jamison. He never wanted any of this."

Iphy said softly, "If you were warned by several people and you still kept on going, it must have been very important to you."

"More important than breathing," Quinn said in a low voice. "I felt like not knowing where I came from was killing me. I had to do something about it, or I'd never have peace.

But now—now I know for sure I'll never have peace. Because Jamison paid for my mistake with his life."

"If you leave, Quinn, the police will come after you. They'll think you're running because you're guilty."

"I don't care."

"No," Iphy agreed in that same soft tone. "You want them to come after you. You hope they'll think you are dangerous because then they might shoot and kill you."

Chapter Nine

A shiver rippled down Callie's spine, as her great-aunt continued, "You also want to die, like Jamison died, because you think it's your fault. But it's not. Whoever killed Jamison killed him for his own reasons. And he will have to take responsibility for that murder. Not you. You don't have to sacrifice your life."

Quinn leaned his head on the steering wheel. "I'm just so tired," he said in a strangled voice.

Callie looked at Iphy. She had no idea what to say or do.

Iphy kept her eyes on Quinn. Her expression was both sad and hopeful. "I know two boys who will be excited to see you. I also think their mother can cook you a wonderful late lunch. With some food in your stomach, you'll feel better."

"Peggy will never want to see me again," Quinn said. "She'll think it's my fault."

Callie quickly intervened, "Peggy was at the police station this morning to plead for you. She asked me to team up with her and find proof to clear your name."

Quinn shocked upright and stared at her. His face went

deathly pale. "No," he said in a croak. "She can't involve herself. She can't poke around. What if the killer comes after her? What if he hurts her or even kills her as well because of what he thinks she knows or could discover?"

He started the engine. "I have to get to her and tell her not to do anything stupid."

"She's at Book Tea right now," Iphy said. "I kept an eye on her all morning. We can all go there, and then you can go with her to her home and have a late lunch and play with the boys. No—no protests. I don't think Peggy will stop worrying about you or poking around, as you call it, until she knows you're all right. You owe it to her to show up."

Quinn stared at her, then said, "Maybe you're right. I need to explain to her how dangerous it is. She can't get hurt. Or the boys."

He looked into Biscuit's eyes. "In the back, boy."

As if the border collie understood how important this was, he jumped between the seats to get into the back. Iphy poked Callie with an elbow, propelling her to the car. "Callie can go with you to restrain Biscuit during the ride. A dog on the loose in a car isn't very safe. We'll meet up at Book Tea."

Callie hurried to get into the back and pulled Biscuit to her. His tongue was out and his tail wagging as if he was excited to hit the road.

Quinn strapped himself in and looked in the rearview mirror. "Aren't you afraid to come with me? In case I'm the killer?"

"I don't think you hurt Jamison. Gut feeling."

"Your friend the deputy doesn't agree. He's dead set on nailing me for it."

"He's just worried about what might happen if he doesn't act." Callie patted Biscuit. "He's not prejudiced. He checked on everything you said during the interrogation. That's how he found out you're no journalist. You told me the truth. Still, as soon as Falk showed up, you lied. Why?"

"To explain my interest in the Monica Walker disappearance. What better cover than being a journalist? Most police officers don't like journalists since they get too close to crime scenes or write about sensitive information—you know how it is. I counted on him not liking me either and buying into my sensationalist interest in the cold case. I have friends who work for news sites, so I could mention a couple of names to make it credible."

"But not credible enough. Falk only had to place a few calls, and your whole story unraveled. You don't have a professional interest in it. It's personal."

Quinn nodded. They were driving now, and Callie wasn't sure how smart it was to discuss a painful topic en route. Quinn needed his attention on the road.

"Why did Falk decide to let you go?"

"I have no idea. But he did tell me he'd need me again and to stick around. I had the impression as I was leaving the station that they were gearing up for something. They were all running around."

"Oh." Callie's stomach tightened at the idea of some big thing in which Falk would also play a part. An arrest? Maybe in another case? After all, the Jamison murder wasn't the only thing on his agenda. If he had to arrest someone on the run, someone dangerous, he could get hurt.

Quinn said, "That's why I thought that if I wanted to leave, I had to do it right away. While the police officers were occupied elsewhere. How did you know I was out, anyway? I assume Falk didn't call in the good news?"

Callie flushed under his probing glance in the rearview mirror. "No, someone called Iphy. Worried about you, it seems."

"How can that be? I don't have any friends here."

"That's what you think."

For the briefest of moments Quinn met her gaze in the rearview mirror and then looked away. His jaw was tight. Callie realized it would take some convincing to get it through his head that he did have friends here and that they would help him solve whatever he had gotten caught up in.

* * *

At Book Tea, Iphy told Peggy she was off for the day and could take Quinn home for a meal. Peggy seemed a little insecure now that Quinn was suddenly out and about again. She asked Callie, "Do you want to come as well? You can help me whip up a salad."

Callie wasn't sure if Quinn would be more forthcoming if he had Peggy all to himself, but she was so curious about his story that she couldn't say no. They took along Biscuit and Daisy and set out for Peggy's house.

It lay along a road off Main Street just where the heart of town ended, with all the shops, the community center, and the church, and the coastal road began that took traffic from Heart's Harbor to neighboring towns.

The house was painted a soft blue, and fishing nets decorated the porch. Seashells formed a colorful mosaic above the door, and a miniature wooden boat hung beside it. On the boat's bow it read, in neat lettering, "Greg Peggy Jimmy Tate."

Callie glanced at Quinn and saw his gaze lingering on the names, on the representation of the happy family Peggy had had before her husband died at sea during a Coast Guard rescue mission. Three young lives had been saved that night, but his had been lost, and his boys had been left without a father.

Jimmy and Tate arrived at about the same time as they did, coming from the other direction. Judging by the kite Jimmy was carrying and the ball Tate had, they had been on the beach. Tate yelled as soon as he saw Quinn. He dropped the ball and ran for him.

Quinn caught him and lifted him high, holding him up as if it took no effort at all. Tate squealed and laughed. Jimmy squatted to pat Biscuit. The dog rubbed his head against Jimmy's shoulder and barked as if he wanted to say hello.

Peggy, her hand on the key to unlock the front door, smiled at the four of them.

Callie saw something in her eyes that hadn't been there before. A sort of tenderness.

But what kind of man was Quinn Darrow really? He had just told her and Iphy that he had had spent his life running away from trouble. Now he had landed headfirst in a murder case. Not exactly the sort of stable man you wanted to see a widow and her two young sons get involved with.

"You play a little, and I'll make something to eat," Peggy said, brushing through Jimmy's hair. He tried to dodge her hand, saying "Moooooom!" in a reproachful tone. Grabbing Biscuit by the collar, he led him around the house. Tate followed, with Daisy hard on his heels, Quinn bringing up the rear.

Peggy gestured to Callie to follow her inside. The large kitchen with yellow curtains and lots of stainless steel had a wooden table with four chairs in a corner. The fourth chair was marked with a paper plaque, handwritten in bright marker with "Ace."

Looking at his name so suddenly there, Callie felt uncertain as to what she was doing here. Falk wouldn't like her any better for not just letting Quinn be. For bringing him to Peggy's house and near the boys.

Peggy opened the tall fridge and began to collect lettuce, cheese, cooked potatoes, cold cuts, and other things that could go into a salad. She also took bowls and plates out of a cupboard and put them on the table. Her expression was pensive, even tight, and Callie wasn't sure how to start a conversation. Her own head was swimming with confused questions and fragments of information.

As Callie mixed the salad, Peggy cut up bread and put grapes on a separate plate. Rearranging the fruit, she asked slowly, "So how is Quinn? I mean, is he really angry about being arrested by my brother?"

"I don't think he's angry. He understands why Falk started to suspect him. He's more worried about how this will all turn out. But let him tell you that himself. Can we take all of this outside?"

"Sure. The weather is nice enough for it. Last night there was terrible rain."

"I didn't hear a thing. I was exhausted."

They all sat down at the long outdoor table and ate in silence for a while. The dogs basked in the sunshine on the lawn, Daisy curled up into a ball, Biscuit stretched out, half on his back, with two paws up in the air. Jimmy mentioned, between bites of salad and bread, that they had flown their kite really high, and Tate added that it had almost gone behind the clouds. They seemed too restless to sit at the table long and begged Quinn to play soccer with them, but Peggy said they had to play by themselves for a while and let Quinn eat in peace. Then he would then join them and play with them for the rest of the afternoon.

Quinn seemed to want to protest, but he couldn't be heard over the excited cries of the boys. They jumped up from the table and ran off inside to get things they wanted to show to Quinn later. The backdoor slammed shut. Biscuit, who had jumped up to follow them, stood on his hind legs against the door, gazing in through the glass pane to see if they were already coming back.

Quinn looked at Peggy. "Are you sure you want to do this? I'm under suspicion of murder."

"Yes, but that will all be cleared up soon."

"Not by any of your doing. I don't want you to go

sleuthing. Not with a killer around. Jamison knew something, and now he's dead. A big strong man, killed like it was nothing."

Peggy said, "Do you have any idea who did it?"

Quinn shook his head. "If I did, I would have told the police, believe me. But I have no idea. I didn't think Jamison knew all that much. Yeah, he got nervous about me asking questions, but that might have been because he hadn't been able to get very far with the case at the time. He's editor-in-chief now—I mean, he was—and so he might not have wanted to be reminded of old failures. His wife did tell me a thing or two about those early days in her husband's career, but nothing significant. I can't see why Jamison had to die."

Callie played with a bit of cheese on her plate.

She had wanted to ask before, but with Quinn being so emotional it hadn't seemed like the right moment. Now, however, it couldn't be avoided any longer. "You said a personal interest in the Monica Walker disappearance brought you here. I don't mean to pry, but it could be essential to solving Jamison's murder."

Quinn looked up at her. "Can't you guess? I told you already that my parents turned out not to be my real parents. On her deathbed my mother told me that she wasn't my birth mother. She also told me that I shouldn't try to find my real mother because it would only make me unhappy. I didn't listen to her."

Callie's mind raced. "You mean you know that . . . Monica . . ."

"Not know. Suspect." Quinn swallowed hard. "I didn't

listen to my mother's sage advice, and I dug into my past. I managed to establish that my mother is an 'M. Walker.' Now, Walker isn't exactly a rare name, but I also found out more about the circumstances of the birth, and it happened at a clinic not far from where Monica Walker lived as a teen. I pieced several things together before I dared conclude that Monica Walker could have been my mother. I knew vaguely who Monica Walker was, but when I looked closer at her story, and read about the disappearance here in Heart's Harbor, I was sure there was more to it, there had to be. I mean, my real mother couldn't just have vanished off the face of the earth. I searched online, and then I decided to come here in person and see what I could find out."

"I'm so sorry for you," Peggy said. "I mean, it must have been a major shock to find out you were adopted and then to discover your real mother just disappeared."

Quinn sighed. "The accepted story was that she eloped with a lover. I was sure I could trace her. I mean, she had to have gone somewhere, lived there. People need money, they have ID, they use credit cards. But I found out right away that she left her ID in the hotel on the night she vanished. She didn't take any of her things. Had she planned to take on a new identity? Had she already secreted away some money into an account someplace where people asked no questions? If she sailed away from here calling herself by another name, then how would I ever find her?"

He knotted his fingers. "I admit I got pretty frustrated looking into the whole thing. Nobody seemed to remember anything beyond the details I already knew from the newspaper reports. Still, Jamison seemed to be keeping something back."

Callie nodded. She didn't want to tell Quinn that Jamison had asked her to keep an eye on him.

Had Jamison known that Monica had a child she had given up years before she ever became famous? Had he suspected that Quinn was that child?

No, that seemed unlikely. There had never been any mention of Monica Walker having a child in any of the news reports. So how would Jamison have known about that?

Jamison must have been worried for some other reason. But what could that be? Just his gut feeling about the case, which had never been good? In spite of the evidence he claimed to have that Monica left Heart's Harbor alive and well and started a new life somewhere else. If she had done so, and there had never been any crime committed of kidnapping or murder, why did Jamison have to die?

Peggy urged Quinn to take some more salad, but he shook his head. "I can't eat now." He looked past their faces. "I just wanted to know the truth about my mother. I never meant for anyone to get hurt. But the frustration is even worse now. Jamison is dead, and now I'll never find out what he knew. If he knew anything about me. I mean, he might have been killed because he had an idea about who had been in league with Monica to make her disappear. She can't have done it alone. She needed a new ID, a boat . . . Can you see Monica Walker stealing a boat from a local fisherman? In her glittery top and her high heels?"

Callie almost had to laugh. "It doesn't seem likely. But

who knows how charming she was? Maybe she only asked the fisherman to lend it to her."

"Then why did he claim afterward that it had been stolen?"

"Because he was afraid to be associated with her disappearance, suspected of some crime."

Quinn pursed his lips. "Possibly, but I think the boat was really stolen. By Monica's accomplice."

"The man she wanted to run away with?" Callie asked.

"Yes. There must have been an affair of some kind at play. Some reason why she couldn't just come out into the open with this new man in her life."

Callie said, "I heard all kinds of things from people, like maybe Monica was seeing a married man or maybe she was considering quitting the series she had become so successful with." She frowned, thinking of Dave Riggs's revelation to her that Monica had been in Heart's Harbor to prepare for a new part. In a series about rural life, in a small coastal town, something a world away from the glitter of *Magnates' Wives*.

Callie said slowly, "Suppose there was a clause in her contract that said she couldn't leave. So the only way out was to vanish."

Quinn sat up, eyeing her. "Who told you she considered quitting the series? Someone within the company who made it?"

"No, of course not. She didn't want them to know anything about her plans. Mr. Bates, the former owner of the Cliff Hotel, told me that the night it happened, Monica seemed very happy and glowing, excited, like she was going to do something she had wanted to do for a long time. That must have been her escape, her start on a whole new life."

"So we can exclude a crime." Quinn leaned back with a relieved expression.

Callie shook her head. "Unfortunately not. We still have to take into account that it's possible that someone who Monica thought knew nothing about her plans did know and didn't want her to get away. That person might have come to town to keep an eye on her, perhaps confront her? Imagine the scene. After dark, Monica runs away from the Cliff Hotel without taking any of her things. She goes to a lonely place where the boat is docked. The stolen boat. She wants to get on it, and suddenly someone is there to confront her. There's an argument, maybe a blow. Monica falls, hits her head and dies. It could have been an accident, but one with far-reaching consequences."

"You think Monica is dead?" Quinn asked in a thick voice. "My mother is dead?"

"I don't know. Jamison mentioned to me that he had proof that she started a new life somewhere. I don't know what that proof was or how he came by it. He seemed to believe she had engineered her own disappearance. At the same time, he said he had never had a good feeling about the case. And his need to know more, even after all of those years, suggests he was never completely sure about Monica's fate."

Peggy said softly, "Would it be possible for someone well known to live somewhere for decades, going undetected?"

"Of course," Quinn retorted at once. "Why would any-body recognize her? If she left the state, maybe even the country, who would think it was her? If she lives in Paris now, who would know her there? *Magnates' Wives* was a hit series here, not in Europe. In those days the internet didn't even exist, and people overseas might not have heard of the disappearance. She could have changed her looks, dyed her hair."

Peggy reached for Quinn's clenched hands. "Of course you want to believe she's still alive. And she could be. Callie just said that Jamison claimed to have proof she started over somewhere new. But with Jamison dead, you have to consider the other option. That Monica died around here and that her killer is still among us."

Peggy swallowed. "That he or she felt threatened now that the old case is being dragged up again and decided to silence Jamison."

"But that doesn't make sense at all." Quinn leaned heavily on the table with his elbows, gesturing with his hands to underline his point. "Jamison claimed to have proof Monica had left Heart's Harbor alive and well. If that's true, what crime would there be to keep hidden? And if there was a murder and if Jamison knew something that could endanger the killer, why didn't the killer get rid of Jamison before? Whatever way you look at it, Jamison's murder makes no sense."

Callie played with her fork. "Maybe Jamison never knew that he held a bit of vital information. Maybe now that there was new talk about the case, he went back through his notes and things on file and drew a conclusion he had never drawn before. He called someone about it, to ask for clarification maybe, before he turned to the police. That someone asked for a meeting, came to his office, supposedly to talk it over, and—*bam!*—killed him."

Quinn shook his head. "You just suggested that the person involved could have been connected to the company who created the TV series she was a part of. Those people don't live around here. How would they know that we were digging into the case again? How could any of them just pop up here in Heart's Harbor and kill Jamison?"

"Let me make a call." Callie pulled out the card that Mr. Bates had given her and dialed his number.

He answered on the fifth ring. "Yes?" It sounded disgruntled.

"Sorry if I'm disturbing your painting. It's Callie Aspen. I was with you earlier today. I wanted to ask if you have any idea if people who were staying in Heart's Harbor around the time of Monica's disappearance are staying here again. Does the hotel ever notify you of old guests, or do you stay in touch with them to . . . ?"

Mr. Bates's breathing rustled down the line. It sounded as if he had run fast to get to the phone before the ringing stopped. "I go to the Cliff Hotel every Thursday night to play bridge. I usually walk around and look at the old place, the guests. Just for fun. Sometimes I do see familiar faces. People who have been guests with me for decades. We have a chat, a laugh. But if guests were with me for a single time, I doubt I'd remember them."

That made total sense. "Could you give the hotel a call and find out if they know about any people having stayed with them during the disappearance and now? I mean, they trust you, and it would be so much easier for you to get that information than it would be for me."

Mr. Bates didn't respond at first. Callie was sure he'd just hang up and think she was rude to even ask.

But he said, "All right, I can do that. But what's in it for me? I mean, I'll be taking a risk. We have a killer about, you know."

"If we can solve the old disappearance and find out what really happened at the time, you can tell about your part in it. The part of your hotel."

Bates laughed softly. "You know how to tempt a vain old man. I'll make a few calls and let you know how I get along."

"Thank you very much. I appreciate it. Bye."

Callie lowered the phone and looked at Quinn. "Mr. Bates is going to find out more for us. If there's anything to find out, that is. He said, and he's right of course, that if someone stayed at the Cliff Hotel years ago, just for a single stay, he won't remember that face or a name."

"Is it even likely that someone who wanted to talk to Monica about her plans to leave the series would come to the Cliff Hotel?" Peggy asked. "And stay there? Why not meet her away from the hotel and people who might remember something later about an argument, raised voices?"

Callie nodded. "I know. We'll have to wait and see."

She folded her hands in her lap and focused on Quinn. "You, uh . . . do you have any idea who your father is? I mean, at the time of her disappearance, Monica had just ended a high-profile relationship. But, doing the math, that can't have been your father."

Quinn shook his head. "I was born when Monica was just a teenager. Before she ever had a part in any show, let alone in a hit series like *Magnates' Wives*. Her parents are no longer alive—her father died when she was just a toddler, and her mother died a few years ago—and she didn't have any known siblings, so I couldn't turn to any close relatives for information about a possible teenage pregnancy and a baby given up for adoption. There are more distant family members, but I doubt they would have known about something so sensitive. Of course, I did look into her boyfriends, hoping I could find my father there, but those relationships didn't make the front page until she got famous. It seems she never managed to fall in with the right kind of man. It was always an athlete, an actor, a magnate of some sort. And it never lasted long."

Callie frowned. "Mr. Bates mentioned to me that there were flowers delivered for her at the hotel. Several bunches, all with the same card attached, reading *'You are my life.'* That sounds pretty obsessive."

"Meaning she had a stalker?" Quinn said. "Some fan who believed he could woo and marry her?"

"Possibly. Monica was upset about the flowers and didn't want to accept them. So they didn't come from the man she possibly eloped with."

Callie pointed at Quinn. "Can you get me a list of men she was involved with? Just so I know a little about them.

And who knows, Mr. Bates might come back with information about guests at the Cliff Hotel that we can compare to the list."

Quinn nodded. "I'll have to look at some paperwork in my luggage."

The boys came back out, carrying half their toy collection. A brick castle with a drawbridge, wooden farm animals, fluffy puppets, and a race car.

Quinn rose from the table and went to meet them, kneeling in the grass to look at everything. He calmed Biscuit with one hand, patting him and ensuring he didn't snatch a toy, while with the other he moved the race car, imitating the roar of the engine. Then he turned it over and explained something, pointing at the wheels.

Peggy studied him with that same glimmer of tenderness in her eyes that Callie had noticed before.

She remarked, "Quinn hasn't had an easy life. And this murder is making all of it even worse."

Peggy sighed. "I know. I guess he won't stick around here as soon as Ace says he is free to leave."

"Maybe if he had a reason to . . ." Callie leaned toward Peggy and said in a low voice, "Quinn is going through so much right now that he probably thinks he shouldn't involve you and the boys in it. But if you like him and if he likes you, you should give it a chance."

Peggy flushed deep. "It's been just a year since Greg died. I'm not looking to—"

"I'm just saying that Quinn might think he has to leave right away when it might be good for everybody if he stayed around. Just some free advice." Callie rose to her feet. "Thanks for a fab meal. I have to run now. I just remembered the Historical Society and Swing It! are rehearsing at Haywood Hall this afternoon, and I want to see how everything is coming along for the Fourth of July party. Enjoy your afternoon off." She winked at Peggy, who was still red in the face and looking confused.

Callie left with a spring in her step. Despite the complications of the case, she had a feeling something good could come out of this for Quinn and Peggy. Neither had had the easiest of times lately, and maybe they could understand and support each other now.

Chapter Ten

Arriving at Haywood Hall, Callie remembered how different the house had looked in December, wrapped up in a layer of snow, with all the evergreen and sparkly Christmas decorations on the pillars and the railing leading up to the front door. Now the house's front looked rather sleepy in the summer heat, the curtains drawn against the bright sunshine and the weathervane on top sparkling so brightly Callie had to half-close her eyes to be able to look at it. She parked the station wagon with a bunch of other cars to the left of the house and walked around to the back, lured by the upbeat tunes of woodwind instruments and a double bass.

On the large back terrace, several couples consisting of men in evening wear and ladies in bright tasseled dresses and feathered headbands moved to the music, whirling around at a dazzling pace. Callie was surprised they didn't collide with one another.

A dancing instructor had climbed onto the stone wall surrounding the terrace, to get a better view, and was trying to shout instructions over the music.

A quartet, equally divided between woodwinds and strings, sat in the open doors leading into the house, giving a tantalizing glimpse of the nineteenth-century interior with its gold-leafed wallpaper, large mirrors, and delicate chairs with embroidered cushions and twirled legs.

The dance came to an end, the couples freezing in a dramatic final position, the ladies slung casually backward over their partners' arms, their pearl necklaces dangling almost to the floor.

The instructor clapped his hands together, shouting, "Wonderful! Take a short break, and then we'll do the two-step one more time." Turning his head, he spoke to someone Callie couldn't see, "This ambiance works wonders for the crew. It's invigorating."

"I'm sure that with an audience they will be even better," a fragile but warm voice replied. A figure moved in the shadows of the house, and Dorothea Finster stepped out into the light, blinking her eyes and smiling.

Callie rushed past the dancers to greet her. The elderly owner of Haywood Hall had always had a special place in her heart, from the day she had first come to the house to play on its grounds with Dorothea's sole relative and future heir, Stephen Du Bouvrais. Just a girl at the time, spending her summers in Heart's Harbor with Great-aunt Iphy, Callie had loved the house with its many corridors full of old paintings, rooms with large cupboards full of china and crystal glasses, and the library, full of leather-bound volumes in languages she couldn't read. They had drawn maps of the forest, giving every clearing and old oak a mysterious name and history. And they had fantasized about the people who had lived here and who had thrown parties where live orchestras had played and carriages with distinguished guests had rattled up and down the drive.

Being able to bring to life some of the history of the house now was amazing, already fulfilling in Dorothea's lifetime what she had asked Iphy and Callie in her new will: to ensure Haywood Hall would be preserved for future generations. Ever since accepting this momentous task at Christmastime, they had made plans to open up the house for events: cooperating with the Historical Society, a theatrical company looking for a location to perform an Agatha Christie play, and musicians looking for an original venue for a performance. The first-ever summer-night concert recently had been a great success, and Iphy and Callie were making plans to do more concerts the following summer and have more intimate performances indoors all through the year.

"Callie!" Dorothea stood on tiptoe to hug her. Her grasp was quite firm for such a breakable-looking old lady. But she had enough willpower to have survived many heartaches in her life and still be full of energy for the future of her beloved house. "How good of you to drop by and make sure everything is going to plan. Your furniture arrived safely and is in the old stables."

"Thank you for keeping it for me. I feel rather guilty for not having shown my face sooner," Callie admitted. "But things have been so crazy since I came back to town. Iphy rented a cottage for me, so there are some decisions to make about decorating it, and then the handyman I hired to help me with it got into some trouble." She fell silent a moment.

Dorothea nodded gravely. "Joe Jamison's murder. I've known him for so long it seems odd he's no longer there. He used to come here, you know, when he wanted to look up something in a book I own. He knew a lot about local history. I think he also wrote about it in the Historical Society's quarterly magazine."

"So the members of the Historical Society knew him well?" Callie asked, nodding in the direction of the people who were busy on the lawn. Some of them were dressed up in fishermen's clothes, others in uniforms from World War Two.

"Pilots," Dorothea explained, following her gaze. "Heart's Harbor delivered a few young men who went to Europe to fight against Hitler. The plane they are bringing in is going to be a real attraction. It's an original fighter plane, now owned by a private collector. I'm delighted we have the space here at Haywood Hall to make something like that possible."

Callie's smile at Dorothea's enthusiasm faded when she detected a familiar tall, sunburned figure among the pilots. Dave Riggs, her new neighbor. She couldn't help wondering why he had been so eager to report to her that he had met Monica Walker while also assuring her that he didn't know all that much about the woman and that her visit to the lighthouse had been purely for research purposes.

Nobody else had mentioned this alleged new series Monica had been working on. Had Dave invented it to explain her visit to the lighthouse?

Dorothea touched her arm. "I hope, with all the unrest just as you're moving here, you're not sorry about your decision."

"I'm not sure." Although Callie felt reluctant to mention her feelings to Iphy, who had prepared everything for her move here and seemed so delighted with it, she felt comfortable sharing them with Dorothea. Perhaps the astute elderly lady could give her some advice. "It's a big step, you know, giving up my job and my apartment. I loved all the traveling and telling my stories to people."

"You could do guided tours here, at the Hall. There's so much to tell people about it. And I'm sure we have international tourists staying nearby too, so you could even keep up your languages. Iphy gushed to me that your French is *magnifique*."

"My French is passable." Callie nodded in the direction of Dave Riggs. "I couldn't translate historical novels like his wife does. Do you know Elvira? Dave mentioned to me in passing that she didn't have an easy life before she married him, and . . . well, I was curious what he was referring to."

"I wouldn't really know. I've met her on several occasions over the years, and she's always been charming and friendly, but not someone you get close to easily, if you know what I mean. *Guarded* might be the best word to describe it."

Dave had insisted that Elvira hadn't yet come to Heart's Harbor when Monica Walker had vanished. But had he been lying? Had she arrived unexpectedly and seen her husband with another woman? Perhaps she had freaked out, thinking he was betraying her, with a TV star no less, and killed Monica. Had she hidden the body, stolen a boat, and made it disappear as well, to suggest that Monica had sailed off to start a new life?

"Do you know if Elvira is handy with boats?" Callie asked Dorothea.

"Oh yes, she and Dave have had their own boat for years, taking people out for trips. That was before she had the translation work, I think. They really took on everything they could get back then, to make ends meet."

So both of them knew their way about a boat. Interesting.

Dorothea pointed in the direction of a group of trees. "That's where they'll put the table for the sweet tea contest. Every participant is allotted a number, and the jury won't know who made which tea. To prevent another wedding cake debacle."

"Wedding cake debacle?" Callie queried.

"Two years ago an influential couple wanted to get the best wedding cake for their daughter's wedding. They asked several local bakers to present a cake and several local sweet tooths to test the samples. It turned out later they had all voted for the same cake because they knew who had made each entry, and the winning baker had bribed them. We won't have any of that in our sweet tea contest."

Dorothea leaned over and added in a whisper, "Mrs. Keats is also participating. I talked her into it. You know how she is, never asking attention for any of her accomplishments. I think her creation with raspberries is quite special."

"I'm glad I'm not on the judging panel. It's going to be very hard to find the grand winner."

Dorothea hadn't seemed to hear her. She was looking

around her with a smile of deep satisfaction. "This is how Haywood Hall should be, you know. Alive and full of activity. Just what I wanted when I made the new will." She squeezed Callie's arm. "You helped to make my dream come true."

* * *

Having lingered a little while longer in the bustle at Haywood Hall, Callie came back to Book Tea rather late and offered Iphy some help cleaning up after closing time. "You go and sit down for a bit. I bet you intend to stay up late to redo those macarons that didn't turn out exactly the way you wanted them to."

"The taste was all right," Iphy said with a frown. "But they fell apart too easily. I want to use them to decorate the rim of the base tier of my three-tiered cake for the Fourth of July party." She walked off, muttering to herself, while Callie took the vacuum cleaner out of the closet.

Despite the vacuum's hum and other sounds as she pulled chairs away from tables to clean underneath, Callie became aware of some action in the street near the newspaper building. A police car had arrived, and several men were going in and out of the building. She couldn't help peeking out the window every once in a while, trying to determine what they were doing.

Once all the tables were in perfect order for the next day's guests and she had even straightened every book on the shelves along the wall and picked out dead flowers from the centerpieces that weren't really all that dead yet, she couldn't take the tension anymore, so she slipped into her coat, and headed out into the street. She walked down the sidewalk casually as if she was just enjoying the summer evening and kept her eye on the group of locals gathered on the pavement, watching the action.

A woman on the edge saw her and waved at her. Taking this as her cue, Callie went up to her at once. The woman, in her late fifties, with ash-blonde hair swept back by a gemstone-studded headband and carrying a Pekingese on her arm, enthused, "You're Iphy's grand-niece, right? I saw you at Book Tea the other day when I was in with friends. You do have the best brownies I ever tasted in my life. And I try the brownies wherever I go. I've been trying to tease the recipe out of Iphy for as long as I can remember, but she won't budge."

"I have no idea what she does when she's baking," Callie said quickly. "She won't let me in on her secrets either. She's even up and about at night, when no one can disturb her."

The woman smiled. "Too bad. But what a terrible thing this is with Joe Jamison. Known him all my life. He used to pull my pigtails in school. And he wrote a really nice piece about my husband's upholstery business for the eightieth anniversary. Dug up some old black and white photos of my father-in-law, fresh out of school, working outside his tiny workshop when he first started here in town. We had never even seen those photos. But Joe knew the photographer who had taken them, or rather his grandson, who's now in charge of his archives. Oh, Joe was a treasure trove. Not much he didn't know about or couldn't find out about through some connection." She sighed ruefully. "Now they're turning everything inside out to look for more on that boat."

"What boat?" Callie asked innocently.

"The boat they found this afternoon."

"You mean, they found the boat that was stolen right after Monica Walker disappeared? The one that the fisherman lost and reported stolen?"

"Gill Gillespie. Yes. He always talked about that boat. About who could have taken it and where it could be. Well, now he can add another chapter to the saga. They found it."

"Where?" It seemed likely it would have to be nearby, but Callie didn't quite see how it had gone unnoticed for all of those years.

"On the bottom of the sea." The woman widened her eyes. "For some reason, Deputy Falk knew exactly where to look. They sent divers in, and then they had it in an hour or so."

"The boat sank?" Callie's heart pounded. "So Monica Walker left on a boat that had an accident and sank?"

Did that mean she was dead? That Falk could be recovering her body or whatever was left of it as they spoke? How terrible for Quinn.

The woman said with a frown, "It was a quiet night back then, as I remember it. No major storm or anything. They would have looked for wreckage then right after it was known that a TV star and a boat both vanished in the same night. But they didn't expect anything had happened to any boat on such a quiet night. How could a boat just sink?"

Callie held her gaze. "Foul play?"

"I suppose they think so. Why else look for evidence

there?" The woman nodded at the newspaper building while shifting the weight of her dog in her arms. The Pekingese yapped and licked her cheek. "I wonder what they think Joe knew. All along, mind you. He investigated the disappearance at the time. Claimed not to have found out a thing. And now he's dead, but otherwise, I would go over and give him a piece of my mind."

Callie was surprised at the emotion in her tone. "But we don't know for sure that he knew anything."

"He's barely dead and the police found the boat they couldn't find for thirty years? That tells me enough." The woman nodded firmly. "I wonder why it never occurred to me before. Joe knew about everything. Why not about this case? The biggest thing that happened in Heart's Harbor during those years. We have burglary here, all right, damages done, or kids joyriding. But serious crime? A disappearance—of a celebrity too. It must have grabbed him. Oh, I can't help feeling Joe knew something."

Callie remembered her talk with Jamison, his discomfort, the distinct feeling he had been hiding something. Had his request for her to keep an eye on Quinn been less innocent than she had assumed? Had he been part of Monica's disappearance, anxious to keep the secret safe?

Suspecting a dead man of a serious crime made her feel terrible, so she said quickly, "We shouldn't speculate as long as the police are busy. It would be so painful for his wife. His widow now."

Callie wasn't sure her words were carrying any weight, as the woman simply turned her back on Callie and started to whisper to another spectator. Of course, the recovery of a boat that had been missing for three decades was a sensation. You couldn't really blame people for having their own thoughts about it—and perhaps suddenly suspecting that an innocent neighbor might not have been so innocent after all.

Shivering despite the warm evening air, Callie walked off, her mind reeling at this turn of events. The boat recovered. From the sea. Sunken. By accident? Or on purpose?

Had Monica been lured into a trap? Had she believed she was sailing into a new future when, in reality, she was cruising right into sudden death?

Callie shivered even more. She had to talk to Falk and find out what had happened to that boat. Quinn's mother might have been on it. Quinn's mother might have been—

Murdered? Just like Jamison?

By the same person?

* * *

Her hands tightly gripping the wheel, her jaw clenched, Callie drove along the coastal road. She could see the place where the action happened from afar. The area was secured with police tape, and officers were keeping curious tourists at a distance. A van from a local TV station was parked on the shoulder of the road, the reporter talking into the camera as Callie passed. She was determined to stay away from any press for the moment, and as she got out of her car, she pulled up the collar of her coat so her profile would be less recognizable.

She went to the nearest policeman and asked if Deputy

Falk was on the scene. "I have some important information for him. Please tell him Callie Aspen is here, and he'll want to talk to me."

The officer looked doubtful, but he backed up to go look for Falk, and Callie was glad that this prompt response at least suggested Falk was still on the scene. She couldn't see much, as white canvas barriers had been erected and the action was taking place behind those. Her throat constricted, thinking of Quinn and the possibility that his mother's remains were somewhere behind those cold white walls. He had been controlling his emotions with great effort that afternoon. Another shock on top of that might make him snap.

Falk appeared and came toward her with long strides. "Important information, huh?" he called across the distance. "This better be good."

Callie waited until he was even with her and then asked softly, "Is it just the boat or . . . ?"

Falk held her gaze. His features were tense, probably also from exhaustion, as he had been working for hours now. She noticed that the legs of his pants were wet to the knees, as if he had waded into the water, maybe to meet a boat racing to the shore with news?

She expected him to bark at her that it was none of her business and tell her she had to leave again, but then he sighed and relented. "The divers found remains on board the wreck. We think somebody went down with the boat."

Callie dug her nails into the palms of her hands. "And the reason why it sank?"

"Experts will have to look at that."

169

"Of course the remains could belong to a thief who stole the boat. It might not be . . ."

Falk's expression betrayed nothing of what he thought. Callie had no idea if forensic experts could immediately see whether remains were male or female and how long they had been in the water.

She shuffled her feet. "What Monica Walker wore that night was pretty distinctive. Sequined top, high heels. I can imagine those don't just dissolve in water. Do you think . . . ?"

Falk tilted his head. "What's your interest in the events? The Fourth of July party? This has all turned from a call for information about a disappearance into something far more serious. Sinister too. You won't be sharing this at a family event."

"I know. It's . . ." Callie hesitated. Quinn had shared his story with Peggy and her, obviously not intending for the police to know, or he would have told Falk himself when he was arrested.

On the other hand, if the remains were of Monica Walker, it might be better if this news was broken to Quinn in the gentlest possible way.

She whispered, "Quinn told me that he came here for the case because he thinks Monica Walker might be his mother."

Falk stood motionless. She saw something of understanding flash across his features as pieces fell into place, and then a hint of compassion lit his brown eyes. He exhaled in a huff. "That's the last thing I would have thought. And it's bad luck for Quinn. You're right. Some things are easy to recover, even after years of being submerged. We have every reason to believe that . . . The clothes suggest that—"

"The remains belong to Monica Walker?"

Falk nodded. "Of course we need more than just a few sequins and a pair of shoes to go on, but the clothes recovered fit the description of what she was wearing on the night she vanished."

He rubbed his face. "Look, this might sound a little grim, but it could be really helpful. If Quinn is indeed related to Monica Walker, we could test his DNA and that of the remains to establish . . . to make sure . . . I mean, there isn't a lot left to ID."

Callie grimaced. "I see. I have no idea how Quinn would feel."

Falk nodded. "I understand. I'm just thinking aloud. It's great that we now have the boat and that we have some evidence to suggest that Monica Walker was on board when it went down, but I don't want splashing headlines proclaiming her dead before we have something official to go on."

"I totally understand. I'll ask Quinn how he feels about a DNA comparison." Callie nodded at Falk with more firmness than she felt. Quinn had been so emotional when he had wanted to run away from town.

"How do you think the boat went down?" she asked. "Bad weather, poor boating skills?"

Falk scoffed. "More like an explosion that made it sink."

Callie's stomach shrank. "And that explosion also killed Monica or whoever that dead body might have been?"

Falk shrugged. "I can't tell. I'm just going by what the divers told me. They have experience with salvaging crafts that went down, and they were sure there was damage from an explosion of some kind. Could have been the engine over-heating or some electrical trouble. It might not have been foul play. Especially when you're not familiar with boats, you can make a mistake, you know."

"I see. Well, you're right that we need a lot more informa-tion before any of this can get into the papers. They'd specu-late like crazy and only hurt people who are personally involved."

"I'm sorry for Quinn. I mean, he must be . . ." Falk fell silent and shuffled his feet.

"He spent the afternoon with Peggy and the boys. I think that cheered him up a bit."

Falk nodded. "I can't leave here. Could you go and ask him if—"

"Yes, of course. I'm sure he'll want to help. I mean, he came here looking for his mother."

"What a way to find her." Falk looked up at Callie, a frown darkening his eyes. "If we had found this boat before Jamison died, I would have concluded that Monica Walker had tried to escape the pressures of her high-profile life and had simply been unlucky in doing so. But with Jamison murdered . . ."

"You think Monica was murdered as well?"

"I can't figure out why anybody would want to keep this"—he gestured to the white canvas screens—"boating accident a secret if there's nothing fishy about it. I mean, Jamison must have known something."

"Because the map indicating the spot where the ship sank was on his desk?" Callie asked. It had been the question singing around in her head ever since the woman with the Pekingese had told her a boat had been found and the police seemed to know exactly where to look.

Falk studied her. "You knew?"

"I couldn't see the map very well. But I can put two and two together. A boat that has never been found is suddenly recovered. The map in Jamison's office must have led you here."

"Yes. I wanted to act right away before the press got wind of it and started to muddle things by maybe trying to dive for it themselves. I know it's been decades, so perhaps I'm paranoid when I say I worry about traces getting disturbed, but I do feel better now that we've salvaged the boat and the remains on it."

"I understand, and I think you did a great job."

"It isn't that hard when the place is mapped out for you." Falk rubbed his hands together. "I wonder, though, what happened in Jamison's office that night. Did Jamison have the map with the spot marked on it? Did he take it out of the file cabinet to show to someone? Did that someone then kill him?"

"But they didn't take the map?" Callie queried.

Falk pointed at her. "Bull's eye. That's been bugging me ever since I saw it lying there. If the map is a bit of vital information related to Monica Walker's death, something worth killing Jamison over, why not take it along? I mean, if Jamison had this locked away, and he took it out into the open so the killer had access to it, maybe for the first time since that summer night on which Monica vanished, why not grab it and take it?"

"Who says the killer came for the map? Or maybe they killed Jamison and were then so upset that they ran without it?"

Falk shook his head. "If the person who killed Jamison was involved in Monica's disappearance all those years ago, we're not dealing with someone who gets upset easily. We're dealing with someone who is cold and calculating, who can plan, who can organize things, who has knowledge. That person wouldn't make such a crucial mistake as to leave the map there."

"I tend to agree, but what do you conclude then?"

"I'm not sure. Maybe Jamison didn't put the map there while the killer was around? Maybe he denied having it. Maybe the killer struck out at him, and he crashed to the floor. The killer thought he was dead and left. But maybe Jamison was still alive and with his last breaths managed to put the map on his desk as a clue for the police."

Callie pursed her lips. "Sounds a little far-fetched to me."

"Well, the killer certainly didn't put it there as a clue," Falk said. "Look, I have a lot left to do. Also to keep the press off my back." He nodded in the direction of the TV van.

"I understand. I'm leaving." Callie stepped back. "Good luck."

Chapter Eleven

Callie woke the next morning with a dull headache behind her eyes. Slowly the memories came back of the past day's events and especially Quinn's agonized determination to help right away with IDing the remains that had been recovered from the sunken boat. He had gone to the police station with Peggy, who insisted on supporting him while a friend of hers watched the boys.

Callie sat on the edge of the bed, wiping her sandpaper eyes. She hoped with everything inside her that the remains didn't belong to Monica Walker so Quinn wouldn't have to work through the fact that his mother had died all those years ago and perhaps had even been murdered.

But on the other hand, she knew very well that the remains could hardly belong to somebody else. Not only had the boat vanished on the same night as Monica, but Falk had said the remains had been dressed in what was left of a sequined top and high heels: the exact outfit Monica Walker was wearing when Mr. Bates had last seen her at the Cliff Hotel.

Having showered and dressed, Callie dragged herself

downstairs to breakfast. Daisy ran ahead of her, entering the kitchen first and bumping into Iphy's legs as she was putting a stack of pancakes on the table.

"Good morning!" her great-aunt called. "Sit down. They're still hot. I put some homemade butter there and several kinds of jelly. I think strawberry is best, but please feel free to differ."

Callie's stomach felt the size of a ping-pong ball. "I can't eat pancakes now."

"Nonsense, you need your strength for the investigation." Iphy eyed her. "You can't help Quinn by feeling sorry for him. I'm sad too that the remains on the boat might belong to his mother. But Monica Walker vanished thirty years ago, long before Quinn even knew he was adopted. That's a given fact. We can only try to support him as he attempts to unearth the truth about that night."

Callie knew her great-aunt was right and nodded. Iphy's brisk practicality brought back some of her own spunk. "Pancakes it is, then."

She looked at the counter, where there was an array of cut-out colorful shapes. Fondant, probably.

Iphy caught her look. "I wasn't quite happy with the fondant fireworks I made to put on the three-tier cake. They're supposed to go all around the top two tiers so that you can look at it from different angles. I'm using slightly thinner stripes so it looks more realistic. I also need to think about the color scheme. Red, white, and blue, or something more flashy?"

Iphy tilted her head in concentration. "I'm glad I've at

least decided on the flavors for the different layers of cake. The base will be pecan banana, the middle tier chocolate fudge, and the top one raspberry white chocolate."

"I can't wait to taste them all. When will you be doing the full try-out bake?"

"Sometime next week. I need a couple of hours for it." Iphy was still studying her fondant. "I wish I could think of an ingenious way to shape it better."

Callie seated herself at the table and buttered her first pancake. "I heard the phone ring quite a few times late last night."

"Yes, people heard about the search in the water and the canvas barriers and a boat being found, possibly, and you know how it goes. Everybody had heard a different story. They all called me to tell me their take on it."

"Oh. Interesting. Anything worthwhile?"

"Well, most seem to be convinced that Monica left with a man, and they wonder, if there's only one dead body aboard that boat, where the man vanished to. They seem to think he killed her."

"Her new lover?" Callie's eyes went wide. That idea hadn't occurred to her, but with only one dead body aboard the sunken vessel, it did make a lot of sense. "But what on earth could have prompted him to kill her if he loved her and wanted to start a new life with her?"

"Well, consider this." Iphy pointed at Callie with the whisk in her hand. She had washed the things used for baking the pancakes and was now clearing them away. "Monica left her ID behind. She knew she needed money for a new life. She might have been carrying a large sum of cash. Or she might have already put cash in a place only she and her lover knew about. Maybe he killed her for the money. He might never have loved her and only suggested they run away together to gain access to her funds. After all . . ."

Iphy held Callie's gaze. "Monica earned a fortune with her role on the successful TV series. But after her disappearance, not much of it was left. I called Falk to tell him about the money theory, and he confirmed that, at the time, everybody was surprised that Monica's bank accounts held so little money. She must have funneled it away to use in her new life. But now that she's probably dead, I'm afraid her killer has been living off it."

Callie cringed. "That's terrible."

She chewed in silence while Iphy poured coffee for her and encouragingly moved the bowl with blueberry jelly closer to her.

Inhaling its sweet scent, Callie spread the jelly thick across her second pancake. Nobody made blueberry jelly quite like Iphy, and the taste was even better on something warm. "So we're not just talking about a woman who went missing, but about her fortune that went missing as well. I hadn't realized, although it makes perfect sense to assume she had put money aside to use once she had run away. How else would she live?"

"And stay undercover," Iphy added. She sipped her own coffee from her favorite daisy-spattered mug. "Very clever, but not so clever when you share your plan with a killer."

"Right. Quinn gave me the list last night of men Monica

had been involved with, as far as he could find any. He emphasized again that the men she might have dated before she got famous are, of course, not on it, as there was no interest from the media in her life then. I was wondering if maybe after her last relationship ended in heartbreak, she turned to one of her old lovers for support. Let's have a look."

She produced the list and smoothed it on the table, running a finger down the names and the brief notes Quinn had put after them. "Okay, this one was only a short relationship and a long time before Monica vanished. I doubt she'd turn to that man for support. Hmm . . . here's someone she was with for four years. That could create a bond of confidence even after it ended, right? And here . . . Wait—what?" Callie stared at the last name on the list. "Her last relationship was with a man named Roger."

"So?" Iphy asked, refilling her coffee mug.

"The flowers she got and didn't want to accept came from an 'R.' *You are my life,'* signed 'R.' What if they came from this Roger? Not a fan stalking her, but her ex. Making her feel so insecure and threatened that she wanted to vanish."

Iphy nodded. "Possible. You hear a lot of cases where exes can get quite obsessed."

"And more often than not those cases end in violence." Callie leaned back against the chair. "We need to know if this guy Roger had been sending her flowers before, which she refused to accept. Maybe somebody who worked with her on *Magnates' Wives* would know about unwanted deliveries arriving for Monica?"

Iphy nodded again. "That would make sense. But how

can you trace that person? The series ended years ago. How would you even know who handled such things as deliveries for the stars at that time?"

"Yes, that's a problem." Callie ate her third pancake, turning the question over in her head. How to contact someone relevant, how to find someone who would actually want to cooperate now that the story was getting hot again? Not all publicity was good publicity, she supposed, and former employees on *Magnates' Wives* who still worked in the business might be reluctant to touch anything potentially damaging.

Iphy leaned against the sink. "Mr. Bates was going to ask around the Cliff Hotel, you said last night before turning in. Did he get back to you yet?"

"No, but I suppose it's too soon. He needs some time to gather information, I'd say." Callie used the last of her pancake to wipe the remaining jelly off her plate. "Delicious breakfast—thanks for cooking. You know what? I think I'll look up Dave Riggs. He met Monica. He might know something about this Roger. I wanted to go see my cottage anyway. I need some measurements to order curtains for the various rooms. I'll also get wallpaper and paint. I think Quinn needs to do something physical to take his mind off the case."

"Great idea. But I don't see what Dave Riggs could contribute. Even if he met Monica, she wouldn't have shared her relationship troubles with him."

Callie wanted to protest that sometimes it was easier to confide in a stranger, but Iphy said, "She was a public figure. She couldn't trust someone she'd just met."

That seemed right. Still, Monica had told Dave she was

going to do a new series. Something she might not even have been supposed to mention. Weren't such things usually kept a secret until the last instant?

Odd.

Callie called Daisy, who had just finished her own breakfast and was eager to come along. Waving goodbye to Iphy, Callie smiled down on the dog. "Let's go see our new home, girl."

* * *

"That should be it." Callie stared at the scribbled notes of measurements for curtains, calculations for enough paint to cover all the wooden surfaces and for wallpaper for the bedroom and living room walls. Her shoulders ached from reaching up to run the tape measure along the top of the windows or get it into a far corner. But at least she had now tackled this necessary chore and could focus on actually choosing colors. Seeing Peggy's home had inspired her. That blue was gorgeous. Maybe combined with some sunny yellow and touches of lime green?

Or pink?

She did also love gray and purple. Dark purple or lilac. Wouldn't that look great in the bedroom, combined with wallpaper with some botanical pattern?

Her cell phone beeped, and Callie almost dropped her note paper. She reached into her pocket for the phone. It was an unknown number. "Hello?"

"Callie Aspen? It's me, Kay Tucker. I'm in Vienna with the group."

It took Callie a moment to work out that this was her replacement at Travel the Past who was presently in Austria's capital showing a group of senior citizens the famous architecture, parks, and white horses. "Yes? What's the matter?"

"I lost someone!" Kay's voice was panicky. "Last time I looked, everyone was still here. But now we're short a group member."

"Have you asked the others whether they've seen him or her?"

"It's a she. She was snapping some pics. Now she's gone!"

"People don't just vanish. She must have wandered off. Is there something interesting to see nearby? A landmark she might have wanted to photograph?"

"I don't know. It's full of old buildings here."

"Have you agreed on a rendezvous place where you'd go in case group members got separated from the rest?" Callie had always worked with such a rendezvous place, whether in a large museum or a city center, choosing a well-known spot that a lost tourist could easily ask for.

"No. I forgot." Kay breathed hard. "Everything has been going wrong. In restaurants, they don't speak English, and we get the wrong orders. Someone broke her heel stepping into a hole in the pavement. We couldn't find a shoe shop so she could buy other shoes. And now this."

"Kay, stay calm." Callie wished fervently that she was in Vienna right now to take charge and solve this. "The wrong orders and the broken heel don't matter. You have to find this missing woman. Now think hard. Where could she have gone to?"

"Someone else in the group is waving at me. Wait a moment. What? Where? Oh, I see." Kay sounded relieved. "They spotted her. She's on the other side of the street, snapping pics of some old banner on a building."

"When you have everyone together again, tell them to notify at least one other group member if they're going to wander off. And decide on rendezvous places wherever you go."

"Yes, I will. This is just so much harder than I thought. I wanted a nice trip, having a drink here and there, chatting with fun people. They're all asking questions I don't know the answers to."

Callie couldn't remember feeling quite so lost on her first trip, but then it was a long time ago, and the routine had settled in so much she had been able to do things on autopilot. "It will be fine," she said to Kay. "It's just your first trip."

"And maybe my last if it keeps going like this. I don't need all this stress." Kay hung up without even saying goodbye.

Callie stared at the phone in her hand. If Kay quit, would her former boss ask her to come back? Was she going to decorate a home she wouldn't be living in at all if she moved back to Trenton to start in her old job again?

Right now that prospect seemed inviting. Heart's Harbor was once more the scene of a murder case, whereas Vienna offered beautiful sights, wonderful meals—if you did get the right order of course—and the freedom Callie had always craved. What had she done moving here?

Confused, Callie left the cottage behind and walked with Daisy to the lighthouse. She was determined to talk to

Dave about Monica Walker, something quite natural, she supposed, with the boat having been found, but at the same time she was sort of worried she'd run into Elvira instead of Dave and would have to make up some reason for her presence.

But, to her relief, the tall man was busy on a ladder leaning against the base of the lighthouse. He clambered down to greet her.

"Hi, Callie. I saw you at Haywood Hall yesterday, but I didn't have time to come up and chat. Did you like what you saw? The dancing and all. Swing It! is really good." He held his hand over his eyes to shade them against the sun. "Is there something you need for your cottage? I could lend a hand. This"—he gestured at his ladder—"isn't urgent and can wait."

"Monica Walker," Callie merely said.

Dave flinched. "I didn't tell you about my encounter with her to get more questions about it. I just want it to stop." He rubbed his left hand over the paint stains on the right.

"That won't be possible now that the boat has been found on which Monica allegedly left Heart's Harbor. There might be remains on it." She didn't want to say for sure that there were. and assumed it was natural to speculate about it. "Monica Walker might be dead. Killed. Like Jamison."

If Dave was shocked by these suggestions, he might be open to a conversation.

There was a moment's hesitance in his features as if he was weighing the circumstances and coming to some kind of a decision. Then he nodded, more to himself than to her it seemed. "Let's walk on the beach."

He went on ahead of Callie and Daisy, his hands folded on his back. As she came to walk beside him, he was staring ahead in deep thought, a frown settling over his features. "What do you want to know exactly?"

"Was she afraid of someone? Did she feel . . . persecuted?"

"By the press, of course. What celebrity doesn't?"

"And her previous boyfriend? Roger Aames?"

Dave scoffed. "Him? Yes, he kept sending her things. Also here at the hotel."

"She told you that?" It seemed Monica had been very forthcoming to the keeper of a lighthouse she was just visiting for a taste of coastal life.

Dave shook his head. "No, I had heard about it from someone who worked there. It seems Monica was quite upset about all the gifts that kept arriving and had asked for them to be thrown away. That does tend to draw attention among the hotel staff."

"Of course. You felt like she was eager to start fresh?"

"She was looking forward to this new series she was going to do. A clean break with the old, she called it." He glanced at her. "I really can't tell you much. I only met her once. And it was so long ago. With all the things I heard when she disappeared and the stories going around now, I'm not even sure that I remember what she actually said to me or if I'm changing what I remember because of what I've learned after the fact. If that makes sense."

"Perfect sense." Callie sighed. "Look, I don't want to make this hard for you. You said you didn't want Elvira to know a thing about it, and I want to respect that. But there's been a murder, and now a boat has been found that might tie in to Monica's disappearance. We can't deny that something is going on here."

Dave nodded. "I know."

He fell silent when a figure came up to them from the dune path, waving cheerfully. It was Elvira, her hair drifting on the wind, her face relaxed, her eyes smiling. She put her arms around Dave and hugged him, then said to Callie, "So how is your cottage coming along?"

"Coming along might be an overstatement." Callie forced a laugh. "I still have to buy so many things for it, you know. I was just over there making a list. I can't really decide what color scheme I want. I had hoped to be organized sooner, but . . ."

"You don't need many things to be happy." Elvira leaned down to pat Daisy. "You've got this cutie."

"Well, I do want some wallpaper on the walls. I'd better go and shop for some. Thanks for telling me all about lighthouse history," she added to Dave, to give some reason for her presence. "I can use it for the Fourth of July party. Dorothea will be very pleased with all the local tidbits we've managed to include."

"Sure, no problem. Give my regards to Mrs. Finster when you see her."

"Will do."

Callie turned and walked away from the couple. As she looked back to call Daisy to follow her, she saw the two of them standing a foot apart, Dave looking down, Elvira studying him as if she didn't believe for one moment that her husband's conversation with Callie had been about the lighthouse and the upcoming Fourth of July party.

Callie bit her lip. If Dave Riggs wasn't very careful, his wife would start to suspect him of something. And when she found out about his meeting with Monica Walker, even if it was just a one-time occurrence like he claimed, there would be even more trouble.

Why had he not simply told her that he had once met the TV star?

Was Elvira so jealous that she would get upset about a simple meeting so long ago?

Or was there more to it? Something that Callie couldn't quite fathom?

*　*　*

Quinn straightened up and pushed the upper half of the wallpaper piece against the wall while Callie used both of her hands to flatten it top to bottom so it would stick without bubbles. After having bought wallpaper, paint, and other supplies, she had called Quinn to come and help her at the cottage. He had been eager to accept, arriving looking rather worn and explaining he had taken a long run on the beach to clear his mind. The exercise had left Biscuit calm and sleepy, so he was snoring away on the porch, with Daisy by his side, while Quinn and Callie dove into the chore of getting the wallpaper on straight.

It was harder than Callie had thought, mainly because the wallpaper's pattern had to be matched up, and the long sections were difficult to handle.

And as she watched row by row of purple irises take their place along the walls, she wasn't even sure if a room full of those flowers wouldn't be a bit much in the end. Maybe she should have picked something more neutral?

"Now I remember," she huffed to Quinn, "why I rented an apartment that was all ready to move in to."

Quinn grinned. "But this will all be your own effort."

"Yes, my own less-than-straight-and-smooth effort." Callie squatted quickly, to run her hands with enough pressure across the lower section. "Don't let go yet."

"I wouldn't dare."

She pushed her flat palm hard on a particularly uncooperative spot. "There. Stay put, you silly paper. I hope when the glue dries it won't all come down again. I'm not even sure these walls are straight. They seem to be crooked in places." Hoping it might be easier to talk about while they were not face to face, she asked softly, "Did Falk tell you when he would have results from the DNA test?"

"Well, normally it takes some time, but since this is part of a criminal case involving two deaths, they promised him to do it as fast as possible."

She tried to read the tone of his voice. "Are you nervous about it?"

"I'm not sure. On the one hand, I would love to know for certain who my mother is. On the other hand, if those remains were once my mother, it doesn't help me much. I can't ask her anything anymore. About my father or why she gave me up."

"Hmm." Callie took her time using a sharp tool to cut off the surplus at the bottom and throw it into a bin. "When you came here to look into Monica's disappearance, did you really hope you could find her alive?"

"Of course. Otherwise, I would have thought twice about what I was starting."

"But if you believed she was alive, weren't you starting something as well? She ran to escape, to build another life. Could you just have walked into it, saying, 'Hi, I'm your son'?"

"Of course not." Quinn stepped away from the wall and swung his arms. "I only wanted to know why she had run away and how her life was now. If I had discovered she was happy, I wouldn't have barged in to tell her who I was. What for?"

Callie stood up and looked at the table, stacked with more wallpaper that seemed to smirk at her. She sighed. "Can we call it quits for the day?"

"I'll keep going by myself. I feel like working all night. I don't want to think about what might happen when the results of that test come in."

"Maybe the remains they found didn't belong to Monica Walker."

Quinn scoffed. "I don't believe that. And you don't believe it either. Too coincidental."

He started to put glue on another section of wallpaper. His movements were so wild that glue splattered on the floor.

Fortunately, they'd be putting in new flooring later. Callie hadn't decided what it would be yet.

Choices, choices. So much left to do.

Callie's phone beeped. She dug it out of her pocket and answered it. "Hello?"

"Good afternoon. Mr. Bates here, bringing your fresh results."

The pet painter's brisk tone made Callie snap to attention. "Yes, Mr. Bates? I'm listening."

"An old crew member of *Magnates' Wives* has a cottage here in Heart's Harbor. He stays there every summer. He has to be there now too. He dined at the Cliff Hotel a few nights ago. His name is Otto Ralston. I think he can tell you much more about Monica Walker than I ever could."

"Thanks so much. Can you also give me the address of his cottage?"

She scribbled it down on a paper napkin left over from their break earlier and thanked Mr. Bates again.

Quinn eyed her. "News?"

"Just that an old crew member of *Magnates' Wives* has a cottage here in town. Seems to be his favorite holiday hideout."

"How odd."

"Maybe not. Maybe he mentioned it to Monica, and she came here because of his recommendation. I want to talk to him. It's not far from here. I'll go and see if he's home now." She checked her watch. "About dinner time—should be perfect."

Quinn rubbed his dirty hands. "Should I go with you?"

"No, I can do it by myself." Callie called Daisy and put her on the leash. "I'll be back in an hour."

"Okay. Be careful."

* * *

Callie heard the sound of the pruning shears before she could even see the cottage. It was hidden behind a bend in the path. The sounds grew louder, and Daisy stayed behind Callie, her ears flat. She didn't like metallic sounds.

Callie pulled her along and came to a man standing just behind his garden gate, pruning some yellow roses. He was deep into his chore, not hearing her approach until she was beside him. Then he looked up. "Oh, good evening. You must be lost. Not many people come this way unless they take a wrong turn. There's nothing out there."

He gestured with the tool down the path. "Just a dead end."

"I'm actually here to see you." Callie smiled, reaching out her hand. "Callie Aspen."

"Otto Ralston. Let me guess. You want advice on how to grow these amazing roses."

Callie laughed. "That would be useful, as I don't have a green thumb and I did just rent a cottage with a garden. But no, it's not about the roses either. I'm part of a local team preparing a tea party for the Fourth of July, at Haywood Hall. We're focusing on key events from town history, and I'd like to talk to you about Monica Walker."

Ralston looked her over. The relaxed expression on his slightly sunburned face didn't alter at all upon hearing the name, as if it had been but a few days ago since he had last seen her, worked with her. Not as if she was a missing celebrity with a ton of secrets. "What about her?"

"You did work with her, didn't you? On *Magnates' Wives*?"

"That was a long time ago. After the show got canceled, I did a lot of other things. But people always remember *Magnates' Wives*."

Ralston laughed softly, somewhat disparagingly it seemed. "It didn't go deep maybe, but it was a hit series. Mainly because of Monica. She was a natural. When she acted a highly emotional scene, even the crew was crying."

He took a rose in the palm of his hand and studied it. "She had this way with people. She got what she wanted, in a very charming way."

Callie tilted her head. "You mean she was manipulative?"

"Very. You never knew with her where the acting started. Sometimes I think everything she did was acting. For the sake of results, applause, her own satisfaction. She thought she was very clever."

Callie studied this man, the first person she had heard say less than complimentary things about Monica. All the others had seemed to like, even adore, her to some level, but Ralston didn't mince his words. He had to be about sixty, sixty-five. Physically fit, tanned, an outdoor person with a love of his garden, his hands full of scratches from thorns and his fingernails full of dirt. She couldn't quite imagine him on the set of a TV series. But then, as he had put it, it was a long time ago.

Ralston said, "Don't get me wrong. I liked her. We all did. She was charming, funny. She lit up a set with her presence.

When she was off for a day or two because the scenes we were shooting didn't include her, it was dull, and even the prop boys asked when Monica was coming back. The moment she walked in, the set came to life again, and all was right with the world. But we knew, without ever saying it to one another, that Monica got what Monica wanted. When she started dating Roger, he was still engaged to another girl on the show. That didn't matter to her. She wanted Roger, so Roger had to be hers. How the other girl suffered didn't mean a thing. And we didn't tell her to look at what she was doing. We wanted to keep her on the show. So we all just smiled at her."

He shook his head. "You know, Miss Aspen, I see it now like it really was, but back then I was so caught up in what we had created, in our success and in maintaining it, that I was blind to what Monica did. I liked her and I protected her. I catered to her every whim. I sent her here, you know."

He looked at Callie as if waking from his memories. "But how impolite of me—you must want a cool drink. Come on in. The dog is welcome too."

"Her name is Daisy."

"Well, welcome, Daisy. Just don't dig in my flower beds."

Ralston opened the gate and let them into the garden. The warm air was full of scents, and when Callie looked around, she discovered hydrangeas, more roses, fruit-bearing bushes, and a shaded seating arrangement where some children's toys lay in the grass.

Ralston followed her gaze and said, "My grandkids' toys. They're also staying here for the summer. At the campgrounds. They like it a little more rustic than I do."

He waved at the seats. "Have a seat, and I'll be back in a moment or two with the drinks. White wine?"

"Why not?" Callie didn't like alcohol much, but she wanted to maintain the light, chatty atmosphere that would induce this man to tell her more about Monica Walker.

Apparently, he had observed her well, and the relationships she had with other crew members. This girl he had just mentioned, who had been with Roger Aames before Monica had taken Roger away from her—could she have wanted revenge? Could she have followed Monica here to kill her and dispose of the body in such a way that it would seem she had run off with a new lover? That would be extremely hurtful to Roger, perhaps even driving him back into his old love's arms.

Daisy wanted to pick up one of the toys, and Callie lifted her and put her in her lap, brushing back her ears and whispering to her about the nice roses until Ralston came back, holding two wine glasses in his hands. He gave one to her and then toasted her with the other. "To Monica. May she be happy wherever she is."

Callie lifted her glass and repeated the toast, even though her mouth was sour at the idea that Monica was very dead and her remains currently under forensic investigation.

Ralston sat down and stretched his legs leisurely, crossing his ankles.

"You said Monica came here on your advice," Callie picked up where they had left off.

"Advice, advice . . . She asked me for a quiet place to unwind for a few days. She had ended the thing with Roger because she was tired of him, a typical Monica thing to do, and he kept pursuing her, so she wanted to get away. I told her about Heart's Harbor, walks on the beach, going out on a boat bird-watching. That sort of thing. Monica was more into parties and skiing in the French Alps, but if she wanted quiet for a change, I wasn't going to stop her."

"Did she seem anxious about Roger? Was he pursuing her in a nasty way?"

"Well, Roger was engaged to be married when Monica stole him. So he was upset when she dumped him like a brick. He wanted her back, whatever it took. Also to prevent others from laughing about him behind his back."

"Meaning he stalked her?"

"He sent gifts to the set, yes, left flowers at her apartment door. 'You are my life,' or something like that, he kept writing to her. A bit over dramatic, if you ask me."

"And you never felt like something violent was brewing?"

Ralston stared at her, his green eyes lighting. "What are you saying? That Roger hurt Monica? He didn't even know she was here."

"Yes, he did. He also sent her flowers here. The hotel owner at the time noticed and told me about it."

Ralston whistled. "I had no idea. I thought Monica hadn't told anyone where she was going."

"Roger knew. So he could have come here and—"

"You think he was involved in her disappearance?" Ralston shook his head. "Look, I knew him well. He was angry, yes—humiliated too—but foremost he still loved her. He might have done something silly like come out here to try and persuade her to come back to him, but he would never have hurt her."

"Not even if she had refused to come? What if she told him to his face that she was running away? Maybe even with another man?"

Ralston sipped his wine with a pensive expression. "I've never quite considered it that way. That he knew that she was here. That he might have kept an eye on her. Have seen her prepare her departure."

"Maybe even seen her with another man?"

"Yes, now that you mention it, he might have not liked that." Ralston emptied his glass and rose. "I need more of this. You?"

"No, thanks."

Callie watched Ralston walk off. He seemed shocked at the idea that Monica's ex might have come after her here. Callie wasn't quite sure herself whether it fit. If Roger Aames had followed Monica to watch her, why let her know he knew of her hideout by sending the flowers to the hotel? Giving himself away like that?

Ralston returned with his glass and a bottle of wine. He sat down and poured liberally. Taking a few sips, he sighed. "That's better." He glanced at her. "Roger was here, you know."

"When?" Callie asked, confused.

"Just the other day. I saw him on Main Street. I wondered what he was doing here, but I didn't feel like going up to him to ask. We lost touch and . . . well, I like my life quiet now."

"He was here in town?" Callie echoed, a chill running down her spine. So he could have killed Jamison. "At the time of Monica's disappearance, a local journalist called Joe Jamison looked into the case for the local newspaper. Did he ever contact you?"

"Oh, he contacted each and every one of us on the show. We were all tired of him. Couldn't stop digging."

"Still he came up empty."

Ralston turned the glass over in his hands. "Those things happen. I'm sure it wasn't for a lack of trying. He was a super snoop. He even came to the studio to ask questions. I think someone complained that a reporter had been inside his dressing room. But hey, the press was hot on the story at the time. It could have been someone other than this Jamison."

"Have you ever talked to him again? He lived here too."

Ralston shrugged. "It's not such a small town that you can't avoid each other. I'm here most of the time, tending to the garden, or I take our little boat out and do some fishing. I don't need to breakfast in town."

"So you have no idea how Jamison felt after all these years?"

"I supposed he had moved on. The story wasn't news anymore." Ralston lifted the wine bottle. "Some more?"

Callie had barely touched her glass yet and waved off his offer. "No, thanks. It's a very nice wine, but I had a busy day, and too much alcohol gives me bad dreams."

Ralston refilled his own glass.

Callie had noticed his wedding ring and asked casually, "Is Mrs. Ralston also a fan of gardening?"

"Mrs. Ralston isn't with us anymore." Ralston glanced down at his hands. "I suppose that's why my daughter insists on coming to stay in summer, so she can keep an eye on me. She thinks I don't eat enough."

"It's not very nice eating alone," Callie said, smiling at him. The man was probably lonely. "But it's good to be near family during the summer. I'm sure your grandkids love this garden to play in. About Roger Aames, when you saw him in town—do you have any idea where he's staying now? How I might reach him? I'd like to get the best possible picture of Monica for our Fourth of July party." She was quite sure already that with the recent developments, the Monica Walker story didn't lend itself for a presentation at a fun, family-oriented event, but she didn't want to explain to Ralston that she was looking into things for Quinn's sake.

"You aren't going to say I told you she was manipulative?" Ralston looked worried. "The public loved her. It won't do any good to show them what she was really like. Let them believe what they want. I'm fine with that. I just needed to talk about the old days."

He smiled sadly. "There aren't many people who want to hear about it. Certainly not my daughter. She's glad I got out of that world."

He sat up and added, more lively now, "Roger, well, I don't know where he might be staying, but you could contact his agent. Roger's still acting, so he needs someone to get him parts." Ralston stood and pointed at the house. "Can write it down for you. Give me a minute."

Callie sat and watched the tranquil garden while the

bumblebees buzzed about her and Daisy chased a butterfly. This was a perfectly peaceful little place. She hoped it could bring some contentment and consolation to the lonely widower's heart.

Ralston came back with a note for her, holding the agent's name and phone number. He accompanied her to the garden gate and shook her hand. "Very nice talking to you. Do stop by some other time."

As Callie walked back with Daisy, she called the agent. In California it was still within working hours. A secretary answered who was reluctant to connect her until Callie said it was very important.

"Yes?" A male voice came on the line.

"I want to get in touch with Roger Aames. It's very urgent. It concerns the disappearance of his former girlfriend Monica Walker."

It was so silent on the line for a few moments that Callie feared the connection had been broken. Then the agent said, "That was a long time ago, Miss Aspen. What can you possibly want to know about it?"

"I want to get in touch with Mr. Aames. I know he's around these parts. Heart's Harbor, Maine?"

"Most certainly not. He's filming on location in Canada."

"He was seen here the other day."

"That can't be. Thank you. Bye." And the agent hung up.

Callie exhaled and put her phone back in her pocket. Roger might, of course, really be filming in Canada. Maybe Ralston had been mistaken about seeing him here. People changed over time. Or people looked like someone else. How likely was it anyway that Roger Aames had been here?

Unless he was involved, of course, and had been asked by Jamison to . . .

She called the police station. Falk was still there. "I was wondering," Callie said, "if you checked on phone calls going out from Jamison's office at the newspaper before he died. If you found out if he might have called someone asking them to come see him or—"

"Of course. We looked into that right away. Both his cell phone and his office phone."

Callie waited, but Falk didn't seem to want to give her any more. "I wondered," she pressed, "if he maybe called a Roger Aames? That was Monica's ex at the time, and I heard he was seen around town the other day. He could have been in touch with Jamison before he died."

"Interesting."

Callie couldn't stand the tension anymore and asked outright, "Did he call this Aames or not?"

"I don't need to tell you that." Falk added in a friendlier tone, "Look, Callie, the media are all over this, and I've told all of my people that we're not saying anything to anyone until we have some firm results. Until we know for certain if the remains belong to Monica Walker and how the boat sank, for instance. I can't tell them to keep their mouths shut and then go and share information myself. You understand?"

"Of course. But the phone calls could be important. I keep thinking Jamison must have invited the killer into his office."

"That suggests Jamison knew who was involved in Monica's disappearance. That he invited him over to confront him with information he had or wanted to tell him he was going to go to the police."

"Not necessarily. Jamison might have thought about the case anew and remembered something he found odd. He called an involved party to talk about it. The party in question came along and then killed Jamison, either in cold blood because he was dangerous, or in anger or emotion over the turn their conversation took. Jamison might have seen the light during the conversation, and the other person knew nothing better to do than to grab something and lash out. Do you already know what the murder weapon was?"

Falk exhaled. "Doesn't that also go under the heading 'we are not giving out any information'?"

"Yes, I see. I do understand. I just want to help."

"And I appreciate that. Look, why don't you stop by my cabin later tonight? We can sort of . . . catch up."

Callie's stomach was suddenly full of butterflies. "Tonight?"

"If you have something else to do, we can do it some other time."

"No, no, tonight is fine. Around nine?"

"Good for me."

"See you then."

Callie disconnected and stared at the phone as if she could read something special from it. Falk's invitation had come out of the blue. She had no idea why he'd want this. It threw her off-balance, and she didn't like that.

Even worse: if the case was off limits, what could they talk about? Her mind seemed to be blank just imagining them sitting together with the log fire burning. The only questions going through her head would be:

Are we friends or not? Is there more or not?

Did you miss me or not?

Do you even still want me to come and live here?

Of course, she hadn't decided to come to Heart's Harbor for Falk. But for Book Tea, Haywood Hall, a new life in a place she had loved ever since she was a kid. But in December, in that warm atmosphere of togetherness, when she had made her decision to quit her job as a travel guide and settle here, Falk had been a part of that equation. And she wasn't sure anymore how he fit in.

Especially if he didn't want to fit in any longer.

* * *

Around nine, Callie, dressed in a pale pink blouse straight from the laundry and her favorite jeans, with gray sneakers, walked up to Falk's cabin, feeling as nervous as a sixteen-year-old on a date. The door was open, and she hopped up the porch steps and peered in. No one in sight. "Falk?"

Maybe it was about time she started calling him Ace, but since he had never invited her to . . .

She knocked on the open door and walked in.

In December the cabin had looked much the same as it did now, since Falk wasn't into Christmas decorations. The thing she hadn't noticed before was a Tiffany lamp on a side table. It was something out of tune with the rest of the decor.

She felt her stomach clench involuntarily, imagining he had a girlfriend now who came here every now and then and had started to change little things.

But if Falk was seeing someone, Iphy would have told her, right?

Callie held her hands behind her back and called again, "Falk? Are you here?"

Falk appeared from the kitchen, holding up two metal sticks with marshmallows on them. Pink and white ones. "To roast on the fire," he announced. "Here, hold these." He handed them to her, their fingers touching for a moment. "Do you like iced coffee?"

"Love it."

"Great. Let me get it."

She seated herself on the sheepskin and stared into the fire, holding both sticks with marshmallows.

Falk came back, closed the door and handed her a tall glass filled with iced coffee. Clinking his against hers, he said, "Much the same as last time, huh? Murder case."

Callie nodded, handing him his marshmallow stick. "Better weather, though."

Falk nodded at the rocking chair. "I'd sit there, but to roast these marshmallows I need to get close to the fire. So . . ." He sat down right next to her.

Close to the fire, hmm. Callie didn't dare look at him as she focused on holding her marshmallows where they would get roasted, but not burned. Falk sat so close his shoulder was touching hers, and she could smell the scent of his spicy aftershave. "I have the results from the DNA test. I wanted to tell you first so you can tell Quinn. I don't want to tell him myself as our relationship hasn't exactly been . . . friendly."

Callie nodded. "Okay."

Tension swirled in her stomach. What could she hope for? That the dead body wasn't Monica? That would be a relief to Quinn, but it would explain nothing about her disappearance that night.

Falk took a swallow of his coffee. "Quinn is related to the remains we found on the boat. In fact, closely related. In the first degree. So I guess he is indeed the son of this dead woman who sank with the boat."

Callie bit her lip, clutching the cold glass. "That will confirm what he thought but also confirm what he doesn't want to hear. That his mother is dead."

"Yes," Falk said. "But I have a corker coming that will turn this entire case around."

Callie looked at him. The fire threw light on his intense expression, reflected in his deep brown eyes. "What?"

"The remains on the boat can't be Monica Walker's."

"*What?*" Callie stared at him. "They must be wrong about that."

"No, they're not." Falk turned his stick to prevent his marshmallows from turning black. "I don't know all the ins and outs about it, but they can detect a lot of things from remains these days. Mostly if people have been in contact with toxic substances."

"The victim on the boat was poisoned?" Callie asked, completely confused now.

Falk shook his head. "Chemicals that enter the body can

get into the tissue and remain there. They can determine for instance, from a person's hair, if he has used drugs in the past. In this way they have also been able to determine from the remains the divers secured from the boat that the victim was a drug addict. And we know for sure that Monica Walker never used drugs. That wasn't just what she said or the media believed, but also what we can prove from her medical records. To be part of the series, the actors had to be tested regularly for substance abuse. It was in their contracts. Monica was tested and tested again, for years. The tests all came back negative. It's impossible that she was using drugs and was never caught. But the team looking at the remains is certain that this person—this woman, because it was definitely a woman—had been using drugs for years. The abuse, combined with eating lots of sugar, as addicts often do, caused damage to her bones. They say this woman must have been in pretty poor health."

"I see." Callie stared at him. Her mind worked at top speed to process this new and perplexing information. "But she was wearing a gold sequined top. High heels. That's what you told me after the body was found. So she looked exactly like Monica Walker."

"That's just it. My question is now, how did a drug-addicted woman come to be wearing Monica Walker's clothes? And how did she end up on the boat that disappeared the same night as Monica? The boat we have been assuming was supposed to take Monica away from here?"

Callie refocused on her marshmallows. She withdrew the stick and blew on a pink one to cool it down. "Maybe

Monica wanted to fake her escape? Maybe she paid this woman to pretend to be her and leave on the boat. And the killer who was after Monica killed the wrong woman."

"Yes, my thoughts exactly. The skull was damaged, suggesting she received a blow to her head. Knocking her unconscious, or perhaps killing her before the murderer sank the boat. Remaining question: Where's the real Monica Walker?"

"Since the boat vanished without a trace, Monica must have believed her plan had succeeded. And she must have left town in another way, believing that the press would follow the false lead. Which they did."

Falk nodded. "There's another possibility though. Monica Walker might have killed the woman."

"What on earth for?"

"To make sure she could never come back to ask for more money or tell her story and give Monica away?"

Callie shook her head. "If Monica had to be on the boat to kill the woman and sink it, how did she get away from it?"

"She might not have had to be on the boat to sink it. Incendiary devices can be controlled remotely."

"Would Monica have had the technical knowledge to set it up like that?"

Falk shrugged. "Her lover might have set it up for her. Perhaps Monica had only intended to use the woman as stand-in, but her lover killed the other woman as a more permanent solution. But no matter how we construe what might have happened that night, we have to tell Quinn that he's the son of the woman on the boat but that she wasn't Monica Walker and wasn't a successful TV star, but a heavily addicted woman. Whom, I might add, nobody missed. I've looked into missing persons cases around here from that time, but nobody reported a woman of that description missing. So either she came from somewhere else, in which case we'd have to check all missing persons nationwide, or she came from around here but had no one to care for her."

"Homeless maybe?" Callie suggested.

Falk nodded. "My guess is that when Quinn was born, she was already in trouble. The adoptive parents must have believed they did the best thing possible taking the baby away from this woman, who was perhaps already into drugs or on the verge of being so."

"But Quinn told me his mother was called M. Walker. Isn't that really coincidental?"

Falk shrugged. "Maybe this woman was also called M. Walker, and after having seen Monica in a newspaper, she thought she could approach her and ask for money. Then Monica saw a likeness between them and thought up this escape idea."

Callie pursed her lips. "A woman who used drugs for years can't have looked like Monica Walker."

"You can do a lot with makeup."

Falk thought in silence for a few moments and shook his head. "I feel so sorry for this poor woman who was used in a clever scheme and ended up dead because of it. I don't very much like Monica Walker anymore."

"It's in line with what Otto Ralston told me about Monica's manipulative character."

Callie told Falk all she had learned from the former

Magnates' Wives crew member upon her visit to his cottage garden.

Falk ate his marshmallows and listened, washing down the stickiness with the occasional sip of iced coffee. After Callie had finished telling him the story, he said, "So a manipulative woman, who created a problem for herself by stealing someone else's fiancé and then dumping him for another man, decides it's time to leave the stage in a dramatic scene that could have come right out of *Magnates' Wives*. Woman on the run, stolen boat, explosion. *Bam*— everything over. Did Monica count on the victim dying in the blast and the debris being spread so that we could never reconstruct what happened? Was the woman never meant to get away, but to die in Monica's stead? The newspapers would write about a tragic accident and Monica Walker would be officially dead and done with."

"I don't believe that. Monica worked in TV. She would know from scenarios she had read or seen in other series that forensics are so good that they would sooner or later discover that the victim on board the boat wasn't Monica Walker. It didn't happen in the twenties, when you could just put a body in a car, run it off a cliff, and have the police believe that the owner of the car had died in the accident. Besides, I think the boat was never meant to sink. I think Monica was supposed to disappear. Sail away across the horizon. A mystery forever."

"Well, whatever she planned, it went wrong. Her stunt double, so to speak, died."

"But Monica might not have known that."

Falk sighed. "Nobody has been able to find her, so what are we thinking? That we can find her and ask her what happened that night?"

He shook his head. "No, I just see that Quinn is going to have a tough time facing who his mother was and how sadly her life ended with seemingly no one caring whether she was around or not. And I'm left with an investigation that offers too many question marks and nothing solid to go on."

Callie finished her marshmallows and rubbed her sticky fingers.

"Are you already sorry?" Falk asked softly, keeping his eyes on the fire.

"Sorry for what?"

"Having come back here. Another murder case, all this trouble . . ."

"I made a choice to come and live here."

"Yes, of course." Falk rose to his feet. "Want another coffee?"

"No. Maybe a glass of sparkling water or something?"

"Sure. I'll have a water too. Need to keep a clear head in case I have to drive later tonight. They'll notify me if something comes up."

Callie called after him as he walked away, "Do you never get tired of having to be available, and never for something fun, but always for things like bar fights or accidents or robberies and cattle theft?"

Falk came back from the kitchen with two glasses of water. He handed her one and said, "Not really. I just love what I do."

Callie wanted to pull the glass from his hand, but Falk held it as he probed, "You loved what you did as a tour guide. Won't you miss it?"

Callie's throat was tight. She thought of Kay's panicky phone call and how she had wished she was in Vienna in her stead. To make sure everything went well but also because she missed the whole adventure of traveling. "I'm not sure yet."

"I see." Falk released the glass. Instead of coming to sit by her side again, he sat in the rocking chair. He seemed to look at the Tiffany lamp, then he drank deeply and stared up at the ceiling.

Callie said, "So now that we know that the woman on the boat wasn't Monica, what does that mean for our understanding of Jamison's death? He had the map marking the place where the boat sank. Did he get that far with his investigation back in 1989, when he was somehow forced to drop it? Did the killer offer him money to keep his mouth shut? Has he been paid off for years? Did he want to come clean?" She shook her head slowly. "I can't believe Jamison had an idea that someone died on that boat. He told me he was certain Monica was still alive. He mentioned having proof. What proof? Have you found anything in his filing cabinet to that effect?"

Falk shook his head. "Beats me what the proof could be that Jamison mentioned to you. I did look into phone calls going out, and I was quite surprised by the name that popped up. The last call made from Jamison's cell phone before he died."

"Yes?"

Falk looked at her. "Dave Riggs, lighthouse keeper."

"What?" Callie shot upright. The mineral water almost sloshed over the rim of her glass. "You mean . . ."

Her mind raced. Dave had admitted to her that he had met Monica. He had been secretive about it. He had been insistent that no one could know.

Had Jamison called him because he knew about Dave's contact with Monica? But why had it been so essential?

Falk said, "Jamison might have called him about an unrelated matter. But still, I want to talk to him."

"Yes, I think you should. He turned up at Book Tea the night Jamison was killed, with an odd story." She told him about their conversation.

Falk leaned forward with his elbows on his knees. "I think"—he checked his watch—"I'm going to talk to him now. This is just too important to postpone. Maybe he knows something that can help us."

Callie rose. "Can I come with you? Dave seemed worried about Elvira, like he had to protect her from something. Maybe it's better if I'm there when you question him. If she gets emotional, I can calm her down."

Falk thought a moment, looking as if he would rather decline her offer, but then he sighed. "All right, then. I'm not eager for a scene."

They left the cabin together. Callie noticed the wind had turned chilly, even though it had been such a great day. She felt cold inside too, thinking of Dave Riggs leaving Book Tea mere hours before Jamison died. In what kind of mood had he been?

What had he felt when Jamison called him? Had he gone to the offices of the *Heart's Harbor Herald*?

Was he the person who knew what the murder weapon had been because he was the one who had used it on the unsuspecting editor?

Chapter Twelve

At the lighthouse, lights were burning behind the windows of the keeper's cottage. They seemed to wink at them from the darkness as they drew near, on foot because cars couldn't reach this place.

This isolated place, Callie thought and shivered again.

"Are you sure you want to do this?" Falk asked.

"Of course. Maybe Dave has an innocent explanation for everything." She caught herself hoping that he would, because she had really liked him—him and his wife and the idyllic existence they had built for themselves here by the seaside.

They knocked at the door, and a few moments later Dave opened it. He was in stocking feet and with his shirt sleeves rolled up. He said at once, "Come on in—the wind is chilly tonight." Elvira sat next to the fireplace, crocheting. Several balls of yarn lay in a basket at her feet. She smiled at them. "Looking for another lost dog? I haven't seen any today."

Falk said, "Jamison called you recently. What was that about?"

The name *Jamison* seemed to cause a change in the room, as if a glass of water had dropped to the floor and shattered there.

Dave rearranged knickknacks on the mantelpiece.

Elvira crocheted even more furiously.

The ticking of the clock seemed to grow louder with every moment that passed.

Falk pressed, "You do remember a call, don't you? We can prove he called you."

"I must not have been here. The phone can ring here all it wants when I'm not around."

"No, you did answer and speak to him. The call lasted a few minutes. We can also prove that." Although Falk's tone was still friendly, his posture was tense, his hands held in front of him as if he expected he might have to jump Dave as he tried to make a break for the door.

"Oh," Elvira said, "now I remember. He called to ask if we wanted to send in some copy for the newspaper about our treasure hunts. I asked him what and how he wanted it sent, and that's why it took a few minutes, I suppose."

"So Dave never talked to Jamison?" Falk asked.

"No, Dave wasn't even at home."

"Then why did Dave go and see him that night?" Falk shot back.

Looking up, Dave said, "I never went to see him." He glanced at Elvira. "He did call me and asked me to come, but I didn't go."

"So he did call you? Elvira just lied that it was about copy for the newspaper." Falk sounded confused, his brows drawn together.

"Of course Elvira didn't lie." Dave spoke fast, his breathing ragged between the sentences. "He called and he talked to her about the copy for the newspaper. In the end, he said I had to drop by. That night. But I never went."

"And why would you have to drop by?"

"I have no idea." Dave's expression was cut out of marble, unreadable.

Elvira said, "Jamison sounded strained, like he was overworked. Maybe he wanted to ask Dave to do some work for him?"

"And he couldn't ask that over the phone?" Falk shook his head. "Look, I'm sorry about this, Dave, but I'm taking you down to the station for questioning. I want some better answers, and I'm going to record them as well."

Elvira clenched her crochet hook. "Why? What did he do wrong?"

"I want to ask him some questions without you interfering and lying for him," Falk snapped at her.

Dave raised a placating hand. "You're probably right. I'm coming." He rolled down his sleeves, then looked for his shoes.

Elvira said nothing. Her nostrils were flaring as if she was worked up and only constraining herself with an effort.

"We're leaving now," Falk said to Callie.

Callie had come in her own car so she could head to Book Tea after they were done, but she was confused now as to what was the best thing to do. Leave and go home, since she knew Falk wouldn't allow her to come to the station and be present at the questioning, or stay here and try to learn something from Elvira.

"I'll leave in a sec. I want to ask Elvira something about the treasure hunts. My former colleagues are looking for a team building activity, and this might be nice."

Falk looked as if he didn't buy her impromptu lie, but he nodded. "Okay. See you later."

Dave walked out ahead of him, his head held high, a calm and assured figure fading into the darkness outside the door.

Elvira said, "A treasure hunt might be a little dull for adults. It's more of a family thing, with the parents playing along for the children's sake."

"I see. Well, then I'll have to come up with something else. They were sorry to see me leave, so I'm still trying to remain part of things from a distance."

"It can be hard to break away from your life and just start over. Especially if you liked what you did." Elvira picked up another skein of wool. "Did you like what you did?"

"Yes, very much. Still I felt like I had found something here that meant even more to me."

Elvira nodded as if she completely understood.

"What did you do before you married Dave?" Callie asked her.

"I worked in a coffee bar. Dave stopped in on a trip abroad."

"Where exactly?"

"Copenhagen."

"Oh, how lovely. Which street was your coffee bar on? I might have been there or, in any case, near there."

"I can't remember. It was a long time ago."

Callie surveyed the woman. Was she even telling the truth? "Did you ever go to Moderna Museet, the museum of modern art? The location on a little island is worth seeing in itself, apart from their collection."

"No. I must have really missed something. I like modern art. Preferably a little realistic, though, not those paintings where you can't recognize anything."

Callie nodded slowly. "I see." She checked her watch. "That late already? Iphy must be waiting for me. Good luck with your crochet project. I'll let myself out."

She rushed to the door, opened it, and stepped into the evening air. She pulled the door shut behind her and used her phone to light her way as she hurried to her car.

While walking, her neck prickled as if she could feel eyes glaring at her. She listened for footsteps, waited for a whoosh of cold air as someone struck her. Her heart was pounding, and her palms were covered in sweat. She was so sure Elvira knew she had tried to lure her into a trap. The museum she had referred to, Moderna Museet, was located in Stockholm, not in Copenhagen.

Had Elvira ever actually worked in a coffee bar in Denmark? Had she met Dave there? Or was she lying because she had something to hide?

Something like a criminal past? Why else was Dave so protective of her? So worried she would learn about certain things?

Did Elvira have a record, for assault for instance, of a woman she considered a threat?

Was that why Dave hadn't wanted her to know about his meeting with Monica Walker?

Nothing stirred behind her. She reached her car without incident, got in, and drove off.

Half a mile away, she pulled onto the shoulder and placed a call to the police station. Falk had just come in with Dave Riggs. She told the deputy she needed to tell Falk something before he talked to Dave. He came to the phone and she told him what had happened between Elvira and her.

Falk said, "Hmm, thanks for telling me that. And keep away from that woman. She could be dangerous. Good night."

Callie put the phone away and looked into her rearview mirror. She saw the headlights of another car in the distance. Her heart skipped a beat, and she clenched the wheel, suddenly eager to get moving. But she kept looking at the lights, as if mesmerized. They didn't come any closer.

The car was also on the side of the road. A distance away from her. Parked.

Waiting?

She turned the ignition and started driving again. The lights followed her. At the same distance. Not coming closer, not intending to pass, even though Callie was driving too slowly for the speed allowed on the road.

Her breathing was ragged now and her hands shaky on

the wheel. She expected any moment that the car following her would suddenly accelerate, come up around her, and try to run her off the road. What would she do then? How would she defend herself?

But nothing happened. Just those lights teasing her from the darkness.

Telling her she wasn't alone.

Chapter Thirteen

"I can't believe this." Quinn sat on the floor of Callie's cottage, with his legs crossed, his hands fidgeting with the sandpaper he was using to smooth patches on the window frame before painting it. He had probably started early, as the other window in the room was already finished. Callie had driven out first thing after breakfast to tell him what Falk had told her the previous night. She had a vague hope he would know something about his mother, anything that might have seemed irrelevant before that might now help them to work out who she was.

He stared up at her, his eyes wide with shock. "The woman who died on that boat all those years ago was my mother, but she was *not* Monica Walker?"

Callie nodded. "Falk explained to me that the experts are pretty certain about it. They can still deduce a lot from the remains apparently. And the woman who died on the boat was not in good health, had been addicted to drugs for quite some time. That doesn't fit with Monica Walker."

Quinn clenched his hands together. "When I set out to

look for Monica Walker, of course I realized in the back of my mind that she might be dead. I mean, come on, vanished, never to be heard of again? How is that possible? So I did accept that maybe she had died in an accident while fleeing or maybe even been killed by someone who didn't want her to leave. But this . . . another woman. Taking her place. I mean, the sequined top, the high heels. That dead woman was wearing Monica Walker's clothes! Clothes she wore on that same evening of her disappearance, so she couldn't have given them away to a homeless person or something. The other woman couldn't have stolen them from her either. No, Monica must have given her clothes to this woman and asked her to leave on the stolen boat. For what purpose? I mean, who actually saw her leave? Why did it matter?"

"Maybe the boat was supposed to have been seen. With the woman in the golden top aboard it. Maybe she was supposed to lay a false trail while Monica herself left in another direction. But it didn't work. It went wrong. And we can only guess as to how and because of whom."

Quinn asked, "Was the woman on the boat murdered?"

Callie pursed her lips. "They're still looking into that. It seems someone struck her on the head. But whether that was fatal . . . maybe she was only unconscious. The boat's malfunctioning may have caused the woman's actual death."

"You mean, an explosion maybe, a fire on board?"

Callie nodded. "If she inhaled a lot of smoke, for instance."

Quinn banged the floor with a fist. "Now I want to find Monica Walker even more. I mean, I need to know how my mother got caught up in this disappearance with her. I need to know if Monica realized she was in danger when she sent my mother out on that boat. I need to know if she cared so little for my mother's life that she just gambled it away. After all, the woman was a drug addict, right? Probably homeless at that. Something far different from the successful, rich, and beautiful woman Monica Walker was. She might have looked down on her and figured she was the perfect victim."

"It wasn't like that at all," a calm voice said from the door.

Quinn and Callie turned their heads to look at the person who had come in without them noticing. Elvira Riggs looked at them with a vaguely worried expression. She said, "Deputy Falk called me. He's holding Dave. He's convinced Dave killed Jamison."

Callie frowned. "Why? What evidence does he have against Dave? Except for Jamison's call to him, of course."

"He found Dave's fingerprints in Jamison's office."

"He also found mine there because I had been there," Quinn said. "So that doesn't say much."

Elvira swallowed. "He claims he found the murder weapon. And he can tie it to Dave. I don't know why. He didn't want to tell me. He just said Dave wouldn't be coming home." She raised her hands to her pale face and swallowed convulsively.

Callie said, "Do you think Dave has anything to do with Jamison's death?"

"Of course not. What on earth for?"

"Dave came to me the night Jamison was murdered. He showed up at Book Tea to talk about Monica Walker. I'm sorry, Elvira, but it seems he knew her. That he met her before she disappeared. He was nervous about it, furtive. Maybe he did know something, and Jamison knew or suspected that and confronted him about it. Maybe Dave panicked and struggled with Jamison to convince him to keep his mouth shut. He might not have intended to kill him but—"

"Dave did no such thing. He's not the sort of person who'd ever hurt anybody."

"You don't know what people are like when they're cornered." Quinn pushed himself up from the floor. "I've got work to do."

"Falk won't let Dave go," Elvira said with emphasis, "unless we can prove that he didn't do it. That someone else did it."

"I have no interest in that." Quinn picked up a paint brush and leaned over to the window frame.

Callie said to Elvira, "This is just a very difficult time for . . ."

She fell silent and then asked, "Why did you just say that it wasn't like that at all? When you came in? We were talking about the dead woman on the boat. How can you know anything about her?"

Quinn now turned back to Elvira. "You know something about her?"

Elvira stood and looked at them, not speaking.

Callie said, "Dave claimed you married abroad and you came over here after the disappearance."

"In a way, yes."

"Don't talk in riddles," Quinn yelled. Paint dripped from his brush to the floor. "I can't stand it. My mother died on that boat. I want to know why and who did it."

Elvira swallowed again. "I can't tell you who did it. But I can tell you why. Because it should have been me who died there."

Callie blinked. "I don't follow. So you were here in town on the night Monica Walker vanished?"

"Yes. Dave and I had been preparing it for weeks. Ever since we married. It was the only way."

Quinn said, "You planned the murder?"

"No, you don't understand. We planned the disappearance of Monica Walker." Elvira stood very still. "And the appearance of Elvira Riggs."

Callie stared at the woman. In her mind she reproduced the pictures of Monica Walker that she had seen in the newspaper and online. She tried to superimpose those pictures over Elvira Riggs's face. Of course her hair color was different, her haircut, and her face seemed broader, and . . .

"You're Monica Walker?" Callie asked in a whisper.

Elvira nodded. "I met Dave in Bretagne when he was visiting lighthouses and I was on vacation. All the tables at the small café in the village square were taken, but Dave invited me to sit at his. I was afraid for a moment he would know who I was, but it soon turned out he had no idea. We got to talking, about the nearby chateau, lighthouses, our childhood memories—just about anything you can think of. It was so natural and it felt so right. We just kept on sitting there, ordering more cheese and wine, and we fell in love. Dave was different from all the men I had met before. Solid, dependable. And he hated the limelight. I was the last woman in the world who should have been with him. But I wanted out. Out of the series, out of the suffocating attention from my ex."

"Roger Aames, who wouldn't let you go."

Monica nodded. "He was hounding me, on set and off. I was desperate. I told Dave. He came up with the plan. Dave was lighthouse keeper in Heart's Harbor. A colleague of mine had a house here and had recommended the place to me. To everyone who wanted to hear about it."

"Otto Ralston," Callie said.

Monica nodded. "Dear Otto. He told me the Cliff Hotel would be perfect for me as it had this vintage feel. So I would visit for an innocent vacation. Then, during my stay, I would vanish. A boat would disappear with me on it and be recovered hundreds of miles away."

"With a dead body on board?" Quinn asked in a disgusted tone. "Where did you find this woman? On the street? Perfect for your purpose?"

"No, she was never part of our plan!" Monica spread both hands in a placating gesture. "I hadn't been in touch with my sister since she ran away from home as a teen. We all thought she was dead. It was such a shock to me when she turned up here."

"Your sister?" Quinn echoed.

"Yes. Muriel turned up here and asked me for money. I was upset and unsure what to do. Dave said she could be part of the plan. She would wear my clothes and take the boat out and make sure she was seen. Then she could earn the money she wanted. I agreed to it. I doubted that she would be true to her word, in the end, but she knew nothing about Dave. She had never met him, and she only knew what I told her: that I was going to leave the States and start a new life abroad. Dave said that if she started talking, the press would look for me far from where I really was. The beauty of our plan was that I would never leave Heart's Harbor. I would live here under my new identity, and nobody would even look at me. It worked perfectly."

"Until I came to town," Quinn said with a bitter smile. "Asking questions, upsetting Jamison. Did he know? Did he inform you that I was dangerous? Did you kill him?"

Monica shook her head. "Jamison didn't know anything. He investigated my disappearance while he sat at a table a few feet away from where Dave and I were sitting having coffee. It was nerve-wracking, but it worked. The more we just went about our normal business, the less suspicious we were. Jamison never knew it was me. Listen, even Otto Ralston never knew it was me. He has a cottage here, and he comes here every year. He worked with me on the series, and he's never recognized me."

"So if you didn't kill Jamison and Dave didn't, then who did?"

Monica shrugged. "I don't know. If I knew, I would have told the police. Instead, I'm telling you that I'm Monica Walker. Dave will be furious because we vowed to each other that we'd never tell. But I want to get him out of the cell. You have to help me."

"Why would we?" Quinn said. "You didn't care for the fate of your own sister."

"I didn't know she died. I heard today that the boat was found and that there was a dead body on board. I suspected it had to be my sister."

Monica knotted her fingers. "It was a terrible shock to me. For all that time I believed that she got away and sold the boat and lived off that money. I was worried for her, because I knew she had been using drugs, and I was pretty sure that if she kept doing that, she wouldn't see old age, but my sister had always been on the wild side. Nobody had been able to change her. How could I, from so far away? I had no idea where she was."

Monica looked Quinn straight in the eye. "I never knew she was followed to the boat and killed. If I had known that my plan would put her in any danger, I would never have asked her to do it. I certainly didn't know she had a son."

"I didn't know I was her son until the DNA test just now," Quinn said. "I only knew that my birth certificate listed an M. Walker."

"I can't remember reading anywhere that you had a sister," Callie said.

"Like I said, she ran away from home when she was a teen. She never showed up anywhere with me. I think the press simply didn't think about her existence. It didn't matter to them. They were more interested in my boyfriends."

"You had a string of them," Quinn said.

Monica didn't flinch. "I always chose the wrong men. I was looking for security, but I chose men who were adventurous and fun. It always brought me heartache. When I met Dave, I was tired of that life. The series was wearing me out, Roger's relentless attentions were driving me crazy, and to be honest, I was done with it. I told Dave that for all I knew, I would rather not be alive at all anymore. He was concerned for me and tried to cheer me up. He showed me the stars at night and took me out onto the water so I could experience the quietness and power of the sea.

"Before Dave, I thought everybody lived like me, running from one empty party to another, trying to forget how hard life was by taking another drink or finding another way to spend money. He showed me that he didn't care for what people thought of him, for what he owned or how he would be remembered when he died. He just wanted to live a full life. He convinced me in a few short days that what he had was everything I had always been looking for."

She looked at Quinn. "I don't blame my sister for getting addicted. I was addicted as well. To fame and applause, the fans who adored me. I couldn't live without that, I believed. But Dave showed me that I was everything without those things. He changed my life. For him I wanted to give up everything I had. Because it didn't really matter."

"Couldn't you have just quit the series?"

"I talked about it once. They responded fiercely, saying I had signed on for two more years and I had to complete those. They were worried about losing money if I quit, so they raised my salary. Just more money to spend, but I was sick of spending. I had to run."

Monica smiled sadly. "It sounds so selfish now, but I was at a breaking point. Either run and save myself, or die."

"Instead, your sister died." Quinn still sounded grim. "We assume that whoever killed her meant to kill you. But what if that's not what happened? What if you realized that she was a threat to your perfect plan? Dave might have killed her to make sure she could never talk."

"No!" Monica cried.

"Or you."

She turned a deathly pale. "Me? Kill my own sister?"

Quinn pressed, "She knew you were here in town. She could have given you away."

"How? She didn't know I was going to stay here or that I would turn into Elvira Riggs. She believed I wanted to leave the States and go to Europe. She even said she wanted that for herself too and would go if she had the money. I gave her that money. I believed she had done that, left to start over."

"You say that now, but how can we be sure? Your sister popped up unexpectedly—she was a problem, a danger to your plan. She was unreliable."

"She knew nothing to give away." Monica stood firmly, her feet planted, her hands on her hips. "I would never have killed anyone for my escape. I wanted to start over, make things better. How could I have made anything better if I had started my new life with blood on my hands?"

Callie said, "When you were here, Roger sent you flowers at the hotel. Do you think he might have been watching you?"

"I was afraid of that. I was very careful. I met Dave only

once at the lighthouse like I was visiting it as a tourist. We didn't kiss then or act close; we acted like perfect strangers. I'm sure that anybody watching us never noticed a thing."

Callie sighed. "How does the map Jamison had fit into everything? On his desk was a map with the spot marked where the boat sank. How could he have known? Did he sink the boat? Did he kill your sister? Did he then investigate the case to solve it miraculously and take credit for it?"

"If that was his plan," Quinn said, "then why didn't he go through with it?"

"Maybe he was afraid he would get caught. Maybe over time he believed he had made some kind of mistake that would give him away. His career wasn't worth the risk of spending his life in prison for murder."

Callie thought hard. "It doesn't gel somehow. If Jamison thought he had killed Monica Walker on that boat, why did he call Dave before he died? He had no idea you're Monica, right?"

"Nobody knows that," Monica said, "except for Dave, and you two now."

She held Callie's gaze. "What are you going to do about it?"

Callie shrugged. "We can't do much about it. If we reveal it, there'll just be a media sensation, and it won't solve the two murder cases. Besides, I assume you don't want the world to know you're living here and have been since the day you vanished."

Monica nodded. "I want to continue the life I have now. It's quiet and peaceful and just what I need."

"But your disappearance caused your sister's death. My

mother's death." Quinn's whole body was tense. "I can't just ignore that. I want to find out who killed her."

"I know. And I also want you to find out. That's why I'm here. I decided to tell you the truth, even though Dave will be disappointed that I broke my promise to him. I want you to know the full story."

"So far you haven't told me much that's of any use to me. You don't know anything about her life. You can't tell me who killed her. That is, if you're not lying about you and Dave having nothing to do with it."

Monica's jaw pulled tight. "I told you what I know. I can't give you anything I don't have. I believed I was doing the right thing."

"Doing the right thing would have been getting your sister treatment for her addiction. Not giving her money to pretend to be you." Quinn crossed his arms over his chest. "You didn't care for her at all."

"I hardly knew her. She came here to blackmail me. She told me she wanted money or else she would go on TV and spread lies about me. About our childhood, our parents, whatever came to mind. She laughed and said that people would believe her. I hated my life already. What would have happened if she had made good on that threat? She was a ruthless, self-centered person. There was nothing in the world that mattered more to her than her need for drugs and the money to pay for them."

Quinn jutted his chin up as if to resist Monica's explanation, but Callie saw in his eyes that he realized it was probably true.

Monica said, "I know I should have treated her better. And over time I've often wondered if I could have helped her. But I know that it's very hard to help people who are addicted and who don't want to change. My sister didn't want to quit. She just wanted me to supply the money for her to keep on going."

"And you did." Quinn's voice was suffocated. "You gave her enough that she could have killed herself."

"But she didn't kill herself. Someone killed her. And I want that killer found. Not for me. I could have stayed hidden in my cottage, saying nothing."

"You came here because of your husband. Not because of your sister!" Quinn shouted. "It's about you, you, you— never about her. It wasn't back then and it isn't now."

He stormed out the door.

Monica ran after him, calling, "Where are you going? What are you going to do?"

Quinn didn't reply. He dove into his car and drove off.

Monica watched him leave, then turned to Callie, who had followed her out. "What will he do? Tell the press I'm here?"

"I can't say. He's very upset. He only just learned that his parents weren't his real parents when his adoptive mother died. Then he looked for you. Now he's found you, but the story isn't what he thought it would be. That's been very hard on him."

"I know." Monica stood and surveyed Callie. "I lied. When I said the police had found the murder weapon and could tie it to Dave, that's not true. They haven't found it yet. Falk called me to tell me that he released Dave. He might be home already, wondering where I am."

Callie held her gaze, perplexed by this revelation. "Then why did you come here? Why did you tell us the truth? You didn't need to."

Monica smiled. "I wanted to. I realized that for all these years I've tried to tell myself I did the right thing. For survival. I told myself that if I had let down the studio and the crew of my hit series, they had gotten past it and turned the series into an even bigger success without me. I told myself over and over that in the end nobody's lives had really gotten any worse because of what I did. Until the boat was found with the body on it. Then I knew my sister had died. Not by my hand. Not because of anything I did directly. But still . . ."

She swallowed hard. "I involved her in my escape. And she died while I kept on living. I already had the better life of the both of us. Our father died when we were little, and our mother had to make ends meet and wasn't at home a lot. Muriel, as the eldest, felt responsible to bring in some income, so she was doing newspaper rounds and washing dishes at restaurants—anything she could really.

"I was the youngest, protected, getting all the extras, like new jeans or a birthday present. Then Muriel ran away from home, and it was just Mom and me. She put everything she had into my future. I got to study, model, act. After my big breakthrough, I had money, fame. I bought my mother a nice house and made sure she never had to work again or worry about money.

"But I couldn't do anything for Muriel. I had no idea where she was or what her life was like. She told me when we she came here all those years ago that she had given up her baby because the father had left her, and she couldn't take care of a child on her own. I felt so sorry for her." Monica's voice trembled. "Guilty too. But I didn't see how I could help her. I involved her in my plan so I could quiet my conscience with the idea of having given her money. But it was no solution. And now I know she died, and I feel even worse. I can't keep the secret anymore."

She hung her head and stared at the floor. "Dave will probably hate me for what I did just now. But I can't ignore Muriel's death. I can't go on living my life like her death didn't happen. All of those years I didn't know. But now I do."

Callie said, "You should have told Quinn. Then he would have understood you better. He would also have known you that you had some information about his past. The things your sister told you about her baby, why she had to give him up. He wants that information so badly. Now he's run off and—"

Monica said, "It's my fault. I pretended like Dave was in danger and that was I acting because of him. It seemed to be a plausible reason, and I didn't want to say that I felt guilty about my sister. It seems so cheap after I let her down so badly."

Callie squeezed Monica's hand. "We all have things in our lives that we regret. Things we can't undo. But I think it's very brave of you to come forward. I think we should go to Falk and tell him what you told us. He should know. Especially if Quinn is somehow going to make this public."

Her stomach tightened at the idea. "I hope he's not, but this is a very hard time for him, and he's not himself."

Monica nodded. "Let's go to the police then."

Chapter Fourteen

At the station, Falk was surprised to see them but got them coffee and then listened patiently while Monica told her story again. He took notes and asked some questions to get things clearer in his head. "It would be helpful if you could give me a time line for that evening. When you exchanged clothes with your sister. Where she was to go, how she would find the boat, and so on. Maybe we can find a point on that time line where the killer got involved."

Just then the door opened and Dave stormed in. He stopped in the middle of the room and looked at Monica. His voice was strangled as he said, "Tell me you didn't do it."

Monica's lips wobbled as she whispered, "I did it, Dave. I had to. I can't just let Muriel—"

"Muriel was after your money. She wanted to destroy you. She never cared for you, just for herself." Dave's hands were clenched into fists by his sides. He glared at his wife. "She was cold and ruthless and dead set on ruining everything for you. Your career, your spotless reputation. And if she had understood what we had planned, she would have ruined us too. Our chances of ever being happy together."

Monica sat with her head down, tears trickling down her cheeks.

Callie said, "Sit down, Dave. It's too late to change it now. Monica has already told us. She also told Quinn. He got angry and stormed off. We're not sure what he intends to do."

Dave stared at her. Then his eyes flashed to Monica. "Come on. We have to leave. We have to get out of town before the press comes after us. They can't know how you look now. We have to run. We can leave the States. We'll go see Venice. You wanted that, right? We'll go today."

"Sit down, Dave." Falk rose from behind his desk and pointed at the empty chair beside Monica. "Now."

Dave repeated to his wife, "We have to leave. They can't find us. They can't destroy all we've worked so hard for."

"Monica isn't leaving town," Falk said. "We need her for the investigation. Now you sit down, or I'll make you sit down."

Dave sank to the chair. He looked at Monica with wide, disillusioned eyes. "Why did you have to do this?" he whispered.

Monica tried to put her hand on his arm, but he pulled away from her and sat with his back half-turned to her.

"It's convenient that you're here, Mr. Riggs," Falk continued, "because I have some questions about the night on which Muriel Walker died. I want to know exactly what happened. What your part in it was."

"None at all. I never saw Muriel that night."

Dave didn't seem to want to say more, but when Falk just leaned back in his chair and watched him, letting the strained silence linger, Dave seemed compelled to continue, "She knew where the boat was and how to take it out. She knew what to do: Make sure that in the morning she was seen in another town or two. Lay a false trail. Divert attention. Monica paid her enough money to get it right. But she must have been using again and botched it."

"Someone killed her!" Monica cried. "She didn't botch it."

Dave spoke as if he hadn't heard her, "Monica met Muriel to exchange the clothes. Monica then came to me and dyed her hair, changed her appearance, became Elvira Riggs. I had arranged a fake identity for her, through an agency. They delivered everything: birth certificate, passport, diplomas, a complete life to step into. The correspondence was all handled through PO boxes, and they sent me a key to a locker at a bus station where I could find the envelope with paperwork waiting for me. It was expensive, but pretty much foolproof since they didn't know who I was and I didn't know who they were. I had already told people around here about the wonderful woman I had met abroad, about our wedding, and said that she would come over shortly. They were expecting her arrival, so it was never connected to Monica Walker's disappearance. We believed it had worked. Even though there were no sightings and no boat ever turned up. We never thought anything had happened to Muriel."

Falk said, "You knew where the boat was waiting for Muriel."

"Of course. I put it there."

"So you stole it?"

"Yes." Dave glared at Falk. "Are you going to arrest me for that?"

Falk didn't flinch. "You took the boat to that assigned spot, and you knew that Muriel Walker was going there. Who else knew?"

"No one! Is it so hard to understand, man? We made this plan together. Muriel didn't even know I was involved. She thought Monica had arranged for the boat."

"Yes, I see." Falk leaned back in his chair again and leaned his fingertips against each other. "Muriel thought she was dealing with her sister. She thought that after the clothes exchange nobody would be following her around to see what she did. She went out to the boat, not knowing a man knew where it was docked. She went on board unsuspectingly and then you popped up, Mr. Riggs, and you killed her."

Dave scoffed. "What? Why? If someone did follow her and killed her, it was someone mistaking her for Monica. Monica was the intended victim."

"Was she? It's clear you're very protective of your wife. You wanted to take her out of her destructive showbiz life and give her a new start here in his wholesome little town. You had everything prepared, but then her sister turned up. You decided to make her a part of your plan; after all, it was convenient if she could take the boat out so you didn't have to do it and if she could also play Monica. She could even create sightings that would make the elopement more credible. But let's be fair. You knew that her addiction drove her to desperate acts. Lies, manipulation. As soon as her money ran out, she would come back. She would start asking for money again."

"She had no one to come back to. Monica was leaving the States, for all Muriel knew. She didn't know about me. Where could she have gone?"

"That is rational. But aren't a lot of things in life very irrational? You were *this close* to being with the love of your life. To having her all to yourself. You would have successfully severed all ties with her old life, and she would be dependent on you and you alone. That was your idea of happiness. You couldn't risk that. You had come so close. Muriel was a risk. Maybe you even told yourself that with her drug addiction she would never have a really good life. So killing her wasn't really unethical. Perhaps you were even doing her a favor?"

"What are you talking about? I never thought that. I never saw her that night either. I certainly didn't harm her."

"Come on, Mr. Riggs." Falk leaned forward on his desk. "When you came in here just now, you were fuming. You spoke about Muriel Walker in derogatory terms, saying she had been out to ruin your wife's life. You didn't like her. Even after all these years, you can't hide your frustration about her appearance on the scene. And now we know someone killed her. You just told me you put the boat in place. You were the only one who knew where it was. So if Muriel Walker's dead body ended up on that boat, who could have killed her but you?"

Dave was silent. His eyes shot from left to right as he scrambled for an answer to Falk's accusing questions.

Monica said, "Someone must have followed Muriel to the boat. She was wearing my clothes. It could have been Roger or a crazy fan, some stalker who followed me to Heart's Harbor. The dock where we kept the boat was dark and abandoned, an ideal place for a confrontation. The killer might have intended to kill her all along, or maybe there was an argument, a struggle. Then he put her on the boat and sank it to hide her death."

"Not very likely. Someone who had been following her for a longer time and confronted her there would have simply thrown her body into the water or hidden it some other way, but not thought up this entire plan with the boat. No. I think I'm holding Mr. Riggs. You admitted you stole the boat. You admitted you were the only one who knew where it was docked."

"Not quite." Monica's eyes sparkled. "I also knew. I had to tell Muriel, remember? Are you sure, Deputy, that *I* didn't kill my sister? She was a danger to me too. Maybe even more so than to Dave."

Falk looked at her. "A charming way to distract me, Miss Walker or Mrs. Riggs or whatever I should call you now. Is your marriage abroad even valid? I doubt it. If you had married under your own name, the press would have gotten wind of it."

Monica hung her head. Her hands clutched the purse in her lap. "I'm holding Dave," Falk continued. "I want to take a closer look at all the circumstances of the old case and of course Jamison's death as well. You were the last people he called before he died. What was that about? Treasure hunts? I don't think so."

Dave glanced at Monica and sighed. "Okay, so he told me over the phone he had to see me, that he needed my advice on something sensitive."

"Why you of all people?"

"We knew each other through the Historical Society. We got along. He said that he needed someone who could keep a secret. In case he was wrong about what he suspected."

"But you didn't go to him?"

"No. I was worried it had something to do with Monica's disappearance and I didn't want to talk about that. I was already sorry I had gone to Callie. I felt compelled to meddle, to tell her about Monica, about her having wanted to do a new series, and I wanted to steer Callie's perception of the situation, to have her think in a certain direction. But that was wrong. I should never have come forward. It only drew attention to me, to us. Because I had already made that mistake, I was edgy, unsure. I didn't feel up to facing Jamison and risking him maybe intuiting something about my story, finding it suspicious."

"You admit you felt edgy, cornered perhaps even?" Falk hitched a brow. "You had made a mistake approaching Callie, and now Jamison wanted to talk to you. You were worried about what he might know or, in any case, suspect. You did go to him. And then it got out of hand, and you lashed out at him."

"No!" Dave shook his head forcefully. "I never went to the *Herald*'s offices."

"I don't believe you." Falk leaned back with determination etched in his features. "Jamison had the map indicating where the boat was sunk. He must have been on to you. You paid him money to keep his mouth shut. Then Jamison wasn't prepared to shut up anymore. He told you over the phone that he was going to tell the truth. That you killed Monica Walker.

"I don't think Jamison knew Monica was still alive and someone else had died on that boat. I think he believed that the boat held the remains of Monica Walker, and he wanted to come forward and have his moment of glory after all those years of being pointed at as the reporter who couldn't crack the case. He called you and you told him you'd come over to discuss it. Then you killed him."

"You can't prove any of that." Dave leaned back, crossing his legs. "You're just speculating. A good lawyer will have me released in no time."

"Then I suggest you call a good lawyer so we can start the interrogations as soon as possible."

Falk looked at Monica. "You're staying too, to give your side of the story. You can have a lawyer present as well, of course."

"Can we do this discreetly so that it doesn't get out that I'm Monica Walker? Let the people believe you're questioning me, Elvira Riggs, and my husband. Please?"

Falk shrugged. "I don't want a media circus at this station, so I'm fine with that. But you just said this Quinn character knows something and ran off, so he might be telling the whole world right now, for all we know."

Monica sighed. "I should have handled it differently."

Dave shook his head in disbelief. "Why did you have to tell Quinn Darrow the truth? I could have protected you."

"You've protected me long enough. And Quinn Darrow is Muriel's son. I've always felt like I let Muriel down, and I can't do the same to her son. I had to tell him. Please try to understand."

Dave stared at the floor, his shoulders slumped.

Callie looked from the dejected husband to the guilt-ridden wife and wondered if they were telling the truth. Had they really not known that Muriel Walker had died on the night of Monica Walker's disappearance?

Had they really not known that the stolen boat had sunk and been buried under the water, so close to them for all of these years?

Or was it only Monica that didn't know while Dave had known all along? Was he the killer? Did he kill Jamison as well?

Falk gestured to Callie to leave his office. Outside he said to her, "Thanks for bringing her in here."

"She wanted to come and tell you. I didn't make her. I'm sorry about all of this. Dave did what he could to keep her out of it."

"Yes, I wonder how far he was willing to go for that." Falk raked back his hair. "Anyway, I have a challenging few hours ahead of me. I need to reconstruct what happened, and it was a long time ago. Plus they could both be lying to protect themselves or each other or who knows who else involved. So far everybody seems to have been lying about everything."

He sighed. "Well, never mind. I'd just be very happy if Quinn Darrow refrained from making this breaking news on every channel."

He held up his hands and spread them as if unrolling a banner. "'*Actress Missing for Thirty Years Turns up Alive and Well in Small Town Where She Vanished*'—it would be a global sensation."

Callie frowned. "Did you check the map for fingerprints?"

"Of course, but no luck. Nothing on it."

"What? Nothing? Not Jamison's? If he took it from his file cabinet . . . he wasn't wearing gloves, right?"

"No, you're right about that—it's odd. But I don't suppose the killer would have wiped the prints away. He could have taken the map with him. It pointed straight to the scene of the crime. The boat and the remains."

Falk walked away to talk to his other deputy and get things into motion for questioning the Riggses.

Callie stared at his busy figure. He had said before that the killer wouldn't leave a clue. He was saying now that the killer would not have removed fingerprints from the map. But why not?

What if the killer had wanted the map to be found? What if the killer had wanted the police to conclude that Jamison had had the map all along, hidden in his file cabinet?

But what if Jamison hadn't known anything about the

map, the boat, or the body on it? What if Jamison had been killed for another reason?

What if the map had been put there on purpose, to lead the police to the boat and the remains and muddle the waters?

Callie walked out of the station, her head spinning with possibilities. She had to talk to Mr. Bates again. The former hotel owner might be able to help her.

Chapter Fifteen

M r. Bates was glad to see her, as he was just working on Daisy's portrait. He about dragged her into his studio and pointed at the canvas on the easel, where a pencil outline was taking shape. "I'm trying to capture her essentials in my mind as I go," he explained. "A tilt of the ear here, a sparkle in the eye there. But let me not bore you with painting life. Tell me what you're here for. You look kind of beat."

"Thanks—now I feel even more tired." Callie sank into a chair.

Mr. Bates went to a side table and poured some lemonade from a jug. He handed her the glass. "Have a drink. You'll feel better soon."

He sat down himself and asked, "Is it this business about a sunken boat having been found? I heard about it from someone who came to pick up his dog's portrait. Is it Monica Walker's boat? I mean, the one stolen the same night when she vanished?"

"Yes." Callie decided not to say anything about the remains on board. "The police were able to locate it because of a map they found on Jamison's desk after he was murdered. So he must have been involved somehow at the time."

"You think Jamison killed Monica Walker?" Mr. Bates sat down with his own glass of lemonade and sipped. "I do remember he was so fanatical about solving it, but I can't imagine him as a killer. Or as a vain psychopathic personality who kills first and then exposes the killer himself? Who would he have wanted to pin it on? Not on himself, I suppose."

"When you mentioned to me that the cards with the bouquets were signed with 'R.,' you didn't say her ex was called Roger. Roger Aames. You must have known about him."

Mr. Bates stared up at the ceiling with a vacant look as if he was far away. "The vengeful ex—it's such a cliché. I think Jamison also thought so and was looking for something slightly more original. Like, uh . . . a rival in the cast?"

"What?" Callie asked.

Bates smiled at her. "Well, every actress at the time wanted a part in *Magnates' Wives*. And if Monica Walker was no longer available, well, someone would have to take her place. Did you know that only one week after Monica vanished, the studio had already ordered the writers to introduce a new character who could appeal to the audience that had adored Monica? In fact, it's safe to say that this new character rescued the entire series from tanking after Monica's disappearance."

"I see. I can't say I ever watched *Magnates' Wives*, so I really had no idea."

"Ah, Sadie Cooper," Bates said with a fond smile. "A

younger wife, even more beautiful than Monica's character had been—softer, more vulnerable. But also with dark secrets that came to light over the course of several seasons. They really upped their game with her. I doubt they would have gone quite that dark before Monica left."

"Oh," Callie said, "so actually her departure was good for the series?"

"Yes. The news about her disappearance made waves for months, and the series had never attracted so many viewers as it did then. Plus they sold so much merchandise. They had all kinds of items made with Monica's character on them and the new lead, Sadie Cooper, beside her. You could say her career really soared because of Monica."

Callie studied him. "And this actress who played Sadie Cooper, was she here in town when Monica vanished?"

"I don't think so, no. But I can't be sure. I can't say I noticed her at the time, but she wasn't as well known then as she became with the Sadie Cooper part." He held her gaze. "You think she might have . . ."

"I'll look into it. Thank you for the suggestion."

Mr. Bates gestured with a hand. "Don't mention it. I'm probably thinking in the wrong direction anyway. I never was good at solving puzzles. I just wish the disappearance had done my hotel as much good as it did the series. I think the producers should thank Monica for her initiative."

Callie finished her lemonade and thanked Bates for his time. She admired Daisy in pencil one more time, saying she hoped the oil paint version would be taking shape soon. Even though she still thought three hundred dollars was a steep price, she was already looking forward to hanging the portrait of her little girl on the wall of her new cottage. It would make it feel like home.

Mr. Bates accompanied her all the way to her car and waved her off.

Once she had driven a little ways away from his house Callie stopped the car, pulled out her cell phone, and went online. She searched for "Sadie Cooper, *Magnates' Wives*."

She stared at the strikingly beautiful young woman, then read what the entry said about her part. Introduced in late 1989. Played by . . .

Her eyes went wide. *Kim Ralston.*

Ralston? But that was the name of the man who had worked on the series, right? The one who had advised Monica to come out here.

Otto Ralston, who had a cottage here. Who had even told her his daughter was staying here too. His daughter, Kim Ralston? If Kim was Otto Ralston's daughter, he had to be older than Callie had believed when she had met him. Sixty, sixty-five, she had guessed, but with a daughter who had been twenty at the time when she took Monica's place on *Magnates' Wives*, Ralston had to be over seventy. He didn't look his age at all.

Her mind spinning, Callie put her phone away and drove on. Ralston had mentioned in passing that his daughter was staying at the campgrounds. Callie wanted to talk to Kim Ralston right away and find out what she knew about those days thirty years ago.

*   *   *

At the campground's store, Iphy's friend Irma told Callie that Kim and her family weren't tenting, but had a motor home and took her to it. Seeing how large and luxurious it was, with an inflatable Jacuzzi beside it, Callie concluded that Otto Ralston's definition of 'rustic' to describe his daughter's vacation didn't match her own.

A neighbor who was cleaning his barbecue straightened up a moment to reveal that the family were probably at their favorite spot on the beach near the Wavebreaker Beach Pavilion before dipping both his hands into a bucket of soapy water again.

Armed with Irma's directions to the Pavilion and her detailed description of Kim, her husband and their three daughters, Callie exchanged the tree-rich campgrounds for the wide open beach, soaking up the exuberant summer mood of kiting, swimming and sunbathing which eased some of the tension in her shoulders. And when she spotted the family at the water's edge, she was all ready for some innocent conversation.

The eldest daughter, a pretty teen with a slightly bored expression, was swiping through screens on her phone, while two much younger girls built a sand castle. They looked almost identical with blonde pigtails and pink shirts emblazoned with the word princess in glittery letters. Kim was still a striking woman, tall, statuesque, and with the blonde curls that had been her trademark in her days on the show. She wore a simple summer dress now and had bare feet crusted with sand. When Callie asked her if they could talk a moment, she stepped aside with a friendly smile. "Yes? What is it?"

"I'm Callie Aspen from Book Tea, a tearoom in town. I'd like to invite you and your family to the Fourth of July tea party we're organizing at Haywood Hall. We're highlighting town history, and we'll also devote some time to the link between Heart's Harbor and the hit series *Magnates' Wives*."

Kim's friendly smile turned chilly. "That was a long time ago. I had a good time of course, but my life is different now. I don't want to be asked for autographs and all that. I spend the summers here with my family and I'd appreciate it if we could remain more or less anonymous."

"I'm sorry. I talked to your father the other day, and he mentioned his daughter also vacationed here. I had no idea that . . ." Callie tried to look sufficiently contrite.

Kim now thawed a little. "My father is very proud of me. I told him several times not to start on that old *Magnates' Wives* thing again, but it was a highlight in his own career as well. He was responsible for promotion, marketing, merchandise. I think it was one of the series that sold the most merchandise at that time. Of course you can't compare it to the current series, but for the late eighties it was doing great."

"Your father is very proud of you indeed. I can understand that you don't want to come to the tea party. That's fine. I won't point you out to people or anything. I just . . . well, we want to throw a great party, and *Magnates' Wives* is something people remember. Especially with Monica Walker vanishing here."

Kim shuffled her feet in the sand. "Yes, it's a mystery that will probably never be solved. It was odd, filling the empty spot left by her. But I had my own part, my own character. It's not like I had to play her role."

It sounded as if this was something Kim had repeated over and over. To herself?

"Were you already coming here at the time?" Callie asked.

Kim nodded. "With my father. He's always loved the ocean."

"Handy with boats too?"

"Oh, very. He can control anything from a canoe to a catamaran. He always told the series writers what they could do with boats."

Callie smiled, although she felt a little cold inside. "I see. You must have had some thrilling scenes. Real cliffhangers."

"Usually at the season's end. The viewers had to speculate whether somebody was going to die, or . . . I remember one time when we were all aboard a ship, and it was supposed to start sinking. There was only a small dinghy some of us could leave in. What would happen next? The entire summer people argued over who should get into the dinghy and survive."

Kim shook her head. "To them Sadie Cooper and her friends were very real."

"Well, it must be something fun to look back on. Even if you've stepped away from it. What do you do now, if I may ask?"

"I'm a beautician. I have a studio where people come for a facial or a manicure. It's really nice work and an ideal work situation with the kids. After ten years on *Magnates' Wives*,

I did a few other TV shows, but I quit acting after I had my second daughter." She pointed at the teen who was digging through a beach bag. "I just felt like I couldn't fully focus on my work, thinking about my little ones at home. When they were older, I did some work as talk show host, and there were negotiations to get me my own show, but then the twins came along. Rather unexpectedly, but nonetheless very much wanted. They grow up so quickly, you know. My eldest is in Japan right now as part of an exchange program. When I think of her, so far away, I'm glad I have the twins close to hug."

Kim smiled as she watched her daughters bicker over where the sand castle's gate should be. "My father wasn't happy that I quit. He has always said I could get into some big Hollywood production. He's still upset I didn't make it to that level."

Callie nodded. The kids' voices and the cries of the gulls overhead seemed to come from far away. Her mind was racing. Otto Ralston, who loved his daughter. Who was ambitious and wanted to launch her career. Who might have believed that success in *Magnates' Wives* would be the stepping-stone to Kim's Hollywood debut.

A man who knew about boats. Who had been familiar with Heart's Harbor and the area around it.

A man who might have even sensed how unhappy Monica was and how desperate to change her life around.

Had Ralston followed her here? Had he watched her as she met with Dave? Had he found out the two had met before, abroad? Had he seen his chance to get rid of Monica and introduce his daughter in her stead?

It was possible, but to prove it Callie needed a lot more than what she had right now. Assumptions weren't enough. She'd have to prove that Ralston had been in Heart's Harbor that night. That he had known where the boat was. Or that he would have had the chance to follow Muriel, mistakenly believing her to be Monica.

Monica had told her that Ralston lived here in the summers and had never recognized her. So Ralston believed he had killed Monica Walker. He had killed her and sunk the boat. But he had kept a map of where he'd sunk it. As a backup plan? To use in case the matter became news again?

Had he killed Jamison and left the map on his desk as a distraction? To lead the police in circles, ever farther away from the truth? With the boat found and a dead body on board, the police would, of course, have opened up the old case and looked at all the old suspects. Roger Aames, stalker fans, the alleged new love interest. Otto Ralston had never been in the picture, so he needn't fear he would be implicated.

Clever. But if Ralston had left the map on purpose, he had believed the police would find Monica Walker's body. He had not known it would be somebody else's.

That could be their trump card.

Before word got out that Monica Walker was still alive and the remains on the boat belonged to somebody else, they had to confront Ralston. Lure him into a trap.

She thanked Kim hurriedly and walked off, leaving the woman to stare after her in mild surprise.

Callie pressed a hand to her throat as she ran for her car. There was no time to lose. They needed to get to Ralston before he knew what was really up if they were to have any chance of succeeding.

Chapter Sixteen

"**I** don't like this," Falk whispered to Callie.

They were hiding behind a giant tree trunk close to Ralston's cottage. Callie could smell the scents from the blossoming garden. Ralston was working there, quietly pulling out weeds. He had no idea what was about to happen to him.

Falk whispered again, "Dave is in his cell at the station, so I know he can't burst onto the scene to create a mess. But if something happens to Monica, he'll blame me. He might even sue me. This could cost me my career. And where's Quinn? Making this trap work is risky enough without a loose cannon in the equation."

"Do you want to catch a double murderer or not?" Callie asked with more conviction than she felt. Who knew what Ralston might do when he found out he had made a terrible mistake all those years ago?

Footsteps crunched on the gravel, and Ralston looked up. He froze. The weeds he had pulled out dropped from his hand to the ground.

A few feet away from him stood a woman with blonde hair, waving on the breeze that came from the ocean behind the trees. She was dressed in a gold sequined top, black pants, and towering high heels.

Ralston croaked, "Monica! That can't be. You're dead."

Monica laughed softly. "No, Otto. You only believed I was dead. But I never was."

"This can't be." Ralston reached up and rubbed his eyes. He blinked and stared. "It must be the heat. Heat exhaustion. Yes. I need water."

"Stop," Monica said as he started to turn away. "You don't need water. I'm as real as the trees around us."

"I killed you," Ralston said in a shaking voice. "I smashed your skull and I sank the boat. You're dead twice over! Like you deserved."

He stepped forward, waving a hand at her. "You wanted to abandon us. Just walk away. After all we had given you. Your career, your fame, your public. It was ours. We created it for you. You had a little talent, maybe, but not a lot. Others were much better than you."

"Others like Kim?" Monica scoffed. She laughed in a disparaging tone. "You couldn't wait for me to leave so you could set Kim up in my place. You believed she'd go far, didn't you? That she would star in Hollywood movies and win an Oscar. But she preferred to get married, have kids, and play beautician."

"Don't you dare smirk about Kim. She has more talent in her little finger than you do in your entire body." Ralston stared at her, his green eyes flashing with hatred. "That body you so readily gave to any man who could move your career."

"Except to you," Monica said. "Was that it? Were you mad because I never liked you, dated you? Because I chose Roger and—"

"All those oafs," Ralston said. "You always chose the men who hurt you. Like you enjoyed being hurt. I knew Roger couldn't let you go. I knew he sent you flowers and more. But the bouquets arriving at the Cliff Hotel the day you eloped weren't his. They were mine. I sent them to make you edgy, nervous, afraid. And so the hotel staff would know you were being stalked. That would be very convenient once you vanished, right? A ready-made suspect. Poor Roger. The police questioned him for days after your disappearance. They had to let him go eventually. No body means no proof anything happened."

Monica kept her eyes on him. "You sent those bouquets?"

"Of course. I wasn't dumb enough to kill you and trust in the local police to figure it out." Ralston clicked his tongue. "They couldn't figure it out *then*, and they can't figure it out *now*. Jamison's death . . . the handyman's tape measure beside the body. I took it and kept it after he did some work on my cottage. He asked me questions about *Magnates' Wives*. There was this terrier insistence about him I didn't like. At all. I knew he'd be trouble. And Joe Jamison. The man who 'knew' Monica was still alive, as I had provided him with proof. A letter she wrote to me begging me to ensure the public forgot about her quickly so she could have her peace. At the time Jamison believed the letter was real. He took it as proof she had survived the disappearance. That's why he stopped pursuing the case."

Of course, Callie thought. *Everyone had been so surprised that Jamison had all of a sudden stopped investigating further. But he had believed he was following the missing woman's own wishes.*

Ralston continued, "Darrow's questions brought the whole thing back to life again. Jamison started to doubt his earlier conclusions and my proof. He dropped by my cottage and said he had never had a good gut feeling about the case. He wanted to talk to me but I lied that I didn't have time for him right then and was more than happy to come to the newspaper office late at night so we could compare notes at leisure. Because of the hour there was no one in the street who might have seen me. No witnesses. Just the two of us in his office. As he hadn't called me, I knew the police wouldn't find my phone number under his contacts and would never make a connection with me. I pretended like I was fully convinced the letter was real and Monica had survived. It was so easy to get him to open up the file cabinet to show me some witness information he had always kept. He believed that he could convince me to turn over the letter to the police. But I knew, even before I set a foot in that office, that I would kill him. I had to. While he was looking for his statements in the cabinet, I could just walk over and knock him to the ground. I did it with his own paperweight."

Ralston sounded gleefully satisfied. "I thought his secretary would notice right away that it was missing and would tell the police. An impromptu weapon, suggesting the murder hadn't been planned, but committed in a moment of anger. For instance, when Jamison revealed he had known about the boat all along? After all, there was a map on the desk, probably having come out of his locked filing cabinet, which was now open. Of course I brought the map and put it on the desk after I knocked Jamison out. But I knew what the police would conclude from its presence in combination with the open filing cabinet."

He laughed softly. "It's so easy to string people along once you understand their way of thinking. I could just hear the officers discussing the case: 'Jamison had the map all along. He knew where the boat with the remains was. Has he been covering for someone for all of these years? Accepting money to keep his mouth shut? Was he himself involved in the murder? Why not? He dropped the case suddenly, without ever giving an explanation for that. What perfect cover, to report on the murder case in which you yourself are the criminal.'"

Callie dug her heels deeper into the ground, realizing how that reasoning had played in her own head. Ralston had made a correct assessment of the situation.

Leaning closer, Ralston scoffed, "You have to leave the clues all laid out for them. Otherwise, they'll never get anywhere."

Callie felt Falk tense in anger beside her as Ralston's disparaging words sank in. The realization of how this man had played the police thirty years ago with the bouquets and now with the map left on the desk. She hoped Falk wouldn't rush forward to get to the arrogant killer before he had confessed it all.

Ralston continued, "But if I didn't kill you back then, dear Monica, who did I kill? I killed someone, you know. A woman in your clothes. Those clothes." He gestured at her, encompassing her top, pants, and shoes. "But since you're here in the flesh, laughing at me, I assume someone else died? A double, yes, of course, a TV series trick. I should have known you'd know about that."

"Still you never thought you'd killed the wrong woman. Or else you wouldn't have left the map for the police. That was stupid. They have the boat now and the body. Now they'll figure out that the dead woman isn't me. Then what?"

Ralston shrugged. He seemed to have gotten over his initial shock of this confrontation. "Then nothing. They cannot determine who the dead woman is, I'm sure."

"I could tell them."

Ralston laughed. "You're not going to tell them anything. Or else you wouldn't be here. You want something from me. Probably money. And I'm willing to give you some."

"Some?" Monica said. "A lot, you mean. Don't you think I understand why you tried to kill me that night? Because you knew that if I suddenly vanished, if people wondered about what happened to me, you would make a fortune. You created even more merchandise, you put my likeness and the face of my character's replacement, Sadie Cooper, side by side. You struck it rich on the basis of my death. But it's time to pay up now. You will give me what I deserve."

Ralston studied her. "You're right that it was mainly about money. When do records suddenly hit number one? When the artist is dead. When do paintings make a million bucks at auction? When the creator is gone. Especially if the death is sudden and tragic, the public wants to show sympathy by buying. They all want to be a part of this feeling of loss. Connection, togetherness. So I cashed in on your disappearance. To me it has always been your death. Because I was so certain you were indeed dead. You see, I hit you—I mean, whoever that woman was—from behind. I never saw her face clearly. To be honest, I didn't want to look too closely. I'm not a man who enjoys violence. But it was for a good cause. You weren't happy. Roger was hounding you. You were past your prime. The producers were looking to replace you."

"You're lying! They had me sign on for two more years. They didn't want to let me go. That was the whole problem. That was why I had to get away in such a final manner."

"Kim would have replaced you sooner or later," Ralston said calmly. "I just created the perfect moment for her to step up."

"Does she know?" Monica asked.

"That I killed you to get her the role? Of course not. She would never believe it either. She's always told me I was too soft for that business. Too soft." He chuckled.

Monica straightened up. "I want money to keep my mouth shut. Like you said, the local police aren't very smart. They can't work it out. They'll have to give up again this time, just like they did all those years ago. I'm the only one who can hurt you. Write me a check and I'm out of your life."

"All right. Let me go get my checkbook." Ralston stepped back. "Don't worry, I won't run. I'm too smart for that. I don't want to spend my life running. I can see in your face that it's not a good life."

He disappeared into the house.

Monica stood tight, nervous. She didn't make the mistake of looking in the direction where Falk and Callie were hidden.

Callie held her breath. Falk had assured her his men were watching the house and Ralston couldn't escape. But what was he up to inside the house? Would he attempt some kind of smart vanishing trick?

Ralston appeared again. He carried a check in his hand, ostentatiously out in front of him. He walked up to Monica. "This is half of what I earned from the merchandise. It should be enough for a nice couple of years on the Riviera. If you're frugal, it might last a lifetime. But frugality was never in your nature."

As he spoke, pleasantly, sedately, he had come very close to her. Monica reached for the check. Then Ralston's hand came up suddenly and hit her under the chin. She made a soft gasping sound and sagged to the ground. Ralston leaned over her. "You'll get what you deserve, all right," he said through gritted teeth. "The sea grave you should have ended up in thirty years ago."

Falk stepped away from Callie. Her heart pounded for

him. For some reason he hadn't drawn his gun but was going for the man without showing a weapon.

Ralston looked up. He recognized Falk and hissed, "I see. A trap. And I fell for it. Very good, Deputy. You should have gone into the movies."

As he spoke, he jumped with lightning speed over Monica's fallen body and lashed out at Falk. Falk groaned as the old man's fist made impact with his jaw. He staggered back.

Ralston kicked out, almost hitting Falk full in the stomach. But Falk was alert enough to avoid the kick and turn away, throwing himself to the ground. He rolled over and pushed himself up in the same movement. He pulled his gun out and called, aiming at Ralston, "Hands up, or I'll shoot."

Ralston stood, his eyes fixed on Falk's expression. It seemed as if he was trying to determine whether Falk would make good on his threat.

Callie called out, "It's pointless, Mr. Ralston. The house is surrounded. You'll never get away. Just surrender now."

Ralston turned his head to look in her direction. She came forward from behind the tree. "It's over. You, of all people, should know when the game is up. You did very well. You made no mistakes in Jamison's office. You were never suspected all those years ago, and you weren't suspected now either."

"Then how come you're here and I'm being arrested?"

Callie shrugged. "I guess if you had killed the real Monica Walker, you would have gotten away with all of this. But you killed the wrong woman, and the one you suggested come here to Heart's Harbor is still alive. She told me her story, and then it all clicked into place."

Ralston laughed softy. Not a nasty, mean laugh, but a sort of surprised, amused laugh.

"I suppose," he said as he reached to put his hands above his head, "that I should have looked at her face after all."

Chapter Seventeen

Dorothea Finster leaned over the buffet filled with sweet treats and picked up a cupcake decorated with the tiny marzipan picnic basket Iphy had worked so hard on. "This looks delicious."

She turned her head to survey the crowd spread across her lawn—eating, drinking, talking, laughing—and released a happy sigh. "What a wonderful day. I can't wait to see the fireworks."

Callie said, "But first we'll have the Golden Age dances. It fits perfectly with Haywood Hall's grand atmosphere to see those dashing couples whirling across the terrace. I talked to their leader, and they want to do dance demonstrations here more often. It can become a part of our program for fall and winter. Of course, when it's cold, they can't do the dancing on the terrace, but we can do it inside then, restoring the old ballroom to its former purpose."

Dorothea squeezed her arm. "You've come up with such good ideas for the house. And how lovely to see this working out in my lifetime. I had never believed there would be so much liveliness again."

"I'm sorry we couldn't come up with some kind of grand revelation about Monica Walker. But I thought that the whole matter with the remains on the sunken boat and the arrest made recently would be a bit gruesome for a family-oriented gathering."

"Yes, I agree. It would have been wonderful if you could have revealed something happy about her. Like that she really sailed into bliss with a man who loved her very much."

Dorothea sighed wistfully. "It would have been utterly romantic. But I suppose it wasn't meant to be."

Callie bit the inside of her cheek. Monica had indeed become very happy with a man who loved her very much. Right there in Heart's Harbor.

But Monica had asked them not to reveal her identity just yet. She would have to come forward and testify in the upcoming court case against Otto Ralston, but it might take awhile before the case came to trial, and until then Monica wanted to enjoy the last of her undisturbed, unfamous life.

Dave had been livid when he had learned about the risk his wife had taken while he was locked up, but when he had calmed down, he had agreed that it was for the best that an arrest had been made and the whole matter could be put to bed.

Mrs. Keats, Dorothea's faithful housekeeper, appeared by their sides. "The jury is about to announce the winner of the sweet tea contest."

"Perfect. We're coming."

Callie led Dorothea to the long table where the jugs with the participants' creations were waiting. There had been forty-five entries, which the jury had initially narrowed down to ten. Then they had tasted those ten again to determine a winner.

At the table Iphy stood with the chairman of the jury, who held a sealed envelope. He broke the seal with a weighty expression, pulled out a card and looked at it. "The winner of Heart Harbor's Fourth of July tea party's sweet tea contest is . . . number seven!"

Everyone looked at the jug with the neat number seven in front of it, then started to glance round to see whose it was.

Mr. Bates came forward with a high color in his cheeks. He waved off the applause and said to Iphy and Callie that it was really not worth mentioning. But he did beam when his prize—the certificate for a high tea for six at Book Tea—was handed to him and especially when it was confirmed that his creation, called Orange Zest, would be on Book Tea's menu for the rest of the summer season.

"I can't wait to see you at Book Tea soon," Callie said, shaking his hand.

Mr. Bates leaned over and whispered, "I'm glad I'm a better tea maker than a sleuth. I never suspected Otto Ralston. In fact, I rather liked him. Oh, well . . ."

Callie knew he'd be in for an even bigger surprise when he heard that Monica Walker had never left town but had practically been his neighbor for all of these years. She bet he would be the first to support Monica in the difficult time that lay ahead with the publicity, which would no doubt surround the case once it came to court. It was good to know she and Dave would have kind neighbors to fall back on.

Leaving Mr. Bates to accept the well-wishes of his fellow contestants, Callie went to stand with Dorothea, who was just thanking the jury chairman for his efforts. "It can't have been easy to choose from such a wide offering of delicious varieties. Oh . . ." She glanced past the chairman at Falk, who had come up to them. "Deputy! Whatever happened to your face?"

"It'll get better," Falk said in a sour tone. The bruise on his chin where Ralston had hit him had looked much worse earlier, but even now it was still visible against his tan.

Dorothea winked at Callie and led the chairman away to sample some of the three-tiered cake. With its base covered with macarons and top layers full of fondant fireworks, it was the centerpiece of the sweet treat buffet. People took pictures with their phones before accepting a slice and oohing and aahing about the flavors.

Falk said to Callie, "I should have asked my stunt double to take over as soon as Ralston got physical. To be honest, I'm still stunned at how fast he was for a man his age."

"Despair can make people stronger and more resourceful. But I think in his case it was also a matter of rage. He was so mad at Monica coming back from the dead to confront him. Or maybe he was mad at himself for having made the crucial mistake of not checking the face of the woman he murdered. He sank the boat with her on it, never having established that she was really Monica Walker. Of course he had no reason to doubt it. He knew nothing about Muriel's existence."

"The unknown factor that turned everything upside down." Falk picked up the spoon resting in the bowl of fruit punch and filled a cup. "For you. Very creative to cut the fruit into star shapes."

"Thanks. Iphy's idea entirely. She's done so much to make this a memorable day. It's sort of an official start to all of our activities at the estate. Of course there was a lecture or two in spring, the summer evening concert in June, and the library cataloging started last week, but this does feel like a grand opening." Callie took a sip of the refreshing punch and then with her spoon fished for a bite of melon.

Laughter floated their way, and they turned their heads to see Jimmy and Tate playing with Biscuit. Jimmy threw a plastic disc that Biscuit caught mid-air. He made the weirdest jumps and turned his head every which way to get it, and Tate was doubled over with laughter at his antics. Daisy ran with Biscuit to get at the disc as well, but of course the bigger dog was faster and could jump higher. Tate scooped her up in his arms and gave her a cuddle, and she leaned against him, her muzzle in his neck, probably believing that was a good place to be.

Peggy stood under a tree, watching them play, with Quinn by her side. His tanned face was relaxed and quiet. On his bare left arm Callie detected a bit of blue paint left from his final chores around her cottage. He had worked hard, but still he had found some extra things to do, at no charge as he had assured her, and she guessed he was eager for a reason to stay in town.

How Peggy felt about him was harder to tell. She certainly cared but also said it was too soon after Greg had died. Maybe she just needed some time and Quinn's friendship and support to make up her mind.

Callie said to Falk, "Quinn is almost done at my cottage. I guess he'll need to find something else to do now."

"Haven't you heard? The community center needs some maintenance, and Quinn has been recommended."

"By whom?"

"The mayor didn't want to tell me." Falk held her gaze. "I suppose I've got you to blame for that?"

"Certainly not. The mayor wouldn't listen to me either. I just moved to town."

"So you're actually staying? You aren't leaving again when the summer's over?"

"I gave up my job and my apartment in Trenton. There's really nowhere else I can go."

It sounded a bit lame, and Falk grimaced. "That's the most enthusiastic description of a new life I've ever heard."

Callie said quickly, "I meant to say, I came out here to stay. Not to run off again. But I wonder . . ."

She really didn't want to put it into words, not on a grand day like this, when she just wanted to be relaxed and carefree and happy.

"If you're really cut out for small-town life." Falk clenched his cup. "That's exactly what I was afraid of when you said in December that you'd come live here. Then it was all cozy and seasonal, and I was worried you were acting for a sentimental reason. You need more than that to make a big change like this work out. I sort of sensed when you emailed me that as the time came closer to pack up and come out here, you weren't sure anymore that it was the right decision."

Callie bit her lip. It was true that she's had some doubts, and it had been hard to let go of her fun work, her colleagues, her apartment, her whole life as she had known it for so long. Had Falk really sensed that from her emails? Had he read them so closely?

While she had been thinking he hadn't cared at all what she wrote and indeed whether she came out to Heart's Harbor or not!

Falk said softly, "There's no shame in admitting you made a mistake. You did such a good job as a tour guide, I'm sure your boss will want you back. Or you can find work with another tour company. If your heart is in it, you should do it."

He held her gaze with his deep brown eyes. They were concerned for her and even a little sad. "I can't say I won't be sorry to see you leave again, but I don't want to see you here struggling either. You should feel happy about what you do."

"I want to stay here. Yes, it was hard to leave, and I did have doubts, but I love Book Tea and Iphy and the new friends I've made. It's just so easy to get to know new people here, and my cottage is turning into a real home now. Every time I go there, I feel more like it's mine."

She hesitated a moment before adding, "I'd love for you to stop by some time and see it."

Falk nodded. "I'll do that. Soon."

Callie studied his expression. Her heart thundered in her chest at what she was about to say, but she had to do it now or she'd never have the nerve again. "Ace, I . . ."

His dark eyes searched her expression, and her heart pounded even louder. She forced herself to keep looking at him as she continued, "I admit I was a bit put off when the time came to move here, and it seemed like you had no interest in it at all anymore. I felt like you were sorry I was coming."

"Me?" His eyes were genuinely surprised. "No, not at all. I was just . . . I . . . I didn't want to get my expectations up and then hear you were leaving again anyway because this just wasn't the place where you wanted to settle down."

Falk put his cup down with a clank. "I have to leave for a little bit. But I'll be back. Okay?"

Callie stared after him as he rushed off. How about that? The moment they were finally having a serious conversation, and he had to leave!

She exhaled in a huff. Men. She'd never understand them.

Still her head was light with the realization that he had more or less admitted he had some kind of expectations for her new life there and that he had been bothered by the idea that she might regret her decision and leave again.

What did that mean? Why had he not said more?

Why had he rushed off, ending their moment together so abruptly?

Applause pulled her from her frantic thoughts. The Swing It! couples had come from the house onto the terrace. The quartet started to play, and the dancers whirled about doing the Charleston, then the foxtrot.

The women's dresses sparkled in the evening light, the feathers on their headbands ruffling on the breeze. Their energy spread to the crowd at once, and people clapped along or swayed to the rhythm.

Callie tapped her foot in the grass, humming the tune. Too bad they weren't all dancing. She'd love to take a spin with Falk. But he had rushed off, and she didn't even know what for. Somehow he always threw her off-balance and left her confused.

After the dancing, more drinks were handed out, and people flocked to the buffet for savory treats. Iphy had created pizzas in the shape of the number four, which people could customize with all kinds of fresh toppings, which stood at the ready in bowls: pepperoni, mozzarella, vegetables, fruit.

For the kids there were coloring pages to work on at a long low table and sparkling juice that had no alcohol, of course, but still looked like champagne. They were excited that they could stay up past their bedtime and looked in awe at the colorful party lights that were strung between the trees. Their glow seemed to increase as the sun's light faded and darkness closed in, creating the perfect background for the fireworks show that would be their party's grand finale.

Cuddling Daisy in her arms, Callie chatted to Peggy while Quinn was teaching Biscuit to sit. The dog didn't listen most of the time, and the boys were laughing until, as Jimmy put it, their sides hurt.

Peggy said to Callie, "I'm so glad things worked out here for Quinn. Imagine him being able to do such a big job as the work on the community center. I told him that if he's working there and I'm at Book Tea, we should have lunch together some time. It only makes sense, right?"

"Perfect sense," Callie agreed, suppressing her grin of delight that Peggy and Quinn would see more of each other and might get together in due time.

"And he's going to keep Biscuit. He can actually take him to the community center when he's working there. The ladies who volunteer have all taken to Biscuit, and they want to look after him. I hope they know what they're getting themselves into."

"Well, with long walks and proper training he'll turn into a perfectly well-behaved dog. I'm sorry that it didn't work out with the couple who originally brought him here, but maybe, by some weird twist, he ended up with the person he was intended to be with after all."

"You bet." Peggy smiled as she looked at Quinn and her children petting the dog, who lay sprawled in the grass with his four legs in the air.

Biscuit's portrait had turned out to be a stunning likeness, and it was now sitting in Callie's closet; she was waiting for the perfect opportunity to give it to Quinn. Maybe for his birthday? She thought he'd mentioned in passing once that it was in September.

Just as the fireworks were about to start—an official show put on by a licensed company from a nearby town—Falk returned to Callie's side. The bright light of the exploding firecrackers illuminated his face as he came to stand close beside her, his hands behind his back.

"You missed the dance demonstration," Callie groused, "and I don't see what could have been so urgent. I thought you were off today."

"I am. This was personal." He pulled his hands out from behind his back and showed them to her. He was holding a colorfully wrapped box. "For you. But be careful—it's heavy."

Callie accepted it. "You weren't kidding. I'll put it on the grass to unwrap it."

She crouched down on the grass, nervously tearing at the tape while the skies overhead filled with gold, silver, blue, and purple. The oohs and aahs of the eager audience resounded in the air.

What could it be? Last time Falk had given her a present, it was a heart reading "Welcome Home." He had won it in a raffle at the ice-skating rink, and it had seemed to convey a special message for her—for them together. It had felt like the best present ever. Could this new gift be as good?

Or even better?

She slipped the paper off.

It was the Tiffany lamp she had seen in Falk's cabin. The one that had struck her as out of place in his austere interior.

"I bought it for you," she heard him say from above her, "in a little antique shop. Back in February. I meant to give it to you on the day you arrived here in town, as a welcome gift. But I suddenly thought that for some reason you'd leave again. I didn't want you to think I was forcing you to settle someplace when you didn't want to. But now that you told me that . . . well, anyway, here it is."

"I love it." Callie smiled at the lamp's elegant designed foot, the colorful glass fitted into a poppy pattern. It was the perfect thing to claim a place of pride in her new home. Maybe in the sitting room? She had a great oak sideboard there, polished until it shone.

Or beside her bed? Perfect for reading a little before she turned off the light for a good night's sleep.

She got to her feet and hugged Falk, wrapping her arms around his neck. "Thank you. It's wonderful."

Falk's arms closed around her waist as he held her against him. He whispered into her ear, "Happy Fourth of July. My mother always said that when you see all those shooting stars, you should make a wish."

Just then the crackling and light of the fireworks ceased, and Callie let go of Falk in a rush, suddenly conscious that people might see them embracing.

Her cheeks were on fire, and she looked down at her feet.

Jimmy came over and cried excitedly that they could watch while the plane was loaded up to be taken back to its hangar.

Callie nodded and said they'd come over in a sec.

As Jimmy ran back to his mother and Quinn, Callie met Falk's eye. He was smiling at her, his brown eyes sparkling.

She answered his smile with a wide one of her own. "Happy Fourth of July, Ace. And I don't think I need any wishes right now. Everything I wish for is right here."

Acknowledgments

As always, I'm grateful to all agents, editors, and authors who share online about the writing and publishing process. A special thanks to my amazing agent, Jill Marsal; my wonderful editor, Faith Black Ross; and the entire talented crew at Crooked Lane Books, especially cover illustrator Brandon Dorman for the eye-catching cover with Daisy at its heart. And of course to you, reader: thanks for picking up this story: I hope that the warmth and togetherness of the Fourth of July lit up your heart as you were reading. You're invited to join Callie and Iphy again as Heart's Harbor gears up for a Valentine's Day to remember.